DAREDEVIL

DAREDEVIL

A Novel By

Greg Cox

Based on the Motion Picture Screenplay by

Mark Steven Johnson

AN ONYX BOOK

ONYX
Published by New American Library, a division of
Penguin Putnam Inc., 375 Hudson Street,
New York, New York 10014, U.S.A.
Penguin Books Ltd, 80 Strand,
London WC2R 0RL, England
Penguin Books Australia Ltd, 250 Camberwell Road,
Camberwell, Victoria 3124, Australia
Penguin Books Canada Ltd, 10 Alcorn Avenue,
Toronto, Ontario, Canada M4V 3B2
Penguin Books (N.Z.) Ltd, Cnr Rosedale and Airborne Roads,
Albany, Auckland 1310, New Zealand

Penguin Books Ltd, Registered Offices:
Harmondsworth, Middlesex, England

First published by Onyx, an imprint of New American Library,
a division of Penguin Putnam Inc.

First Printing, January 2003
10 9 8 7 6 5 4 3 2 1

PROLOGUE

Forget what you think you know about superheroes. Because this is the real world, and in the real world there is no such thing as "mutant healing" or "spider-sense" to keep a man alive. In the real world, there's just a man in a mask.

And he's bleeding to death. . . .

A drop of blood landed in the greasy puddle at the priest's feet. Father William "Bill" Everett looked up in surprise, his startled gaze climbing the soot-stained limestone facade of the Gothic cathedral looming before him. The church—his church—rose from the blighted urban landscape surrounding it like a fortress, holding fast against the squalid decay of Hell's Kitchen. Through the tireless efforts of Father Everett and his predecessors, the Church of the Holy Innocents had always provided a refuge from the crime, poverty, and bloodshed that had long characterized this most infamous of New York neighborhoods.

At least, until tonight.

"What the devil?" he murmured, stepping back from the bloodstained puddle and crossing himself.

It was well after midnight, but the corner streetlights partially illuminated the western face of the cathedral, wedged between a fenced-in parking lot (now closed for the night) and a storefront psychic and tarot card reader (ditto). Stained-glass windows depicting various saints and apostles looked out from beneath pointed Gothic arches, while ornate stone tracery, sadly corroded by smog and acid rain, adorned the rising turrets and central spire. Father Everett's worried eyes searched the familiar planes and angles of the old church, anxious to discover the source of the blood, yet he was fearful of what he might find.

Please, he prayed silently, *let it not be human.* Although he had witnessed much evil and heartbreak during his years in Hell's Kitchen, his heart had, for better or for worse, never hardened against human suffering. *Let it be some poor bird or beast.*

Steam rose from a nearby sewer grate, and a solitary rat, no doubt attracted by the scent of blood, crept up to the edge of the puddle, only to scurry away as another crimson droplet fell from somewhere above, breaking the surface of the puddle and causing lurid red circles to ripple outward. Father Everett glanced down just in time to see the husky black rat depart, before resuming his fretful quest for the blood's point of origin.

Then, as if to assist him in his investigation, a police helicopter came flying low over the neighborhood. The cold white beam of the copter's searchlight probed the nearby rooftops before turning its incandescent gaze on the church. *Something serious is happening,* the priest realized. But what—or whom—could the copter be hunting for?

Father Everett peered upward. At first, he spotted nothing unusual, just high church walls somewhat in need of a good scrubbing; but then, tilting his head back as far as it could go, he lifted his gaze all the way up to the large marble crucifix rising proudly at the very peak of the cathedral's tall stone spire. His jaw dropped, and a frisson of superstitious fear coursed through his soul at the startling sight atop the cathedral, where the Devil himself could be seen draped over the outstretched arms of the cross!

Speak of the Devil and he will appear, Father Everett thought nervously, recalling a hoary maxim drummed into him at his mother's knee. He blinked his eyes in amazement and crossed himself for the second time in as many minutes. For an endless heartbeat or two, he thought himself genuinely in the presence of the Adversary, until his innate good sense and reason, well honed by decades of ministering to the city's mean streets, reasserted itself. In Hell's Kitchen, he knew from hard experience, the Devil's works were almost always performed by human hands.

Looking again through more skeptical eyes, the middle-aged priest saw that the figure clinging to the spire, exposed by the police copter's incandescent beam, was just a man wearing a devil's costume, dark crimson in color. A mask covered the upper half of his face, and a pair of matching horns sprouting from his brow were silhouetted against the full moon shining above and behind the church steeple. *Some sort of prank?* Father Everett wondered hopefully, more relieved than annoyed. *But it's the middle of summer—Halloween is over two months away!*

The disguised man staggered against the elevated cross, and another bloodred droplet splashed into the puddle on the sidewalk outside the Church of the Holy Innocents. Father Everett knew this was no joke; the man up there was obviously hurt, perhaps seriously.

The worried priest held his breath, afraid that at any moment the unknown stranger would lose his grip on the cross and fall to his death. The spire rose over two hundred feet above the pavement; the wounded man would need a miracle to survive.

Slowly, painfully, the stranger lowered himself onto the roof of the cathedral, eventually disappearing from Father Everett's sight as he fled the glare of the searchlight by dipping below the ornamented turrets of the church. Did the bleeding man mean to enter the Church of the Holy Innocents from the roof? Father Everett couldn't figure out where else he could go.

The priest stared at the locked front entrance of the church, torn between Christian charity and streetwise caution. Who knew what the intruder wanted or why the police were searching for him? What if he was armed and dangerous? A wounded felon could still pose a serious threat.

He looked up and down the moonlit street, hoping for a Good Samaritan (or, better yet, several) he could recruit for assistance. But aside from the whirring helicopter hovering overhead, as frustratingly distant and out of reach as Heaven itself, there was not a soul in sight. New York might be the city that never sleeps, but people in Hell's Kitchen knew better than to brave these lonely, litter-strewn streets at such an ungodly hour of the night. Taxi drivers avoided the whole neighborhood like the plague, especially after dark; only a deathbed visit to a dying parishioner had kept the priest himself out so late. And as for the police . . . who knew when reinforcements for the helicopter would arrive on the ground?

Father Everett took a few halting steps toward the church entrance, then hesitated once more. Despite the muggy August heat, a shiver ran through his body and the sweat on his back felt as cold as ice. He trembled in the cathedral's shadow, afraid to draw nearer. *Aside from the fact that he's hurt,* he asked himself cautiously, *what else do I know about this man?* He tugged nervously at his starched white collar only to remember solemn vows taken years ago and never regretted. He let out a fatalistic sigh and took another step closer to the door. *What else do I need to know?*

Committed now, if no less apprehensive, the priest climbed the steps to the closed double doors barring his way. His shaky hands fumbled with the padlock; as ever, he hated the fact that he had to lock the doors of the cathedral while away after dark, but in Hell's Kitchen, there was really no other choice, aside from letting the church be looted and vandalized every other week or so.

The doors swung open, and he made his way through the vestibule to the nave, where a shocking tableau awaited him.

Moonlight entered the vast cathedral through stained-glass windows mounted high above the marble floor, throwing an eerie spotlight on the figure sprawled in the center aisle, in front of the altar at the far end of the vaulted chamber. Half collapsed, half crawling, the man in the devil's garb gripped the end of the gilded altar in an effort to keep from falling completely onto the scuffed marble tiles beneath his knees. With his demonic horns still protruding from his brow, he resembled a fallen angel newly cast out of Heaven.

Father Everett suddenly recalled a rumor he'd heard, about a costumed vigilante supposedly prowling the neighborhood, putting the fear of God, or at least the Devil, into the local hoods and drug dealers.

What did the papers call him again? The priest
scoured his memory, trying to remember a tabloid
headline he hadn't paid much attention to before.
Devil Man? The Daring Devil?

No. The name came to him at last. *Daredevil.*

A pain-racked groan escaped the injured man, in-
terrupting Father Everett's moment of revelation.
"Hello?" he called out, grateful that his voice shook
only a little. The muffled susurrus of the helicopter's
propellers barely penetrated the cathedral's high
stone walls. He flicked a switch, causing two rows
of lantern-shaped chandeliers to light up above the
varnished wooden pews. The lamps emitted a soft
golden glow that dispelled many of the shadows cast
by the stained glass–tinted moonlight. Drawing
strength from the added illumination, the priest hurried down the aisle toward the other man. "Can I
help you?"

Daredevil, if that was who the stranger was,
merely grunted in reply. Gritting his teeth, he tried
to climb to his feet, only to falter and, gasping, drop
back onto the floor. Blood dripped from what looked
like a vicious stab wound in his right shoulder.

"Careful, my son," Father Everett counseled as he
helped the injured intruder onto the sanctuary floor,
cradling the masked man's head. "Do not exert
yourself."

On closer inspection, he saw now that Daredevil's
bizarre garb was made of sleek red leather, along
with matching gloves and boots. A crimson holster
strapped to his right thigh held a painted wooden
shaft, about two feet long. *A weapon?* Father Everett
guessed, briefly wondering who on earth had dared
to attack such an ominous-looking individual.

The horned cowl concealed all but the bottom half

of Daredevil's face. A white man, Father Everett noted, whose strong chin and chiseled features might have appeared handsome had they not borne the ugly evidence of some recent brawl. Swollen lips, bruised and bleeding, testified that their owner had endured other blows besides the stab to his shoulder. His breath came in ragged pants, and he appeared to be struggling to remain conscious. Father Everett tried to look into the other man's eyes, only to discover a pair of opaque red lenses looking back at him. *How in Heaven does he see through those?* he wondered.

Concerned that his new charge might be suffering from shock or a concussion, the priest gently undid the leather collar around Daredevil's throat and tried to peel back the mask hiding the vigilante's eyes. "No—" Daredevil murmured weakly, raising a hand to stop Father Everett, but his strength deserted him and he surrendered to the older man's kindly intervention.

"Sssh," Father Everett whispered soothingly. "It's all right. I just want to see how badly you're hurt." Confronted with the irrefutable reality of the injured man's weakness, the priest felt his earlier fears slip away. The crimson mask fell away as well, revealing the battered face of a young man in his early thirties. Light reddish-brown hair, slick with perspiration, was plastered to his skull, and dark purple bruises marred his clean-shaven features. Lifeless blue eyes stared past Father Everett at the vaulted ceiling and circular rose window high above them.

The old priest gasped in astonishment. He knew this face—indeed, he had known it for years. It was a face from the neighborhood, one that had withstood more than its fair share of tragedy over the last few decades. "Matt?" he whispered uncertainly, striving to come to grips with this unexpected revelation. "Matt Murdock?"

A single red candle, never extinguished, resided in the sanctuary, symbolizing the eternal presence of the Holy Spirit. Taking care not to drop Daredevil's—Matt's—head, Father Everett reached out and took hold of the candle by its polished silver holder. Without thinking, he brought the lighted candle closer to Matt's eyes, which remained fixed and immobile, not dilating at all.

Of course not, the priest realized, shaking his head. How could he have forgotten Matt's disability? He looked down into the younger man's unseeing eyes, unsure how he would tell if life passed out of them. Dark venous blood leaked from Matt's violated shoulder, dripping onto the marble tiles; his breath came roughly and with obvious strain. *Is he bleeding internally?* Father Everett worried, putting down the candle to apply pressure to the untended wound. He had already administered last rites to one of his flock this evening, an eighty-year-old man succumbing to chronic emphysema; now he feared he might have to do the same to young Matt Murdock.

They say your whole flashes before you when you die, Father Everett reflected, while Daredevil's lifeblood pooled beneath him. He shifted the injured man's weight, hoping to ease his discomfort some small degree. Matt's blue eyes gazed into nothingness.

Is that true even for a blind man?

CHAPTER 1

Nineteen years ago . . .

Twelve-year-old Matt Murdock winced as his finger probed the cut on his bottom lip. *Ouch!* he thought. *That smarts.* A gooey string of blood hung suspended below the split lip for a second before thinning enough to drop into the kitchen sink, joining several earlier drops in a smeary mess at the bottom of the rusty sink. Matt's eyes narrowed as he looked down at his own shed blood. *Is that it for tonight,* he asked the busted lip silently, *or are you just going to keep dripping forever?*

He waited a few more moments, just to make sure the bleeding had really stopped, then turned on the cold water. He splashed a welcome gout of cool liquid against his face while the congealing red blood swirled down the drain. Matt nodded in satisfaction as the evidence of this latest schoolyard pummeling disappeared without a trace. *With luck, Dad won't even notice my lip.*

A pile of dirty plates and dishes was stacked on the counter next to the sink, and the rest of the cramped Hell's Kitchen apartment didn't look much better. Exposed pipes and electrical wiring crisscrossed the ceiling, while a single naked lightbulb hanging over the closet-sized kitchen only made it easier for Matt to see how truly dingy his surroundings were. A plastic bucket rested on the yellowed linoleum floor, catching the unwanted raindrops that periodically dripped from the ceiling. Black plastic roach traps squatted in the corners, to not much avail; Matt caught a familiar scuttling out of the corner of his eye, but the huge brown roach vanished into a crack in the wall before the boy could find something to squash it with.

I'll get you next time, Matt vowed, sure that the elusive vermin would show its disgusting self again. *At least Dad doesn't mind if I whack a roach.*

A raspy snore from the living room informed him that his dad had dropped off in front of the TV again. Matt momentarily considered tackling the daunting pile of dirty dishes, then decided the heck with it. He'd do them later.

The rain outside, visible through the cracked windows of the Murdocks' fifth-floor walk-up, had done little to relieve the oppressive humidity of this unusually hot spring afternoon. A decrepit air-conditioner labored noisily, but it was still too hot and sticky to even think about housework, no matter how urgently it might have been needed. *Time for a nap,* Matt thought, *once I get Dad stowed away, of course.*

He turned off the tap and yanked the chain by the lightbulb, casting the kitchen into murky shadows. Thunder boomed in the distance as Matt trudged into the living room.

He found his father, as usual, passed out in the big easy chair facing the TV. Foam padding peeked through the torn upholstery, and an empty six-pack rested on the bare wooden floor next to the chair. The flickering blue glow of the TV screen cast restless shadows on the cracked plaster walls.

No surprise, there was a boxing match on. Matt heard the ebullient voice of the announcer booming from the TV as the boy approached his dad's chair. "And the winneer, by unanimous decision, Gene 'The Machine' Conlan. . . !"

Matt looked around for the remote, then shrugged and switched the tube off by hand. A flash of lightning lit up the apartment, as if to replace the cathode-ray glare of the tube. He stepped carefully to avoid another plastic bucket, a mate for the one catching raindrops in the kitchen. "C'mon, Dad," he urged mildly, tugging on his father's beefy arm. "Let's get you into bed."

Jack Murdock was a large, muscular man with a boxer's build; his nose had been broken too many times to count. Despite that, his doughy features still held a hint of the good looks he had enjoyed in his youth. On his good days, you could barely see the streaks of gray creeping into his shaggy, light brown hair.

This was not one of his good days.

"Wha—who . . . who won?" he asked groggily, his bleary eyes struggling to focus on his son. Slumped into the easy chair's inviting cushions, his burly frame refused to budge from the chair.

"Conlan. By decision," Matt answered patiently. He flirted with the idea of just leaving his dad where he was, but no, he'd be more comfortable in his own bed, and less likely to wake up with a killer neck ache.

It wasn't easy, but Matt eventually got his father out of the chair and onto his feet. Stepping beneath his dad's drooping left arm, Matt helped him across the floor, guiding him down the nearby hallway to the smaller of the two tiny bedrooms belonging to the cramped tenement apartment. An old poster, thumb-tacked to the wall, touted a long-ago boxing match between Jack "The Devil" Murdock and a tough-looking heavyweight named Tom Sweeney. The crudely mounted fight bill showed Matt's dad wear-ing a dark red boxing robe with two small horns sewn into the hood. The Devil had won that match by a knockout, Matt remembered proudly.

"Yeah, I beat 'em, you know," Jack said.

"I know, Dad."

"Two minutes and thirty-two seconds into the sev-enth round, I went to the body. I see him drop his hands. I knew I had him."

"I know, Dad. I know," Matt said.

But that was quite a few years ago.

His dad's weight sagged against him as they stag-gered into the modest six-by-nine bedroom. At times like this, Matt wished he had a mom like other kids, more to take care of his dad than to look after Matt, but his mother, whoever she was, had exited their lives before Matt was old enough to remember. It was the one thing his dad had always refused to talk about.

There was barely enough room for both Matt and his father in the tiny room. Jack Murdock's bulk landed heavily on the unmade bed. His chin drooped onto his chest as he sat on the edge of the bed, more unconscious than awake. A day's worth of un-trimmed stubble carpeted his listless jowls.

Glad to be out from under his father's heavyweight poundage, Matt knelt to pull off his dad's shoes. As he wrestled with the recalcitrant footwear, which were in no hurry to let go of their respective feet, Jack Murdock opened his eyes and looked down at his son. "Hey," he said, nodding at the fresh cut on Matt's lip. "What's this?"

Damn, Matt thought, *so much for Dad not noticing.*

"Nothin'," the boy mumbled.

His father scowled. "I told you, I don't want you fighting."

"I don't fight," Matt protested, his voice rising from the sheer injustice of it all. "I get beat up."

If only Dad would let me fight back, he thought, for probably the millionth time. *I'd show them. Nobody would mess with me if I gave those bullies a dose of their own medicine.* His imagination savored the image of Dwayne Gleason and his buddies sporting split lips of their own, plus maybe a black eye or three. *I bet I could knock Dwayne out with one punch, like Dad did to Sweeney. . . .*

As if he could read Matt's mind, Jack shook his head. "Matt . . ." He didn't sound angry, just disappointed, which was ten times worse.

"I tried to walk away," Matt insisted. He knew it wouldn't do any good, but he couldn't resist trying to plead his case one more time. "Just like you said. But they kept giving me shit."

"Don't curse," Jack said automatically. "What kind of shit?"

Matt mentally kicked himself for bringing the subject up. Now what was he supposed to say? "Um," he began hesitantly, before fessing up to the truth. "They said you work for Fallon." Matt looked at the floor, unable to meet his father's eyes. "They said you're one of his guys now."

Eddie Fallon was the local Mob boss. Everyone knew that, although the D.A. had never managed to prove anything. In general, the police didn't bother him much. He had connections, and then some. Around the neighborhood, people called Fallon "The Fixer," but he and his boys were just as good at breaking things.

Arms and legs, mostly. Skulls, too.

The very idea that his dad would go to work for a low-life scumball like Fallon was enough to make Matt see red. His dad was a heavyweight, a champion, not a hood!

Wasn't he?

Anxious eyes searched Jack's face, afraid of what they might find. *Please, Dad, don't let it be true. . . .*

His father paused before answering, almost longer than Matt could stand. Then he snorted indignantly at the very notion. "Are you kidding? Think I'd be pulling double overtime if I was working for Fallon?"

Matt smiled, feeling an overwhelming sense of relief. *I knew it wasn't so!* he thought triumphantly. He felt guilty for doubting his dad, even for a second.

But Jack Murdock wasn't finished speaking. A somber expression came over his face, one that Matt knew all too well. *Uh-oh*, the boy thought. *Here we go again.*

"You gotta keep hitting the books—you hear me. I know it's rough on you sometimes, especially in this neighborhood, but it's important. You need to study hard. Be a doctor or a lawyer or something." A trace of bitterness, born of too many years spent making a living with his fists, snuck into his voice. "Not like me."

Matt knew this lecture by heart, but it still got to him. "Dad . . ." he murmured, feeling embarrassed and uncomfortable. *I hate it when Dad runs himself down like this.*

Jack Murdock, fully awake now, looked around the sparsely furnished bedroom, his world-weary eyes taking in the unrelieved shabbiness of the home he had provided for them. Chipped paint peeling off the broken radiator. Water stains on the ceiling. Rusty iron bars over the window, for safety's sake, and the nauseating stench of a dead rat rotting somewhere inside the walls. A stack of bills, most of them marked FINAL NOTICE, piled high on a cheap plywood bureau at the end of the bed.

"You listen to me, Matt," he said firmly, sounding as stubborn and determined as he had ever been in the ring, facing off against the toughest of opponents. "You can do it. You can do anything if you're not afraid. Remember that."

Matt nodded, knowing there was no arguing with his dad on this point. For a moment, he wistfully clung to the glorious prospect of whupping the tar out of Dwayne Gleason, then sighed and pushed that shining image away. *Books, not brawls,* he thought. *I get it.*

Even if it meant being treated like a nerd—a target—every time he stepped outside the apartment. *I won't be afraid,* he resolved, jabbing his sore lip with the tip of his tongue. *I won't let anything scare me.*

Or anybody.

"Promise me, Matt."

Matt knew his dad only wanted the best for him. *How can I let him down after he's worked so hard to give me this chance?*

What was an occasional split lip now and then?

"I promise," he said.

* * *

It was the spring of 'eighty-four, and Michael Jackson's "Thriller" boomed out of every car window and ghetto blaster as Matt cruised on his skateboard through the dockyards down by the Hudson River, between Thirty-fifth and Fiftieth Streets. A breeze whipped past his face, carrying the refreshing scent of the nearby water, and with his wheels beneath him, gliding over the hot asphalt as though he were flying, he felt, for the moment, as free and unfettered as the Silver Surfer.

Having finished his homework early, plus three extra-credit assignments, he could enjoy the rest of the weekend with a clean conscience. The sky was clear and blue above him, and he even thought he saw part of a rainbow peeking through the towering forest of skyscrapers to his right. In short, it was an absolutely beautiful Saturday afternoon.

The last he would ever see.

His speeding skateboard weaved between slow-moving trucks and forklifts as he zoomed up the waterfront, a rolled-up report card in his hand. Sweating longshoremen and stevedores hustled about the wharves, loading and unloading crates, sacks, bales, and boxes to and from the holds of the heavily laden freighters docked along the river. Piles of lumber sat atop sturdy wooden pallets next to sprawling heaps of bagged sugar or bananas. Straining winches and cranes supported slings full of cargo and contraband, sometimes swinging precariously over the heads of the hardhats below. Cargo checkers, armed with clipboards and ballpoint pens, scurried along the docks, trying to keep track of what was coming and going from every scow and rustbucket.

Matt counted out the piers as he skated north; his father was supposed to be hauling produce up by Pier 80 today. He couldn't wait to show his dad the report card, which had arrived in the mail less than an hour ago.

The sudden glare of an arc welder being applied to a stuck warehouse door caught him by surprise, and he squealed to a halt just in time. *Whoa!* he thought, kicking his board up into his hand. Even from where he was standing, the heat of the welding torch toasted his skin. *That was a close one.*

"Hey, kid!" an angry voice called out. Matt realized he wasn't the only one aware of his near collision with the incandescent torch. He turned around to see the dock supervisor, an irritable-looking bruiser with a florid red complexion, stomping toward him. "What's the matter?" he bellowed sarcastically, a clipboard full of shipping manifests tucked beneath his arm. "You blind or something? You trying to get yourself killed?"

Matt gulped and glanced around for his father, not entirely sure he wanted his dad to witness this encounter. A forklift trundled by, bearing a load of metal drums marked with the universal symbol for biohazardous material. *Should they be messing with that stuff here?* Matt wondered absently, before steeling himself to face the irate supervisor.

"Sorry, sir," he said, clutching his report card like a protective talisman. To his slight relief, he saw that the trundling forklift was not being piloted by his father. "I'm just looking for my dad. Jack Murdock."

Puzzlement joined impatience on the man's face. "Murdock? He ain't worked here for months." He gestured back the way Matt had came. "Now beat it."

The supervisor's words struck Matt like a kick to the gut. *Months?* He couldn't believe what he was hearing. *But Dad said he was working here just this morning. . . !*

There was no way around it. His father had lied to him, had been doing so for weeks and weeks. In his shock, the report card, which Matt had been so proud of only moments before, slipped, unnoticed and forgotten, from his fingers. The stiff paper report landed in a muddy puddle, which couldn't have cared less that Matt had scored straight A's across the board.

A perfect 4.0.

Shaken to his core, the confused boy started home. Too distracted to think about riding his board, he plodded along the waterfront on foot. At the back of his troubled mind, an awful suspicion began to surface, despite his best efforts not to admit it. *What's Dad been doing all this time, if he wasn't working at the dock?*

He was only a few blocks away from the pier when a frightened male voice interrupted his anguished thoughts. "Please . . . no," begged the voice, coming from a narrow alley just off Twelfth Avenue. The obvious desperation in the stranger's voice cut through Matt's own distress, drawing him nearer to the alley. Maybe there was something he could do to help?

Rounding a corner, he peered into the alley, where he saw a pale-faced meatpacker shoved up against a wall by another man. Matt couldn't see the second man's face, but his beefy shoulders and threatening posture made it clear that the meatpacker, a smaller man wearing a stained white apron, was in trouble.

"Please," he entreated the menacing thug. "You gotta tell Fallon I need more time—"

Fallon? Matt's eyes widened. He had just been thinking about Fallon, sort of.

Fallon and his father . . .

"You're all out of time," the thug said gruffly. Despite his intimidating manner, he didn't sound angry, just tired and disappointed.

Matt froze in place, recognizing both the voice and its weary, rueful tone. His mouth went dry, and he had to swallow hard before speaking.

"Dad?"

The looming thug stiffened in surprise. His guilty hands fell away from the unfortunate meatpacker's shoulders, dropping limply to the bigger man's sides. His shoulders slumped, and he slowly turned around to reveal the despairing, utterly defeated face of . . .

Jack Murdock.

"Matt . . ." Shame hoarsened his voice, and he looked more miserable than Matt had ever seen him. He held out his hands in a hopeless plea for forgiveness, the same hands that had been carrying out Fallon's dirty work only seconds before. "I'm so sorry. . . ."

Matt couldn't stand it anymore. Tears filling his eyes, he shook his head in stunned disbelief. All of a sudden, his worst fears and suspicions were coming true right before his eyes. *I can't stay here,* he thought frantically. *I have to get away!*

He turned and ran, ignoring his father's raspy cries. "Matt! Come back!"

He threw his skateboard onto the pavement and pushed off with all his strength. He didn't care which way he went, just so long as it was far away from that nightmarish alley—and the broken man chasing after him.

"Matt!"

Blinded by hot, stinging tears, he didn't even realize he was heading straight back toward the busy pier he had visited earlier. Matt's entire world had changed since then. The sky was just as bright and blue as before, but now the sunny weather seemed like a nasty joke. His formerly carefree attitude had been shattered into a million jagged pieces, every one of them tearing at his heart.

Why didn't I realize? he thought bitterly, wiping the tears away from his eyes. *How could I have been so blind?*

A flatbed truck, heavily laden with the same metal barrels he had noticed before, suddenly appeared in his path. Brakes squealed like sirens as the truck swerved to avoid him, leaving long, diagonal skid marks atop the unyielding asphalt.

An oncoming forklift, its prongs up high, swerved as well, only to collide with the truck's environmentally dubious cargo. The elevated forks tore into the ominous metal drums, releasing gallons of stored chemical waste. A slick blue-green fluid, glowing almost like neon, gushed from the ruptured barrels, spraying right into Matt's eyes.

"Aggh!" An inarticulate scream erupted from the boy's lips as the toxic spray seared his eyes. Blazing agony coursed through his optic nerves straight into his brain, which suddenly felt like a seething ball of molten lava. In a panic, he rubbed his knuckles at his eyes, trying to clear the burning goo away, but it was no use; the noxious liquid—and the pain—were everywhere, in his nose, in his throat, inside his skull.

"Ohmigod!" he heard someone exclaim. "The

kid!" Footsteps pounded on the pavement around him as a deafening chorus of agitated voices surrounded him. "His eyes! Somebody get that muck out of his eyes!" Neon blackness beckoned, and Matt slipped mercifully into unconsciousness.

The last thing he ever saw was the bright yellow BIOHAZARD symbol stamped on the side of a toppled metal drum.

CHAPTER 2

Matt woke in the hospital to hear the doctor speaking with his father.

"I'm—I'm sorry, Mr. Murdock. He's blind."

"Are you sure, doc?" Matt could hear the fear and concern in his father's voice. "Is there any chance he'll recover?"

"I'm afraid not," the doctor replied. "The damage is irreversible."

Blind. Irreversible. The meaning of the doctor's words sank in, and Matt understood that they were talking about him.

Blind.

Matt gingerly shifted his hands away from his ears, feeling the thick gauze bandages over his eyes. He tried to peer past the bandages, hoping to catch just a glimpse of light through the heavy gauze, but all he saw was darkness, complete and unbroken.

Irreversible.

To his surprise, he found that he wasn't really shocked by the doctor's dire pronouncement. Over the past few days, ever since the accident on the docks, he had lapsed in and out of consciousness, feverishly tossing back and forth in his hospital bed while his polluted eyes burned and a never-ending parade of doctors and nurses came to peek and probe beneath his bandages. Never had he seen the slightest flicker of light, no matter how many penlights and X-ray machines he heard humming and clicking near his face. Sometimes, uncertain whether he was awake or dreaming, he had heard the hospital workers discuss his eyes, in whispers that were all too easy to overhear.

The poor kid . . .

On some level, he realized, he had known he was blind all along. *Of course*, he thought, remembering the fiery agony of the toxic waste burning away at his eyes. *How couldn't I be?*

But that pain was gone now, thank goodness, and rather than dwell on his life-changing loss, Matt was distracted by the unexpected panoply of sounds and sensations encroaching on his sightless new existence.

Buckets of water seemed to be crashing onto the floor only inches away from his bed, making the perpetual drip-drip-drip of the leaky ceiling back at their apartment seem pitiful by comparison. *Has a hydraulic pipe busted or something?* he speculated. The pounding bursts of falling water sounded close enough to touch, but when he reached out his hand, all he felt was the dry hospital air, smelling oppressively of disinfectant and disease.

Four stories down, and a full city block away, a leaky faucet dripped in the kitchen of an elderly Italian couple who had never heard of Matt Murdock. The sink kept on dripping, the faint, muffled sound being far too quiet to really worry about.

What kind of wacky hospital is this? Matt wondered, as no one came to check on the veritable Niagara

Falls splashing onto his floor. Nothing about this place made any sense. The sheets on his bed felt as rough and coarse as burlap, while every inch of the place smelled as if it had been soaked in ammonia, to the point of almost ridiculous overkill. At first, Matt thought he was in a room of his own, but now that he concentrated, it seemed there were dozens of people crammed into the room, not just his dad and the loudmouthed doctor. He could hear them talking, smell the sweat and the perfume and shampoos. Clothing and curtains rustled all around him, along with the snores and excessively loud breathing of more doctors and patients than he could count.

To his right, a tray of surgical tools rattled like subway tracks at rush hour. To his left, a stinking bedpan assaulted his senses, making his stomach churn. A priest seemed to be chanting in Latin at the foot of his bed, and for a terrifying instant Matt feared he was receiving last rites. Aluminum chair legs pounded like sledgehammers against the ceiling, while a rushing ambulance seemed to be blaring its siren directly under his bed.

"Hey! What's going on?" he called out, but if anyone answered him, he couldn't hear them over the rising din of the overlapping voices, all talking at the same time. Panic threatened, and he heard his own heart firing rapidly like a machine gun. "Dad?"

The harder he listened, the more he heard, until he was positively engulfed in a cacophonous sea of noise. Street sounds, clearly coming from outside the hospital, invaded his room: honking horns, squealing brakes, blaring rap music, shouted profanities, and people whistling for taxis. The volume of the entire city had been turned up to the max, right outside Matt's window.

He could smell the streets, too. The exhaust of a thousand vehicles fouling the air. Heaps of garbage rotting in the heat. A whiff of garlic from an outdoor cafe. Steam rising from a sewer grate. Incense burning at the stands of sidewalk vendors. The lather of a tired horse trotting beneath a mounted police officer. Bacon and eggs frying at an all-night diner. Cigarettes and crack pipes and marijuana. Sweat, blood, perfume, and urine.

It was unbearable. Sonic waves reverberated off the walls, crashing against his ears like a tsunami of sound. Countless odors, both sweet and sour, filled his nostrils and throat, all but choking him. In a frenzy, Matt thrashed wildly in his bed, trying to escape the deluge, only to tumble over the side of the bed and land with a thud on the hard linoleum floor.

The impact of the fall sounded like an earthquake, and still the barrage of noise pursued him. Crablike, he scrambled backward on all fours, seeking some relief from the avalanche of scents and sounds battering his remaining senses. The bumps and bruises he'd acquired in his tumble from the bed were nothing compared to the relentless onslaught. He backed into the nearest corner, his hands clapped tightly over his ears. "Dad?" he whispered, before a frantic scream broke from him.

"DAD!"

Jack Murdock stood in the corridor outside Matt's room, watching the doctor retreat down the hall. He didn't blame the M.D. for the bad news about Matt's eyes. *At least he was straight with me*, Jack thought, his own eyes red and tired. *But how the hell am I going to break the news to Matt?*

Restless feet carried him down the corridor, away

from where his son was sleeping. He headed in the
general direction of the elevator, with a vague idea
of hitting the hospital cafeteria before returning to
Matt's bedside. It was almost six a.m., he noted,
glancing up at the clock over the nurses' station. He
hoped the cafeteria had started serving breakfast
already.

Jack knew the way by heart; he'd been practically
living at the hospital ever since the accident, unwilling to leave his son alone in this place, whether Matt
knew he was here or not. Jack winced as he recalled
the circumstances surrounding the tragedy; it broke
his heart to realize that his son's last sight of him
had been of him leaning on that poor, dumb meatpacker on Fallon's orders. The crushed look on Matt's
face at that terrible moment was forever burned into
Jack's memory.

Is that how he's going to remember me?

Jack frowned, scolding himself for even worrying
about that after all that had happened to Matt. *This
isn't about me*, he remembered. *It's Matt's future that
matters now.*

What about all their hopes and plans? College. A
career. A chance to make something of himself, beyond the squalid confines of Hell's Kitchen. Matt had
worked so hard, studied when all the other kids in
the neighborhood were out wasting time and getting
into trouble. Were all those long hours for nothing?
Had Matt's dreams been washed away along with
his sight?

No, Jack Murdock resolved then and there. A fierce
determination gripped him and he clenched his fists
at his sides. *We're going to get past this*, he vowed.
One way or another, his son was going to have the
future he deserved, no matter what it took. There

had to be books and teachers for the blind, resources to help Matt overcome his handicap. All he needed was plenty of support and encouragement. *We'll start working on it right away*, Jack thought, *just as soon as Matt recovers. . . .*

A hysterical shriek spilled into the corridor, cutting off Jack's plans for tomorrow. Instantly, he recognized his son's cry. *Matt!* His heart in his throat, Jack spun around and raced back down the hall, arriving at the open doorway before any of the nearby nurses and orderlies. He rushed into the darkened room, flicking on the light as he did so. His red-rimmed eyes widened in alarm as he stared at the empty bed where his son should have been.

"Matt!" He skidded to a halt, his eyes searching the room. The sheets on the bed were in a state of total disarray, and a discarded pillow lay carelessly on the floor. "Where are you?"

"Over here, Dad."

An overwhelming rush of relief washed over Jack as he spotted Matt standing by the open window on the western side of the room. For a moment, Jack thought that Matt was looking out over the city; then he realized that was impossible. There was no way that Matt could be enjoying the view, which included a tantalizing glimpse of the Hudson River a couple blocks away, even if his useless eyes weren't completely covered by bandages.

So what was he doing by the window anyway?

I don't care, Jack decided, overjoyed just to see his son up and about, for the first time in days. *Thank you, God!* he thought sincerely. "Are you okay, son?"

Matt held up his hand for silence. "Do you hear it?" he asked quietly. There was strange tone to his voice. A hushed, almost awestruck quality.

"What?" Jack asked, not understanding. He didn't hear anything special, just the usual early morning traffic noises drifting up from the street outside.

Matt turned away from the window, a transfixed expression on his pale, twelve-year-old face, as if he'd just had a religious experience.

"*Everything.*"

"Matt? What is it?" Jack asked, now concerned.

"Something's happening to me. I don't know what it is. But I'm not afraid," Matt replied. "I'm not afraid."

At first, Matt had thought he would go insane. It had all been too much: the noises, the smells, the sheer sensory overload chasing him into the corner of the room, where he had squatted in hopeless shock and terror. Forget being blind—he wanted to be deaf and comatose, too!

Then, just as he realized that he would have to get control of his runaway senses or else crack up entirely, something seemed to click deep inside his brain and he discovered that, if he concentrated hard enough, he could begin to sort through the cascading flood of sounds and smells impinging on his awareness. If he stayed calm and quiet, and listened carefully to all the various noises out there, no matter how loud or disturbing, he could start to make sense of everything his supercharged ears were trying to tell him.

Slowly, awkwardly, he had clambered to his feet and staggered toward the window, somehow managing to avoid the bed or any other obstacle waiting to trip up an unsuspecting blind kid. The voices and odors of the city had drawn him like a sightless moth attracted to an invisible flame.

That loud splashing sound, he comprehended, was

just a faucet dripping after all. And it wasn't dripping here in his room, but somewhere else, outside the hospital and maybe a block or so away.

Matt didn't know why he could suddenly hear and smell so well, but he couldn't deny what he was experiencing. *Is it only my ears and nose,* he wondered, *or are the rest of my senses just as souped up?* Tentatively, he reached out and stroked the folded, cotton curtain hanging beside the window. To his amazement, his fingers could trace every wrinkle and stitch; the swath of drapery felt like a detailed three-dimensional map beneath his fingertips.

He ran a finger along the windowsill, picking up a smidgen of dust, then lifted the finger to his lips. His tongue touched the minute specks of dust and a smorgasbord of different tastes exploded in his mouth. Charcoal and mildew and salt and rust, plus umpteen other flavors he couldn't immediately identify (and wasn't sure he wanted to). His jaw dropped in astonishment. Who knew a tiny bit of grit contained so much variety?

His father ran into the room, calling out to him, but Matt couldn't tear himself away from the window, which now seemed like a portal to a whole new realm of experience. He had to force himself to turn around and face his dad, who registered to Matt as a familiar voice, accompanied by a distinctive scent and heartbeat.

Matt tried to grasp what was happening. He'd read that blind people often developed their other senses to compensate for the loss of their sight, but this was incredible! *I can't believe it,* he thought, even as he offered vague answers to his father's urgent questions. *This can't be normal, but what could have caused it?*

A snapshot flashed across his memory: the yellow warning label on that metal barrel: BIOHAZARD.

Was there something in those chemicals? he wondered. *Something that* changed *me?*

Matt turned back toward the window. He couldn't see the sun over the Hudson, but he felt its comforting warmth on his face. The radiant sunbeams dispelled the anxiety he had felt earlier, making the perpetual darkness much less forbidding.

A new day was dawning.

CHAPTER 3

Jack Murdock's fists pounded the heavy bag. Despite the bag gloves protecting his hands, the rapid-fire punches produced a series of satisfying smacks whenever his padded knuckles connected with the swinging canvas bag. *That's it,* he thought. *One after another, just like old times.*

With Matt's help, Jack had converted the roof of the run-down tenement building into a makeshift gymnasium. The seventy-pound punching bag hung on a chain beneath a huge wooden water tank, whose raised platform provided a welcome oasis of shade on this scorching summer afternoon. Bathed in a healthy sweat, Jack danced around the bag, working on his footwork while delivering multiple combinations of hooks and jabs.

It wasn't easy. This would be a grueling workout for a boxer of any age, and Jack was in his early forties. Already he could feel his energy evaporating, his reflexes growing sluggish, and he still had hours of training to go.

He was out of practice, too, having spent too much time doing Fallon's dirty work and not enough time conditioning his body and honing his skills. *Am I kidding myself?* he wondered gloomily, even as his fists slammed into the bag with steadily decreasing force. He caught himself dropping his guard and had to yank his arms back into position. *Can I still cut it in the ring?*

An egg timer, resting on the sticky, tar-papered rooftop, buzzed shrilly, calling a halt to the three-minute practice round. Jack gratefully stepped away from the hanging bag, taking a momentary breather. His brawny chest rose and fell heavily as he gasped in exhaustion. Sweat soaked through the back of his sleeveless white T-shirt, and he bent over wearily, resting his gloved hands on his knees. His arms felt as if they weighed a hundred pounds each, while his legs were as rubbery as overcooked spaghetti. *I can't do this,* he thought despairingly. *It's been too long.*

Resetting the timer, he glanced over at Matt, who was sitting on a weight bench a few yards away. A pair of newly acquired dark glasses rested on the boy's sunburned nose as he ran his fingers over the pages of a hardcover Braille textbook. Jack could see the obvious effort on his son's face, as Matt was forced to learn to read all over again.

Jack felt a stab of guilt. He had promised Matt, after the accident, that he was through with Fallon, that he was going to concentrate on turning his stalled fight career around. He'd meant it, too. But here he was, ready to throw in the towel before he'd fought a single bout!

Over at the weight bench, Matt slammed the textbook shut in frustration. Cursing under his breath, he looked ready to give up as well.

What kind of example am I setting him, Jack pondered, *if I don't give it everything I've got?*

The buzzer rang again, signaling the end of Jack's one-minute break. Father and son faced each other across the sun-baked urban roofscape, which they shared with scattered chimneys, skylights, TV antennae, and ventilation fans. A ragged beach towel was draped over the seat of the weight bench, to keep the imitation leather padding from getting too hot in the sun. Jack understood that, beneath the opaque glasses, Matt's eyes could not possibly see him, but he knew that his son was "watching" him nonetheless.

Even though Matt had a heightened sense of touch, learning to read Braille was an agonizing chore. Matt felt as though he'd been thrown back into nursery school, compelled to memorize his ABC's all over again. A month ago, before the accident, he'd been reading at a twelfth-grade level, well ahead of his years. He'd even started exploring the adult section of the library, enjoying the likes of Arthur Conan Doyle and H. G. Wells. Now, all of a sudden, he was back to "Dick and Jane" and Dr. Seuss.

It's not fair! he thought. Even the dumbest kid in his class could read better than he could now. *I'll never be able to catch up again.*

Junior high struck him as an insurmountable hurdle, college a total impossibility. Law school? *Hah!* Matt thought bitterly. *Don't make me laugh!*

A buzzer sounded, and Matt heard an almost inaudible groan escape his father as the aging boxer faced the daunting prospect of another three minutes at the bag. He could tell, by listening to Jack's heart rate and breathing, that his old man was almost worn out, after working himself pretty hard. The impact of his fists against the heavy bag had boomed like thunder, while the odor of his father's abundant perspiration overpowered even the choking exhaust fumes from the streets below. He was pushing himself to the limit, just to get back into fighting trim again.

Guess he's kind of starting over, too, Matt thought. His dad had promised not to work for Fallon anymore, and Matt believed him. Jack Murdock was going to be a boxer again, a champion, no matter how hard he had to train to get back into shape. *He's doing it for me,* Matt realized, which meant that perhaps some good had come from his accident on the docks.

The boy's expensive Braille reader, which he had slammed shut a few moments ago, rested on his lap, waiting for him, just as the impervious punching bag waited for his father. Pigeons cooed at the other end of the rooftop, and a warm summer breeze ruffled Matt's tousled light brown hair.

Dad's keeping his promise, Matt thought, his fingertips grazing the individual patterns of dots embossed on the reader's cover, spelling out the book's title in Braille. *How can I let him down now?*

Jack watched, his ragged breathing settling down a bit, as Matt sighed and opened up his textbook again, starting over right where he'd left off before. A smile crossed his rough-hewn face, and he turned back to the heavy bag with renewed determination.

Smack! Smack! Smack! A blistering one-two-three combination battered the punching bag as Jack "The Devil" Murdock found his second wind. Fists up, chin down, in a perfect fighting stance, he whaled on the defenseless bag as though he was going one-on-one with Eddie Fallon himself.

Right, left. Right, left, right. A jab, an uppercut, then a straight right punch with plenty of muscle behind it. Suddenly, Jack couldn't wait to get back in the ring again.

Ain't we a pair? he thought proudly, sneaking a peek at the blind boy at his studies.

A couple of fighters on the comeback trail . . .

Early morning. Matt practiced with his cane as he walked slowly up Ninth Avenue, concentrating on his technique while trying to ignore the embarrassed whispers and sighs of pity that followed him down the block. If only all those people feeling sorry for him knew just how well he could hear them. . . !

To be honest, Matt wasn't completely sure that, what with his ultrasensitive hearing and all, he really needed the cane. But he had decided early on not to worry his dad by revealing just how much the toxic chemicals had affected him. Besides, the last thing Matt wanted was for a bunch of nosy doctors to turn him into a human guinea pig. He'd had enough of hospitals and blood tests, thank you very much. All of which meant that he had to more or less go through the motions of being just an ordinary blind person, which meant wearing the dark glasses and walking with the cane.

A white cane, to be exact, although Matt had to take everyone's word for that. Colors were one thing his remaining senses were no good with. White was the traditional color for blind people's canes, though, so that was good enough for him.

He tapped his way down the sidewalk, swinging the cane from side to side, about two feet in front of him. The idea was to verify that an area was empty, then step into it. You tapped left as your right foot stepped forward, then tapped right as you stepped left. *Kind of like throwing a left jab to the head*, Matt thought, *to open up the chin to a hard right.*

Although his dad had forbidden him to fight, Matt had picked up a lot just by observing his dad all these years and by practicing when nobody was looking—before the accident, that is.

The tip of the cane tapped against an obstacle, and Matt recognized the glassy ring of an empty beer bottle, lying sideways on the pavement. Matt picked it up and thoughtfully carried it to the nearest wire trash container, where the discarded bottle joined an overflowing heap of refuse.

A car honked its horn, maybe five blocks away, but Matt didn't even flinch. He smiled, proud of the way of he had learned to filter out the nonstop clamor of the city. A few weeks ago, that unexpected honk would have caused him to jump out of his shoes. Now he could register the sound without overreacting. He had his supersenses under his control.

Or so he thought.

A city bus, racing a red light, roared through the intersection in front of Matt. The speeding bus sounded like a jet engine taking off. Matt staggered, overwhelmed by the deafening blast of noise. He fell backward over the curb and landed hard on his butt. His cane slipped from his fingers. Startled pedestrians gasped at his clumsiness, and Matt's face flushed red. Refusing all well-meaning offers of assistance, he retrieved his cane and climbed awkwardly to his feet, an angry grimace on his face.

Okay, he thought grimly. *Maybe I haven't got this problem completely licked yet.*

But I will!

*   *   *

The canvas floor was spattered with blood, most of it Jack's. Back in the ring again, for the first time in months, he was taking a beating up against the ropes. Frankie Miller, a hotshot heavyweight six years younger than Jack, had him cornered and on the defensive. Jack shelled up, ducking his head behind his upraised mitts, while Miller lambasted his ribs with a nonstop sequence of punishing body blows.

The crowd hooted and jeered as Jack tried to defend himself. There were no Devil fans in the arena, just a rowdy mob hungry for blood. The smoky atmosphere of the arena was suffused with naked aggression and impatience. This wasn't even the main event, Jack knew, as he felt Miller's pile-driver fists bruise his ribs—just a preliminary match to get the crowd warmed up. Miller landed another punch, and Jack bit down hard on his mouth guard to keep from crying out in pain.

I can't give up, he thought desperately. *If I can't go the distance tonight, I'll never get another bout again.*

He bounced off the ropes, sweeping his right arm out in a clumsy attempt to deflect an incoming body blow. The parry left his right side undefended, though, and he barely snapped his fist back in time to catch a speeding jab to his head. He counterpunched, striking out with his left, but Miller deftly dodged the blow with a sideways slip of his head.

The cocksure young fighter redoubled his attack, driving Jack back into the corner with a blinding flurry of jabs and punches. Jack took the abuse, blocking what blows he could, while waiting to be saved by the bell.

Don't give up! he prodded himself mercilessly. *Stay on your feet. . . .*

For Matt's sake.

*   *   *

Matt was back on the rooftop, struggling through the Braille textbook. After another exhausting training session, his dad had gone downstairs for a nap, but Matt figured he still had a few more hours of study left in him. School would be starting again in September, and Matt wanted to be ready for it.

The wind picked up, causing the speed bag mounted beneath the water tower, across from the heavy bag, to swing back and forth on its chain. The metallic squeak of the chain sounded like a chainsaw to the boy's ultrasensitive ears, which didn't make studying any easier.

Squeak.

Squeak.

The noise gnawed away at his nerves like some sort of Chinese water torture. Matt grimaced and tried to tune the aggravating distraction out, but the creaky chain kept on squealing with every stray gust of wind.

Squeak.

Squeak.

"Shut up!" Unable to take it anymore, Matt hurled his book at the swinging speed bag in frustration. The impulsively flung text flew across the rooftop like a missile—and smacked hard against the inflatable leather bag.

Hey! Matt thought, hearing the book rebound against the speed bag. Nobody could have been more astonished than he was at the pinpoint accuracy of his throw. *I nailed it!*

But how the heck did I do that?

He got up from the weight bench and approached the bag, leaving his white cane behind. When he estimated that he was only about a foot away from the bag, he raised his hands and tried to sense its exact location. His ears focused on the nearby squeaking while his outstretched fingers, which were only just learning how to read, tried to feel the sound waves stirring the air.

Yes! he thought excitedly. Standing there, alone on the roof, Matt discovered that, in a strange way, he could actually "see" the speed bag. The echoes bouncing off the sturdy timber legs of the water tank seemed to outline the teardrop-shaped leather bladder, adding to the impression created by the smell and sound of the punching bag: the erratic squeaking of the chain, the musky scent of the battered leather. Taken together, the varied clues combined to give Matt a clear mental image of the bag, shimmering behind the boy's shuttered eyes like liquid mercury.

It's almost like radar, he marveled. *Like a bat or a dolphin . . .*

Wham! He threw a punch at where he imagined the bag to be, and felt it rebound from the force of his blow. *Yes!* he thought, a grin breaking out over his face. He slugged the bag again and again, ignoring the protests of his unprotected knuckles. He worked the bag with both his fists and his hyperacute senses, until the once-circular bag was just a pitiful streak against his internal radar screen.

Miller was looking cocky, as if he had already won the match. *Don't count me out,* Jack thought, running on nothing but sheer pluck and cussedness, *until I'm flat on my back on the canvas.*

The younger boxer still had Jack trapped in the corner, but now Miller was dancing exuberantly on his heels, wasting energy while he showed off his snappy footwork. Jack blocked and parried, repelling

Miller's blows as best he could, while he reached down inside himself, marshaling what remained of his strength, while he waited for this overconfident punk to give him an opening.

There! Jack ducked Miller's right and countered with a left uppercut to Frankie's chin. The blow caught Miller by surprise, and Jack took advantage of the other fighter's confusion to block Miller's hasty counterpunch and roll off a smooth left hook. Powered by Jack's pivoting back and hips, the hook knocked Miller backward a few steps, almost toppling him onto the mat.

Now it was Miller's blood dripping onto the canvas, and Jack spotted a flicker of uncertainty in the young turk's once-cocksure eyes. *How 'bout that!* he thought triumphantly, feeling better than he had in months, since before he'd let Fallon turn him into hired muscle. *The old man's still got some fight in him!*

The bell finally rang, but it wasn't the Devil who needed saving. . . .

Matt waited at the street corner, at the intersection of Thirty-eighth and Ninth, for that roaring bus to zoom past again. Last time the thunder of the bus's passage had literally flattened him, but today Matt was ready for it.

Maybe.

He heard the bus approaching, less than a block away. Matt grabbed a lamp pole with one hand, bracing himself. Another pedestrian—from the man's gait and heart rate, Matt guessed he was over sixty—brushed by Matt on his way to the crosswalk. "Excuse me," the old man muttered vaguely.

Matt caught the inky smell of fresh newsprint, heard papers rustle nearby, and realized that the old guy had his nose buried in the morning paper. *The Daily News*, it smelled like.

The bus barreled toward them, sounding like a stampeding dinosaur to Matt's ears. Oblivious, the elderly newspaper junkie stepped off the curb.

No! Matt thought. Acting on instinct, he whipped out his cane, blocking the old man's path. A heartbeat later, the massive bus zipped past them at its usual breakneck pace, producing a wall of sound that crashed against Matt's dogged endurance and resolve. He gritted his teeth, standing firm in the face of the deafening racket, but he didn't flinch—and he didn't let the old man walk blindly into danger.

Seconds later, the bus was gone, leaving only reverberating echoes behind, and both he and the other man were still standing, completely unscathed. "My goodness! What—?" the old gent gasped, looking away from his paper at last. Matt felt the man's confused gaze upon him, seeing only a helpless blind child. "How on earth—?"

The light changed, and Matt heard the click of its circuitry, as well as the sound of traffic braking to a halt. He withdrew his cane, granting the old guy free access to the intersection, and calmly crossed the street.

The crowd was bigger this time. Jack wasn't just a warm-up act anymore. "Way to go, Devil!" someone hollered, and Jack realized he actually had fans these days. "Give 'em hell!"

I'll do my damnedest, he thought, facing off against his latest opponent. Dave "Madman" Mack was a major heavyweight contender, not nearly as green as poor Frankie Miller, whom Jack had ultimately beaten by a knockout. Jack knew it was going to take everything he had to stay in the ring with Mack, let alone beat him.

Mack came on strong, closing on Jack to fight inside the strike zone, but Jack held his ground, giving as good as he got. All those hours of training on the rooftop, performing for the pigeons, were definitely paying off; his speed and stamina were as strong as they'd ever been. Jack felt like his old self again, back in his prime.

Thanks to Matt, he thought gratefully, moving his head side to side to avoid Mack's inside punches. *He gave me a reason to turn my life around.* A surge of anger flared in his chest as he remembered the stricken look on Matt's face that day down by the docks. He took that fury and channeled it into a right-left combination that left Madman Mack reeling. *I'm never going to disappoint my son again!*

His fist flew like a battering ram and Mack ate leather. The poleaxed fighter crumpled to the mat, oblivious to the bellowing count of the ref:

". . . seven . . . eight . . . nine . . . ten!"

Mack stayed down, and the delirious audience roared in approval as the ref lifted Jack's glove in victory. The cheers of the crowd rained down on him like a cleansing shower, washing away all the mistakes and setbacks of the last few years.

"Devil! Devil! Devil!"

CHAPTER 4

Matt stood on the ledge, at the brink of the precipice. His dad was gone for the afternoon, so he had the rooftop to himself. Braille texts lay neglected on the tar-paper floor beside his father's weights and jump rope, while Matt eagerly tested the limits of his miraculous new abilities.

He reached out and felt the empty air in front of him. No guard rail protected him from the perilous drop. Matt heard the bustle of the traffic several stories below, and a flicker of doubt undercut his resolve. It was a *loooong* way down.

What if he fell? For a second, he imagined himself splattered all over the sidewalk, a hundred percent dead as well as blind. Then he remembered what his father had always told him.

You can do anything if you're not afraid.

Matt took a deep breath, steadied his nerves, then *cartwheeled* along the edge of the roof. *Yes!* he thought enthusiastically. Instead of falling to his death, he rotated faster and faster, relying on his newfound radar senses to keep him from disaster. Matt couldn't believe how easy it was. *This is fantastic!*

He landed on his feet at the northwest corner of the roof, his heart pounding in exhilaration. The toe of his sneaker probed the corner, finding the top end of a broken rain gutter that plummeted four stories down to the rooftop next door.

"Hmm," Matt murmured. A crazy idea occurred to him. It was insane, but almost too audacious to resist. He crouched beside the top of the gutter and tapped it with his finger, listening to the echo of the aluminum. He felt the vibrations with the palm of his hand. *Would the hanging gutter support his weight?*

Probably.

Don't be afraid, he heard his father coaching him.

He stepped forward, placing one foot upon the top of the gutter. He licked his lips nervously, took another deep breath, and pushed off from the ledge.

Whooooosh!

Matt slid down the gutter like an Extreme snowboarder. His blood was singing in his ears, and a hot wind blew against his face as he zoomed down the rickety slide. A high-pitched whoop burst from his lungs. Gulls and pigeons bolted from their perches in alarm, startled by the boy's unprecedented descent. The soot-blackened roof of the brownstone next door rushed up at him like an oncoming elevator, yet Matt was too thrilled to be concerned. He tried to bail out as he reached the bottom, but he was going way too fast.

Laughing hysterically, he tumbled ass over elbows onto the roof below. His dark glasses went flying from his nose, exposing the wide blue eyes underneath.

Matt lay sprawled on the roof for maybe a minute or two. Then he propped himself up and wiped the soot from his raw, reddened hands. His forehead and palms were scraped, and blood dripped from his nose. One knee of his faded blue jeans had been torn open and he'd skinned the leg beneath.

But Matt was smiling. He thrust his fists into the air in a victory salute.

I wasn't afraid, Dad! he thought proudly. *I wasn't afraid!*

Tonight's the night, Jack thought, as he carefully wrapped his hands in the locker room of the Midtown Civic Center. He pulled the protective strips of cloth tight around his thumb and knuckles, then tied them off at his wrist with Velcro. He flexed his fingers experimentally, making sure the wraps weren't too snug, then smiled at the thought of just how far he'd come.

Six fights, six unexpected victories, had led up to this. He was the odds-on favorite in a televised big-time match against his toughest opponent to date: "Gentleman" John Romita, a former *Sports Illustrated* cover boy and gold-medal Olympic champion.

A few months ago, Jack would never have dreamed he'd be fighting the likes of Romita, let alone be favored to win. But that was before he beat the odds by knocking out Frankie Miller in the fourth round. Now his scrapbook was bulging with gushing articles praising his unexpected comeback. "An inspiration to aging baby boomers everywhere," the *New York Times* had written, while the *Post* had raved, "Give 'The Devil' his due. Jack Murdock has proven that second chances are always possible, if you've got the heart and guts to go for them."

Jack's only regret was that Matt couldn't read the laudatory clippings or see the dramatic news photos of him standing in triumph over the fallen bodies of

Miller, Mack, Robbins, and the rest. *I wonder if there are any fight magazines published in Braille*, he mused, making a mental note to look into the matter if tonight's bout went as well as he hoped. *I wish Matt could see me fighting for him, just one more time.*

Matt was in the audience tonight, Jack knew. Even though he wouldn't be able to see anything, Matt had insisted on showing up for tonight's big fight, and Jack hadn't had the heart to say no. *I wouldn't be here if not for Matt*, he thought. *He deserves to be on hand when, God willing, our hopes and dreams come true.*

All Jack had to do was beat Romita tonight, and they would be set for life. He'd have a shot at the title then, and the big-money endorsements and pay-per-view deals.

I can do it, he thought confidently. He got up off of the bench and threw a couple of practice punches at the pungent locker room air. He'd never been in better shape, or better motivated to win. "Just you wait, Matt," he whispered. He had let his son down for too long; tonight was the night he buried the past and became the man he owed it to his son to be. "I'll make you proud of me."

"Talking to yourself, Murdock?" A sarcastic voice intruded on his dreams of glory. "Don't tell me you're punch-drunk already."

Jack spun around in surprise; preoccupied, he hadn't heard the locker room door swing open. His expression darkened as he saw who it was.

"Fallon," he snarled, all but spitting out the name.

Eddie Fallon, a.k.a. the Fixer, was a cunning-looking sharpie wearing an expensive pin-striped suit. His silver hair was slicked back elegantly, and his cuff links and tie pin glimmered with twenty-four-karat gold. He strolled across the locker room toward Jack, flanked by two glowering thugs whose surly scowls seemed permanently imprinted on their features.

"Jack," Fallon said with a smirk. "It's been a while. . . ."

Not long enough, Jack thought. He wasn't interested in making clever conversation. "I don't work for you anymore," he said bluntly.

Fallon sighed theatrically. "Jack, Jack—you never stopped." He shook his head like a schoolteacher dealing with a particularly slow-witted pupil. "Did you really think you won those fights on your own? Miller, Mack, Bendis—they're all my fighters. Just like you."

Jack felt as if a rug had been yanked out from beneath his feet. *Of course!* he realized, unable to deny the truth of Fallon's smug declaration. Reality crashed down on him like a crowbar, and he dropped onto the bench, a beaten man. *How could I have been such a dope?* he castigated himself mercilessly. *They don't call him the Fixer for nothing!*

Fallon smiled, like a crocodile savoring a bloody meal. "You're taking a dive in the first round, Jack. No arguments." He raised an impeccably manicured hand in anticipation of an angry protest, but Jack was too devastated to make a fuss. "Think about your boy, Jack. That poor blind kid." His eyes glittered as coldly as his polished cuff links. "Shame if he ended up an orphan, too." He turned his back on Jack and, accompanied by the two looming gorillas, headed for the exit. He paused in the doorway for one last parting shot. "I'm sure you'll do the right thing."

Jack just sat on the bench, staring in silence at the uncaring concrete floor.

* * *

He was just as silent later that evening as his handlers, who undoubtedly worked for Fallon as well, led him from the locker room to the ring. His trademark boxing robe, with its flashy crimson satin and pointed devil horns, hung on his muscular frame like a shroud. Peering out from beneath its hood, Jack mournfully searched the bleachers, quickly spotting Matt sitting at ringside. Matt held a transistor radio to his ear, to listen to the on-the-air fight coverage, and his white cane was clutched between his knees. The thrilled look on Matt's face, as the crowd greeted Jack's arrival with hearty cheers and applause, broke Jack's heart.

I wanted you to be proud of me, he thought bleakly. It was all he could do to put one step ahead of the other as he climbed into the waiting ring.

Fallon was waiting, too, only a few seats away from Matt. Ironically, only his retinue of surly bodyguards separated the Mob boss from the unsuspecting boy. Fallon gave Jack a knowing wink, and the unhappy boxer wondered bitterly just how much the Fixer stood to make on tonight's betting. *Probably more than Matt and I could spend in a year . . .*

Busy hands peeled his robe off his shoulders and thrust a mouth guard between his jaws. The bell rang, and Jack plodded into the ring, all his recent accolades and accomplishments ripped to pieces by Fallon's sly insinuations. Jack felt as though he'd been roughly awakened from an impossible dream.

John Romita was ten years younger than Jack, and light-years faster. His mind enveloped by a cloud of choking despair, Jack barely saw him coming. The crowd gasped in astonishment as Romita hit Jack with a vicious upper cut that dropped the Devil to the mat in a matter of minutes.

His skull ringing, his bruised profile flat against the canvas, Jack wondered if he should even bother trying to lift his head. Fallon had said in the first round. *Well, it can't get much firster than this.*

". . . two, three, four, five . . ."

Through a fog, Jack heard the ref counting him out, but he never wanted to get up again. *Maybe if I just lay here,* he thought, *the world will go away and let me die.*

Then a single voice cut through the turmoil and misery. "Dad!" Matt yelled from only a few yards away. "C'mon, Dad! Get up!"

Unable to ignore his son's spirited cries, Jack raised his head, gazing through bleary eyes at Matt's opaque black glasses. For once he was glad Matt couldn't see him, gasping and bleeding on the canvas like the washed-up loser he was.

"That's it, Dad!" Matt urged. It didn't occur to Jack to wonder how Matt knew he had lifted his head. His son's cane clattered to the floor of the arena as the boy leapt to his feet, crying out at the top of his lungs, "You can do it! Get up!"

A couple seats away, Fallon glanced irritably at Matt, then fixed a warning look on Jack. *In the first round,* he mouthed silently, his baleful expression conveying an unspoken threat. Jack felt a cold hand grip his heart as he acknowledged what was sure to happen to him if he defied the Fixer's orders. *I'd be as good as dead,* he knew, swallowing hard. Even with his life and career going down the tubes, Jack was afraid to die.

But what had he always told Matt?

Don't be afraid. You can do anything if you're not afraid.

Matt needed to believe that if he was going to overcome his handicap. Jack knew now that his hopes of the big time, of the championship and all that entailed, were just the pipe dreams of a deluded old pug, but maybe there was still one last thing he could provide for his son.

A good example.

". . . seven, eight, nine . . ."

Jack lurched to his feet before the ref could finish his count. The crowd howled with delight, and Jack saw a flash of genuine annoyance on Romita's handsome face. *Guess he figured he wouldn't have to bother putting me down for real,* Jack thought, raising his mitts before his face and taking the fight back to Romita. He stampeded into the younger fighter's strike zone, tossing jabs and counterpunches at Romita like they were going out of style. *Probably afraid I'm going to muss up his cover-boy good looks.*

The Devil intended to do a whole more than that. Romita danced in to finish him off, but in his impatience, the younger boxer wasn't watching for Jack's legendary left hook. The Devil's knuckles slammed into Romita's jaw, catching him off guard. Blood flew from the onetime Olympic champion's pulverized bottom lip.

Then Romita made his big mistake: he got mad. *How dare this overaged has-been put up a fight!* his body language positively screamed. *Why didn't he just fall down like he was supposed to!*

Romita's face flushed with anger, and he charged Jack like an enraged bull, flailing wildly with his fists. *Bad move, kid,* Jack thought, calmer and more in control than ever before, knowing that he had nothing left to lose except his son's respect. *You don't get angry in a prizefight. Anger makes you sloppy.*

Jack blocked Romita's frenzied blows with ease. The furious young fighter left himself wide open, and Jack took advantage of his carelessness to pummel Romita's body with combination after combination until Romita looked as woozy as a Hell's Kitchen wino after an all-night binge.

"Way to go, Dad!" Matt screamed from the bleachers, and Jack risked a lightning peek at the boy's ecstatic face. Not even those damn dark glasses could hide his son's overflowing excitement and pride. *This is for you, Matt,* he thought.

He didn't look at Fallon.

Time to wrap this up, Jack decided. He dropped his left, luring his opponent in. As Romita lunged forward, taking the bait, Jack bent his knees, dipping beneath Romita's headlong punch and swinging up from below with a rocketing upper jab that knocked Romita right off his feet!

The young boxer hit the canvas with a gratifying thud. Jack stood by, fists raised and ready, until the ref counted all the way to ten. Then a sweaty hand grabbed Jack by the wrist, raising his right hand in triumph.

"And the winneeer . . . Jack 'The Devil' Murdock!"

Except for Fallon and his goons, the entire stadium erupted in a thundering roar. Matt ran up to the edge of the ring, and Jack eagerly pulled him through the ropes. A frowning handler threw Jack his red robe, and he draped The Devil's garb, horns and all, over his son's head and shoulders. He hoisted Matt on his shoulder as they accepted the boisterous cheers and applause of the enthused crowd.

Row after row of hardcore fight buffs gave him a

standing ovation, but the only fan Jack cared about was the one sitting on his shoulder. Jack cherished these magical moments with his son, knowing they were his last.

Later, after the crowd went home, Jack found himself surprisingly alone. His handlers, the fight officials, even the press guys cleared out of the locker room fast. *Guess everybody knows what was supposed to go down tonight,* he realized. *Nobody wants to get too close to a walking dead man.*

He took one last look around the empty locker room. He thought of Matt, who was waiting for him out in front of the arena. In theory, the boy should be safe; after Fallon made an example of Jack, he'd have no reason to go after Matt.

Good-bye, son, he thought solemnly. He hated the idea of leaving the poor kid alone in the world, but there was no other way to keep Matt safe; as long as Jack was of use to people like the Fixer, Matt would always be in danger. *Take care, kiddo. Study hard and don't forget what I taught you.* Emotion tightened his throat, and his tired eyes grew wet. *Hope your life turns out better than your old man's.*

There was no point in putting things off any longer. Jack left the civic center via the rear exit, stepping into a grimy back alley that smelled like a toilet. A black limousine with tinted windows waited in the alley, looking incongruously elegant amidst the greasy puddles, broken bottles and discarded cigarette butts littering the pavement. Spray-painted graffiti defaced the walls, while a rusty green Dumpster, its lid almost completely caved in, failed to contain all the garbage spilling onto the blacktop.

Jack made no attempt to flee the alley. "Go on,"

he said gruffly, addressing the limo's occupants. The purr of the car's engine was deceptively gentle. "Get it over with."

A car door slid open, and Jack gulped as the limousine rose a full six inches off its wheels, as though disgorging the weight of an entire gang.

His dad's robe was way too big for Matt, but he didn't care. He figured he must be presenting quite a peculiar sight—a blind kid wearing an oversized devil costume, complete with horns—but who cared what anyone else thought? *Dad wiped up the floor with Romita!* he thought proudly, reliving that glorious moment. Grinning broadly, he threw an enthusiastic punch at the warm summer air, mimicking his dad's match-winning upper cut. *I knew he could do it!*

Matt paced back and forth in front of the civic center, waiting for his dad. His cane tapped the sidewalk a bit more emphatically than usual. Too bad he couldn't tell his dad just how closely he'd managed to follow the fight; with his radar senses, Matt had kept track of every single punch and parry, even with the distracting clamor of the cheering crowd. He was getting better and better at perceiving specific targets through all the white noise out there.

Several minutes passed, and Matt started to wonder what was keeping his dad. He had heard the reporters and fight officials leave a while ago. It was getting late, and Matt was looking forward to celebrating his dad's victory, maybe over a root beer float or a chocolate sundae.

Smash! Krak!

Without warning, the unmistakable sounds of violence drove all thought of sugary desserts from his mind. With his heightened hearing, he couldn't miss the sickening racket of flesh and blood being pounded on by both heavy knuckles and heavier steel. *What the heck?* Matt wondered. At first he thought maybe another bout had started inside the arena, but no, this was no regulated athletic competition; this was some poor sap being walloped within an inch of his life—and beyond.

Matt hesitated, unsure what to do. Should he call for help?

Then he heard his father groan.

"Dad?" Matt's heart throbbed loudly in his chest. *"Dad!"*

Clutching his cane like a weapon, Matt ran madly toward the alarming noises. The crimson robe flapped behind him like a superhero's cape as he raced around the corner of the civic center, effortlessly avoiding the parking meters and fire hydrants in his path.

Every sense he had left was focused on finding a way into the alley where his dad was being beaten. His blood froze as he heard the crashing blows fall silent—and a heavy body collapse onto unforgiving asphalt. *No!* Matt thought, terrified that he was already too late.

A cruel chuckle reached his ears, followed by a deep, unfamiliar voice that made Darth Vader sound like a soprano. "You should have stayed down," the voice said sonorously.

Matt heard something light and insubstantial—a flower?—fall onto a groaning mass of human tissue whose heartbeat was fading fast. A powerful automotive engine revved up, and Matt listened to an unseen vehicle pulling away, its wheels splashing through muddy puddles and possibly other liquids as well. The coppery tang of spilled blood assaulted his nostrils, adding to the boy's growing fear and anxiety.

His sneakers carried him down the sidewalk, past the side of the civic center, until, finally, he sensed an opening to his left. He swung out with his cane, confirming that there was a gap there, and ran into what smelled like a dirty, trash-strewn alley. He heard the mysterious automobile disappear out the other end of the deserted back street.

"Dad!" His attention was riveted by the demolished carcass lying motionlessly on the ground. A puddle of blood spread outward from the body of the fallen heavyweight. Even over the rotting garbage, fresh blood, and fading exhaust fumes, he recognized his father's scent. "Oh, my God—Dad!"

There was no heartbeat.

The horned robe, emblazoned with the name DEVIL MURDOCK, slipped from Matt's shoulders, fluttering in the breeze like some sort of demonic specter. Matt dropped to his knees next to his father, lifting Jack's head and shoulders and cradling them against his chest. His father's blood soaked through the knees of Matt's best pair of blue jeans, and the dead man's skull sagged against the boy's shoulder. "No, Dad, no . . ."

His fingers sought out his father's face—to no avail. Matt knew every plane and angle of his dad's face by heart, but there was nothing left to recognize, only a shapeless lump of wet, pulpy meat. Shaking fingertips searched for some trace of his dad's familiar features, but this was a stranger's face, barely even identifiable as human. "I can't—I can't see you, Dad!" he sobbed, rendered blind once more by the grisly mess that had been made of Jack Murdock's face. "I can't see you. . . ."

He hugged his dad tighter, unwilling to let go, and was surprised when a solitary flower dropped into his lap. *A rose,* he discovered with a sniff—left behind by his father's killer?

Rage mingled with grief in Matt's tortured heart. He squeezed the rose in his fist, the thorns biting into the palm of his hand. A drop of his own blood fell onto the floor of the alley, mixing with the gory puddle beneath Jack's body.

The Devil's red robe lay on the blacktop, only slightly out of reach.

CHAPTER 5

Nearly twenty years later . . .

"Ladies and gentlemen of the jury, we have come here today to seek the truth. We have come here today to seek *justice*."

Carved in marble, Justice herself looked down upon the air-conditioned courtroom. A sculpted blindfold symbolically covered her eyes, while she held up the scales of justice in one hand and the sword of retribution in the other.

Attorney Matthew Murdock could not see the chiseled goddess, but he knew she was there. After all, they had a lot in common. . . .

A dark red cane in hand, he stood facing the jury. From their heartbeats and mild breathing, he judged that he still had their full attention and that none of the jury members had started to doze off yet. Then again, this trial was just beginning.

The courtroom itself, one of many at the New York County Courthouse, was sparsely populated. Aside from the participants and the various officers of the court, there was no one on hand to witness this particular trial. No curious reporters. No concerned loved ones. Matt found it sad that such an important event in his client's life held so little interest for the rest of the world. With luck, the jury would not prove equally indifferent.

"Lenny Bruce once said that, in the halls of justice, the only justice is out in the halls. But you can change all that. Because today *you* are justice."

To his right, seated at a long table facing the judge's bench, was his partner, Franklin "Foggy" Nelson, and their client, Angela Sutton. Angela, according to Foggy, was a tough-looking woman whose hard life and years of substance abuse made her seem much older than her years. She was still attractive, Foggy said, but no one would mistake her for an ingenue. Matt heard Angela catch her breath as he got to the heart of their case.

"The criminal case against Jose Quesada was dismissed due to the defending officer's failure to read the defendants their Miranda rights. This civil suit is the victim's only recourse."

Matt paced back and forth in front of the jury box, punctuating his remarks with every tap of his cane.

"But Angela Sutton doesn't seek damages. She seeks the truth. And the chance to get on with her life."

He listened carefully to the men and women comprising the jury. No one was yawning or shifting restlessly in his seat. He had kept their attention, but had he elicited any sympathy for his client?

That was harder to tell. Even with radar senses.

Jose Quesada was a short, pugnacious pit bull of a man, with serious Mob connections. His hairline had receded almost to nonexistence, and he wore a tailored blue suit. Seated upon the witness stand, he faced Matt's cross-examination with infuriating calm. He wasn't even breaking a sweat.

"Mr. Quesada," Matt began, "please state for the court the sequence of events leading up to the night of June thirtieth."

"I believe I've already covered this," Quesada said. His tone was polite and professional; clearly, he'd been carefully coached by expensive lawyers.

"I'd like to hear it from you directly," Matt insisted.

Quesada sighed, bored. Matt didn't need to see his face to know how unworried this defendant was. "I stopped by Josie's Bar for a few drinks after work. . . ."

As the accused rapist spoke, Matt focused on Quesada's heartbeat, listening carefully for any irregularity. Josie's Bar, he knew, was a notorious hangout for the city's worst criminal elements.

"Angela was closing up and asked if I wanted to stick around for some fun." Quesada shrugged his shoulders, as if the alleged encounter was no big deal. "Who was I to say no?"

The thug's heart kept on beating steadily.

"Everything that happened after that was entirely consensual."

There! Matt thought. Quesada's heart skipped a beat, and Matt nodded grimly. *Busted!* he silently accused the defendant. *You're lying and you know it.*

Not for the first time, Matt regretted that his radar senses were inadmissible as evidence. "Mr. Quesada," he said sternly, "you do understand that perjury is a federal offense?"

Quesada didn't give an inch. "I know what happened."

"I'm sure you do," Matt agreed sarcastically.

Over at the plaintiff's table, Foggy tapped a stack of photos. Matt traced the sound and scooped the pictures up before passing them out to the jury. The irony of a blind man relying on photographic evidence was not lost on him.

"These are photographs," he explained, "of the victim taken at Mercy Hospital that night." He gave the jury a moment to absorb the grisly details of the photos before returning to his cross-exam. "I wonder," he asked Quesada, "did she ask you for the cuts and bruises as well?"

Matt could practically hear the defendant smirking. "She enjoyed every minute of it. . . ."

A few yards away, Angela choked back angry tears. Matt heard Foggy give her a comforting pat on the shoulder. His partner was good with clients that way; he had a big heart and a reassuring manner, like a friendly, energetic Saint Bernard.

Matt wanted to wring the smirk out of Quesada's smarmy voice with his bare hands, but settled for giving him a warning—for now. "For your sake, Mr. Quesada, I hope justice is found here today," he said darkly, his face as cold and stony as the marble goddess presiding over the courtroom. "Before justice finds you."

Several discouraging hours later, Matt and Foggy trudged down the steps outside the courthouse. The sun was setting and the sidewalk vendors, who catered to the court's teeming workforce and reluctant visitors, were already shutting down their carts.

Foggy did his best to console Matt. "Look, we knew it was a risk going in—" he began.

"Why?" Matt asked bitterly. "Because she's from the Kitchen and not the Upper East Side?"

"Because she had a drug problem," Foggy said quietly. He wasn't being judgmental, just realistic. A stocky young man, perhaps a tad overweight, he had curly black hair and a mild demeanor. He shrugged his shoulders sadly beneath the starched fabric of a conservative gray suit. "Juries don't like their victims to be flawed."

Matt knew Foggy was right on the money, but that didn't make their loss any less galling. His blood boiled on behalf of Angela Sutton, who had just been brutalized all over again. The blatant miscarriage of justice gnawed at his mind.

"Jesus, speak of the devil," Foggy murmured. Matt sensed the presence of Jose Quesada even before Foggy alerted him. The victorious mobster, his heavy cologne as distinctive as fingerprints, paused at the bottom of the steps, in front of a waiting town car. He gave Matt and Foggy a cocky wave, his hand slicing through the humid air currents, before getting into the car and being chauffeured away.

A free man.

Foggy sighed and shook his head. Matt knew Foggy wasn't any happier about letting Angela Sutton down than he was. "You wanna get drunk?" he asked Matt glumly.

Matt appreciated his partner's attempts to raise his spirits. He and Foggy had been best friends ever since they first dormed together back at Columbia University. Foggy was the most decent, good-natured, unassuming guy Matt knew; he often envied his partner's simple, uncomplicated temperament. Unlike Matt, Foggy had no deep-rooted secrets or burning obsessions.

"Yeah," Matt admitted. Part of him wanted nothing better than to go out drinking with Foggy, to try to forget their demoralizing loss in the courtroom. "But not tonight."

Another part of Matt, more fierce and unrelenting, had other plans.

"I've got work to do."

That night, on a lonely rooftop overlooking Hell's Kitchen, witnessed only by the uncaring moon, an unlikely transformation occurred. Matt Murdock, attorney-at-law, exchanged his business suit for a tight-fitting sheath of dark red leather, his opaque glasses for a cowl with ominous red blinds over his eyes. A pair of two-inch horns, protruding from his brow, gave him a literally demonic appearance, while an empty holster was strapped to his right thigh. Leather boots and gloves, the same dark crimson as his jacket and trousers, completed the striking and fearsome uniform, transmuting the blind young lawyer into . . . Daredevil, the man without fear.

Even Matt Murdock's ubiquitous red cane underwent a dramatic metamorphosis. With only a few, crisp, efficient motions, Daredevil converted the blind man's cane into a lethal-looking billy club, gripped tightly in his fist.

He was ready now.

As always, he reflected on the slippery reasoning behind this nocturnal masquerade. Matt Murdock had always promised his father not to fight, to use his brains instead of his fists, and Matt had kept that promise.

But Daredevil had made no such vow.

Trust a lawyer to find a loophole, he thought, behind Daredevil's intimidating mask. He stepped onto the ledge, undeterred by the twenty-story drop in front of him. Solid concrete waited over two hundred feet

below; to jump from this height you'd have to be
blind.

Or fearless.

Or both.

Daredevil swan-dived off the ledge. Gravity seized
him as he plummeted toward the pavement. Ignoring
the rush of air against his face, he reached out with
his senses. His sensitive ears, hearing clearly through
the leather cowl, listened to the *whoosh-whoosh-whoosh*
of nearby fire escapes as he hurtled past them, accelerating at a rate of over thirty feet per second
squared.

Extending his arm, he pressed a hidden stud on
his billy club.

Cha-chick!

The metal claws of a grappling hook shot out and
caught the iron rungs of a fire escape, breaking his
fall like a bungee cord! Daredevil pressed off against
the front of the twenty-story skyscraper, leaping over
a busy downtown street onto the roof of a seedy
tavern across the way. The thundering chords of
heavy-metal music leaked through the roof from the
gin mill below.

Not even winded by his dizzying plunge, Daredevil crept across the rooftop as silently as a ghost.

CHAPTER 6

The interior of Josie's Bar was a cavernous space, housing the worst cutthroats and criminals the city had to offer. Ceiling fans the size of jet propellers spun high above the floor, fighting a losing battle against smoke, alcohol fumes, and stale air. Thick steel beams supported the vaulted ceiling, crisscrossing several feet above the heads of Josie's unsavory clientele. A row of pool tables ran down the center of the saloon, between the booths lining the western wall and the well-stocked bar to the east. A television set, with the sound turned down, was mounted above one corner of the bar, while a jukebox blared noisily nearby.

It was a busy night at Josie's, crammed with mobsters, gang-bangers, bikers, murderers, rapists, and thieves. Everyone present was either drunk, wired on meth, or both.

Jose Quesada felt right at home.

Seated at the bar, celebrating his victory over that bitch Sutton and her do-gooder lawyers, he smiled as Josie, the no-nonsense owner of this particular bucket of blood, poured him a glass of tequila. He dropped a match into the drink and downed the flaming shot in one gulp. *Too bad that stuck-up lawyer,*

Murdock, was blind, he thought. *I would've liked to have seen the look in his eyes when the jury let me off.*

In the excitement, no one noticed a stealthy figure creep along one of the metal beams overhead, like a panther silently stalking its prey.

Having entered the bar via a convenient skylight, Daredevil surveyed the crowded gin mill with his hypersenses. The noxious mixture of sweat, smoke, and motorcycle exhaust offended his nostrils, which only darkened his already virulent mood. His keen ears sorted through the babel of raucous voices, clinking glasses, and colliding billiard balls in search of one particular voice.

A burst of harsh laughter came from the direction of the bar, and Daredevil nodded in recognition. "To the justice system!" Jose Quesada crowed jubilantly, downing another shot of tequila. Daredevil bared his teeth in vengeful anticipation and made his way across the ceiling beams toward the bar. Had anyone looked up from below, they would have seen Daredevil's horns silhouetted against the moonlit skylights—like an enraged bull ready to charge.

Gripped in his fist, Daredevil's billy club bore the metallic face of a devil matched with the cherubic face of an angel on its burnished stainless steel. Daredevil scowled. The blasting heavy-metal music was hell on his senses. He quickly aimed the billy club at the jukebox and pressed its hidden trigger. The far end of the club shot across the saloon like a missile, smashing into the targeted mechanism, which abruptly fell silent. *That's better*, he thought; he needed to completely control every element of his environment in battle.

A high-performance nylon cable connected the

billy club's top half to the handle still clutched in Daredevil's grip. An instant later, the cable retracted, yanking the club back into one piece. Daredevil felt the weight of his weapon resting securely in his hand. He cast a long shadow across the bar, veiling Quesada in darkness.

The startled felon gulped nervously; he had heard rumors about a masked vigilante haunting the Kitchen, but he had never taken them seriously before. Now, as a pair of gleaming red eyes peered down at him like twin windows into Hell, an unaccustomed chill ran down Quesada's spine. Could this actually be . . . Daredevil?

"What do you want?" Quesada demanded, his bellicose tone undermined by the tremor in his voice. Groping under his jacket, he drew out a .44-magnum pistol. A scowling biker, seated one stool over, also pulled a gun on the costumed intruder. The flaunted firepower bolstered Quesada's confidence. "I said," he repeated, more steadily this time, "what do you want?"

A cold smile appeared upon the devil's face. "Justice."

Without warning, Daredevil fired his billy club again. It slammed into Quesada's face, breaking his jaw, then ricocheted into the gun-toting biker's nose. The sound of bone and cartilage shattering was music to Daredevil's ears, as was the thud of their weapons hitting the sawdust-covered floor. The club rebounded back into the hero's hand, leaving two threats disposed of in as many seconds.

Angry shouts and curses swarmed at Daredevil as the saloon's irate patrons reacted to his attack on Quesada and the biker. Daredevil didn't wait for the assorted hoods to come after him; instead he jumped eagerly into the mob, ready to deal out all the punishment these scum had coming to them—and more. His fists, boots, elbows, and club wreaked havoc on the crowd, while his radar senses alerted him to every potential threat, almost as if he had eyes in the back of his head.

Not bad for a blind man, he thought.

His hybrid fighting style, developed through countless hours of practice and training, mixed traditional martial arts with hardcore street fighting. Daredevil showed no mercy. Brutal punches sent blood and teeth flying. Lightning kicks shattered knees and dislocated shoulders. Snarled threats and obscenities gave way to pain-filled moans and whimpers.

The Devil had come to Josie's and there was hell to pay.

His ears caught the hum of the fluorescent lights hanging over the pool tables. The flickering glow of the lights was wasted on him. *Let's save some electricity,* he thought, even as his senses locked onto three bloodthirsty bikers clutching broken bottles in their fists. *Jack Daniel's,* Daredevil determined with a sniff. He grinned wolfishly as an idea occurred to him.

Clutching his fractured jaw in agony, Jose Quesada watched in dismay as Daredevil demolished a barful of hardened crooks and bikers. He couldn't believe that one man could take on the usual night's crowd at Josie's and live, let alone come out on top, but the masked devil was beating the crap out of the roughest crowd in the city.

What's he after me for? Quesada wondered anxiously, remembering the way Daredevil had looked down at him at the bar, his red eyes burning into

the frightened mobster's soul. There had been no
question as to who the devil had come for, only why.
Justice? he thought furiously. *Whose justice? What the
hell did I do to him anyway?*

A flicker of hope sparked in his chest as he saw
three leather-clad bikers advancing on Daredevil,
each brandishing a broken bottle. Perhaps Hell's
Angels would save him from this rampaging devil,
ripping through the invader's own leathers with
blades of jagged glass. Quesada held his breath, praying that someone would kill Daredevil before the
seemingly unstoppable vigilante came after him
again.

His desperate prayers went unanswered as, undeterred by the razor-sharp glass, Daredevil leapt
across the bar and triple-kicked the bottles out of the
bikers' hands. The dislodged weapons spun in the
air and Quesada looked on in horror, seeing events
unfold almost in slow motion, as Daredevil kicked
the flying bottles again, propelling them straight into
the lights hanging over the pool tables.

Craaash!

Sparks and broken glass rained down on the
whiskey-soaked tables, every one of which instantly
burst into flame. The overhead lights shorted and
sparked, creating a strobe-light effect that made it all
but impossible for Quesada to keep an eye on what
was happening. "Hey! Watch out!" Strident voices
added to the confusion as the strobing lights, smoke,
and fire disoriented everyone in the bar.

Except Daredevil.

Oblivious to failing lights, he smiled in satisfaction
as he heard the confused bikers lash out at each other
by mistake. *Where is Quesada?* he wondered, having

not forgotten his primary objective. His radar senses locked onto the wounded rapist, whose heart was pounding like a machine gun, not far from his over-turned bar stool. Only a couple dozen crazed hood-lums stood between Daredevil and his prey.

No problem, he thought. He rose from behind the flaming pool table like a demon come directly from Hell. He snapped his billy club together and spun it around like a bo staff. Bodies went flying left and right as the spinning shaft cleared a path for Dare-devil through the chaotic scene.

A skinhead, too hyped up to be afraid, whipped out a knife and slashed at the rotating staff. Dare-devil deftly pulled the billy club apart, using the weighted ends like escrima sticks to batter the skin-head's crudely shaven skull. The knife-wielding goon collapsed onto the floor, unconscious before he even hit the ground.

Is that it? Daredevil wondered. Fun was fun, but he was getting impatient to finish his business with Quesada. He strode across the tavern, only to find his way blocked by four belligerent Hell's Angels. They glared at him with homicidal intensity, their meaty fists clenched and ready. "You mess with one biker," one of them informed him gruffly, spitting onto the sawdust-strewn floor, "you mess with all of us!"

I don't have time for this, Daredevil thought. With his fists wrapped tightly around each end of his billy club, he cross-threw the versatile weapon, whose di-verging ends rebounded off the saloon walls like boomerangs on speed before taking out all four Angels in a matter of seconds.

Both ends of the billy club sprang back into Dare-devil's fists. He didn't even look down as he stepped over the bikers' prostrate bodies. His clashes with the skinhead and the bikers had barely slowed him, and never for a moment had he lost track of Quesada. Over the pitiful gasps and groans of the brutalized bar patrons, he heard Quesada's breath rattling through the terrified crook's broken jaw.

He might as well be wearing a bell around his neck, Daredevil thought, a merciless smile on his lips. Quesada was crawling over the broken bodies of his fellow crooks as he clumsily tried to get away from the crimson devil pursuing him. In the dim, sporadic lighting, he stumbled against the edge of a smoldering pool table, bruising his elbow. A choked-off yelp of pain rang as clear as a pealing church bell to Daredevil's hypersensitive ears. *Forget it, Jose,* he thought grimly. *You're not getting away from me tonight.*

Angela Sutton's bitter sobs echoed through Daredevil's memory as he quickened his pace. Then another sound demanded his attention: the distinctive *cha-chunk* of a steel magazine being loaded into an automatic rifle.

Even with radar senses, he couldn't dodge hundreds of bullets at once. . . .

Daredevil reacted instantly. Raising his arm, he fired his grappling hook into one of the industrial ceiling fans above the bar. The spinning fan yanked Daredevil off his feet as it wound the hook's cable around itself. Daredevil used the fan's momentum to flip up past the whirling blades and onto the base of the fan, only a heartbeat before the anonymous gunman opened fire, spraying the ceiling with a barrage of high-caliber ammunition.

The bullets struck the fan's heavy iron blades, ricocheting back in an explosive hailstorm of hot lead. Daredevil heard wood and bone splinter beneath him, as well as the sickening impact of multiple bullets striking human flesh. Whiskey bottles exploded like firecrackers as Daredevil leapt from fan to fan, keeping one bound ahead of the bullets chasing him.

For a second, he dared to hope that one of the ricochets would take out the gunman himself, but no such luck; the blistering fusillade kept on coming. Daredevil knew he couldn't evade the hail of gunfire forever.

Tuning out the clamor of misdirected fire, he concentrated on locating the gunman himself. His ears locked onto the clatter of the automatic's firing mechanism, while his nose traced the source of the gunpowder he smelled. The sound of discharged cartridges raining onto the floor drew his focused senses toward the southeast end of the tavern. *Right,* he determined swiftly. *Over there by the front booth.*

Reaching the last of the overhead ceiling fans, and with a nonstop salvo of gunfire nipping at his heels, he dropped off the base of the fan and grabbed one of its spinning blades. The fan whipped him around and he waited until precisely the right moment to release the blade and let it send him flying across the bar toward the nameless gunman.

Daredevil felt the hot lead blaze past him, only a few inches below his airborne body, but kept his focus on the man behind the gun. He practically heard the man's jaw drop as Daredevil came hurling toward him like a meteor. The Devil's boots slammed into the gunman's head and shoulders as Daredevil split-kicked him into the nearest wall.

The automatic thudded onto the floor, and the onslaught of bullets ceased. Daredevil allowed himself a second to pause and take his bearings.

He was the last man standing. The floor of Josie's

Bar was littered with broken bad guys, clutching their injuries and whimpering weakly. Footsteps clattered on the streets and alleys outside as smarter or luckier hoods beat a hasty retreat from the wrecked gin mill. Liquor from dozens of spilled cups and broken bottles made the trashed saloon smell like an explosion at a whiskey factory. Smoke from the charred pool tables hung like a haze over the entire scene.

So much for Josie's place, Daredevil thought, figuring the devastation couldn't have happened to a more deserving location. But what about Quesada? For a moment, he feared that Quesada might have slipped away while he was dodging bullets.

Then he heard a broken jaw rattling only a few yards away, coming from beneath one of the smoking pool tables. "Quesada," he said loudly, letting the slimeball know that he hadn't forgotten him. Quesada's heart was racing like a thoroughbred, and his bloodstained suit rustled every time he trembled.

Daredevil stepped toward the pool table, hearing broken glass crackle beneath the soles of his boots. Quesada was breathing hard, nearly hyperventilating. Daredevil could literally smell his fear. *Good*, he thought. *That's just how I want him.*

"Time to give the Devil his due."

The undisguised malice in Daredevil's voice was more than Quesada's fraying nerves could take. Realizing that his hiding place had been exposed, he bolted from beneath the pool table and ran madly for the tavern's back exit. His fractured jaw shrieked in agony with every step, but the panicked hoodlum didn't let that stop him from racing across the floor.

Gotta get away! he thought frantically. *Can't let him catch me!*

The back door led to a grimy alley, where Quesada was shocked to discover a huge red DD spray-painted onto the wall facing the exit. Had Daredevil himself tagged the wall or had one of the local gangs? Either way, the overlapping D's carried a definite warning: You have entered the Devil's neighborhood.

Damn it! Quesada thought, fleeing the alley and its foreboding graffiti. The humid night air made his sweat-drenched clothes cling to his trembling body. *We* owned *these streets—until that horned freak came along!*

He tripped on a chunk of broken pavement and fell into a slimy puddle, barely throwing out his hands in time to keep from landing face-first into the muck. He scrambled clumsily to his feet, looking around desperately for an escape route. Closed storefronts, protected by louvered steel grates, offered no refuge. A speeding subway rumbled beneath his feet, teasing him with the promise of deliverance, if he could just find the goddamn entrance to the station. He ran madly after the sound of the departing train, past the boarded-up windows of a defunct topless bar.

At Thirty-fourth and Eighth, a subway entrance beckoned invitingly, and he half ran, half stumbled to the waiting steps. With luck, maybe he could catch the A or the E train. At the top of the stairs, he heard unshakable boots splash through the puddle behind and looked back over his shoulder to see Daredevil in hot pursuit. The crimson demon was right behind him.

Quesada ran down the concrete steps. Adrenaline gave him the energy to jump the turnstile at the bottom, over the indignant protests of the token clerk in her sealed-in box. Like he was really going to fumble in his pockets for a token or MetroCard when the Devil was hot on his heels!

He staggered down another flight of steps. The subway platform was completely deserted, most people knowing better than to ride the subways through Hell's Kitchen at this time of night. Graffiti covered the concrete pillars supporting the ceiling, while rats scurried along the tracks on both sides of the platform. A squawky P.A. system, producing mostly static, made incomprehensible announcements regarding tonight's service—or the lack thereof.

To his dismay, there were no trains waiting at the station, on either side of the platform. Quesada paced back and forth across the empty platform, hoping to spot the headlights of an arriving train. Uptown, downtown, express, local—he didn't care as long as it was going away from here, and the relentless devil out for his blood. *C'mon, c'mon!* he thought, his toe tapping impatiently upon the floor. *If only a train would show up right now. . . !* He might still have a chance of getting away with nothing more than a broken jaw.

The sound of determined footsteps, descending toward the platform, magnified his sense of urgency.

Where the hell is that friggin' train?

Daredevil realized he'd made a mistake the moment he stepped down onto the platform. *I should have never let him reach the subway,* he thought, scolding himself for his carelessness. *I don't belong here.*

The underground station acted as an enormous

echo chamber, confusing his radar senses. He scanned the desolate station, searching for Quesada, only to pick up the echoes of *four* identical Quesadas, hiding behind separate subway posts. It was the audio equivalent of a house of mirrors, and just as baffling to this particular blind man.

Better clear this up with some echoes of my own, he decided, striking his billy club against the nearest iron railing. A loud, metallic clang rang out through the station, the rippling sound waves striking each of Quesada's four possible locations in turn before rebounding from the all-too-solid form of the real Quesada back to Daredevil's attentive ears.

Got you! he thought triumphantly.

Terrified, Quesada pressed his back against the concrete pillar, trying to hide from the avenging demon on his tail. He tried not to breathe, but a whimper escaped his lips as he heard those unyielding footsteps drawing ever nearer. The excruciating pain from his broken jaw ran a distant second to the overpowering dread those hellish footsteps instilled in him. He reached instinctively for his .44, only to remember that the gun was lying somewhere on the body-covered floor of Josie's Bar.

Fortunately, he still had one more weapon left, one that he had almost forgotten in his fear-stricken flight from the devil's wrath. . . .

Before he could reach for it, however, a heavy baton whipped across his throat, pinning Quesada to the concrete post. Daredevil stepped around the pillar to look the trapped felon in the face, his soulless red eyes only inches away from Quesada's own bulging orbs.

The club pressed against Quesada's windpipe,

making it hard to breathe. He whined hoarsely, his fractured jaw making every syllable a torment. "I'm innocent. Didn't you hear?"

He couldn't know for sure, but he guessed that the devil's insane vendetta had something to do with that Sutton broad and her pathetic lawsuit. But why would anyone care about that junkie tramp?

Daredevil increased the pressure on Quesada's throat, choking him. "I—I was acquitted. . . ."

"Not by me," Daredevil said, without a trace of mercy or compassion in his tone.

Quesada's face was turning blue. He could barely breathe, let alone speak. "Who . . . made . . . you . . . judge?" he somehow managed to croak.

A least a foot taller than his prisoner, Daredevil looked down on Quesada, icy contempt dripping from his voice. "You did."

Quesada thought he was done for, even as a sudden gust of hot air heralded the arrival of a subway train barreling into the station. An express train, it didn't even slow down as it zoomed past the platform, but the tremendous roar of the train's passage had a surprising effect on Daredevil, who reeled backward suddenly, clutching the sides of his head as though unable to endure the deafening noise.

Quesada didn't get it—the subway was no louder than usual—but he saw his chance. The choking club fell away from his throat and he snatched a loaded .38 from an ankle holster beneath his pant leg. He took advantage of Daredevil's inexplicable moment of weakness to press the snub-nosed barrel of the .38 right up against the devil's forehead. He snarled venomously, amazed that he was still alive.

"Go to Hell, diablo. . . ."

*   *   *

The express train charged out of the station, taking its unbearable caterwauling with it. Daredevil felt cold metal press against his brow, heard a single bullet roll into a waiting chamber. Jose Quesada angrily consigned him to perdition.

"You'll beat me there," Daredevil replied.

With lightning reflexes, he ducked beneath the gun barrel and lashed out at Quesada's leg with his billy club. Bone cracked like a rifle shot, and the mobster stumbled backward, tumbling off the platform. He landed hard on the tracks, across the way from the iron rails used by the express train.

Daredevil stood up and walked over to the edge of the platform, contemplating Quesada's fallen form. From the pulsing of the mobster's circulatory system, and harsh rasp of bone fragments scraping against each other, he deduced that Quesada's crippled leg was bent at an ugly angle. There was no way he was going to be able to crawl back onto the platform by himself.

Now you know how Angela Sutton felt, Daredevil thought, *after you were through with her.*

Another gust of hot wind entered the station, propelled by the nose of an oncoming train. Daredevil didn't need to see the train's headlights to know that they were shining brightly.

"That light at the end of the tunnel?" he informed Quesada calmly. "It's not heaven."

Quesada's heart sounded ready to explode. He gasped in fear as he struggled, unsuccessfully, to get back on his feet. "Help me!" he shrieked. "For God's sake, help me!"

Daredevil didn't budge. He heard the speeding train drawing nearer and braced himself for the din of its arrival.

"Okay, I'm guilty!" Quesada blurted. He squirmed helplessly on the tracks, unable to get away from the blazing headlights bearing down on him. "I confess! Show a little mercy, for Christ's sake!"

Once again, Angela Sutton's despairing sobs echoed in Daredevil's mind. He wondered how many other lives had been blighted by the wanton cruelty and violence of the man now lying in the path of the train.

The red-clad figure might have been a statue, just like the immobile sculpture of Justice back in that lonely courtroom.

"I'm guilty! I'm guilty!" Quesada screamed.

The echoing roar and screeching brakes of the 1 train filled the station.

CHAPTER 7

A strip of yellow crime scene tape cordoned off the subway platform. Reporter Ben Urich tossed away a smoked-out cigarette butt, extinguishing it beneath his heel, before ducking under the tape. A short, middle-aged New Yorker wearing tinted amber glasses and a tan felt cap, he scoped out the scene with a pair of highly observant eyeballs. *This looks promising,* he thought, smelling a story. *Wonder if our horn-headed friend has been up to something tonight?*

"Hey! You can't go past there!" a uniformed cop objected, moving to block Urich's path. Urich flashed his press pass, and the cop reluctantly stepped aside. A mischievous smile appeared on the reporter's face as he glimpsed the squat, familiar form of Detective Nick Manolis standing by the edge of the platform, supervising the investigation. Urich lighted up another Camel and headed over to see what was what.

Manolis groaned and rolled his eyes as he saw the reporter approach. "You're wasting your time, Urich," he growled, in a futile attempt to discourage Urich's curiosity. "There's nothing to see here."

Yeah, I bet, Urich thought skeptically. He glanced past Manolis to see one of the forensics guys pulling a sheet over the face of a lifeless body laid out on a stretcher. He caught a peek at the face before it was covered completely.

"Jose Quesada . . ." he muttered, recognizing the corpse. *Funny, I thought he was taller than that. . . .* It took him a second to realize that the stretcher carried only Quesada's torso. A team from the coroner's office carted the truncated remains away, followed by a second stretcher bearing the lower half of the bisected mobster. "And the rest of Jose Quesada."

He watched the dual stretchers disappear up the steps to the street, then peered over the edge of the platform. A gory splash of blood on the tracks below spelled out the exact manner in which Quesada had, er, split the scene. "That's a whole lot of nothing, Nick," he challenged Manolis.

The detective made a sour face, like maybe his ulcer was bothering him. "You keep running those stories and we're going to end up with a bunch of copycat vigilantes getting themselves killed."

Urich held up his whirring tape recorder. "You're confirming that Daredevil is responsible for this, Detective?"

Manolis leaned forward to bark into the recorder. "There's no proof that your so-called Daredevil even *exists*. Got it?" He shook his head as if the whole idea was too ridiculous to take seriously.

Hey, I don't write the headlines, Urich thought. It seemed to him, though, that Manolis was protesting too much. He sniffed the air, catching a faint wisp of lighter fluid, and knelt down to run his finger along the concrete floor of the platform. Just as he expected, he found an invisible line of gassy liquid. A knowing smirk greeted his discovery. *Pulling this trick again, are you, Horn-Head?*

Stepping back, he flicked his lighted cigarette butt

onto the cement. With a sudden *whoosh*, a line of flame raced across the floor, forming two large overlapping D's made of bright red fire. Urich recognized Daredevil's singular signature, as did every cop on the platform, whether they admitted it or not. Manolis looked like Bill Clinton confronted with Monica's dress.

"Got it," Urich said.

Dawn was still a few hours away when Daredevil returned to the rooftop of Matt Murdock's weathered brownstone in Hell's Kitchen. The backside of a nearby billboard helped to hide his arrival from sight.

He was glad to be home. If he was lucky, he could still get in a few hours of sleep before heading to the office. Chances were, Foggy would be sleeping in this morning, too, at least if he'd stuck to his plan of going out drinking. Daredevil hoped Matt's partner wouldn't be too hungover.

An impregnable steel door, with no less than four combination locks, barred the exit from the roof. Daredevil spun all four locks at once, knowing every click by heart. With his heightened senses, he could have been the world's greatest safecracker, had he been more criminally inclined. He reached out and stopped each of the spinning locks at precisely the right moment.

Chuk-chuk-chuk-chuk!

The solid steel door swung open, and Daredevil descended the stairs to Matt Murdock's apartment.

Appropriately for a blind man, the apartment was as spare as a monastery, with no stray coffee tables or lamps to bump into. The only art decorating the walls was a large bas relief featuring a tangle of angels and devils, locked in eternal contention. The tactile sculpture also served as a sound baffle, cutting down (but never completely eliminating) any distracting echoes bouncing around the apartment.

Daredevil peeled back his cowl, revealing the bruised and cut face of Matt Murdock. As he walked down an unobstructed hall toward the kitchen, he passed a pair of aging boxing gloves mounted on the wall. Jack Murdock's gloves, worn the night of his greatest victory—and untimely death. Matt touched the gloves reverently, as he did every time he returned from a mission of vengeance.

Four more billy clubs, identical to the one in his hand, hung on pegs beyond his father's gloves. Matt returned tonight's club to its peg as well, then continued to a low table where three plaster busts watched over the hallway. Spare masks rested on two of the sculpted heads, flanking a naked bust in between. Matt dropped his sweaty cowl onto the middle head.

The kitchen was spotless and impeccably organized, every item in its place. Matt's acute sense of smell gave him a low tolerance for dirty dishes and rotting food particles; he never missed a speck when cleaning up.

Matt shed Daredevil's leather jacket, exposing an athletic torso marred by scars and scratches both old and new. Lines of stubborn scar tissue crisscrossed his body, making it look like some sort of flesh-toned patchwork quilt. His fingers traced the network of old wounds: badges of honor from a never-ending street war.

An answering machine rested on the far end of the kitchen counter, next to the phone. Matt wearily pressed a Braille button on the machine. An electronic beep informed him that he had at least one message.

A woman's voice—strained, unhappy—reached his ears. "Matt, it's Heather."

Matt winced, and not because of the cut on his cheek. A twinge of guilt stabbed his conscience.

"Are you there?" the voice asked. Matt heard a plaintive sigh. "Of course you're not there. You're never there. At least not for me."

Heather's bitter words followed Matt as he walked over to the kitchen sink. Blood dripped from his torn cheek.

"I didn't want to do this over the phone. But it's not like you give me a choice."

Matt listened to his blood swirl down the drain and experienced a distinct sense of déjà vu. A visual memory, of bright red blood eddying at the bottom of a rusty sink, surfaced from his childhood.

"I mean—it's been three months now and I've never even seen your apartment."

Probably just as well, Matt thought. He opened a wooden cabinet next to the sink, which held several shelves of first-aid supplies: disinfectants, Band-Aids, gauze, and peroxide. Essential supplies for any serious urban vigilante. *Too bad I can't deduct them as business expenses.*

He dabbed a bit of peroxide on his cut cheek before swabbing it with orange Betadine. The peroxide only smarted a little.

Heather's voice stung more. "Every time we sleep together, I wake up in the morning alone."

He heard a sob catch in her voice and opened another cabinet. This one contained a small pharmacy's worth of painkillers.

"I mean, Jesus, where do you *go* at three o'clock in the morning?"

Trust me, you don't want to know, Matt thought. He contemplated the array of analgesics before him, assessing the extent of tonight's aches and pains. The Tylenol? No, not strong enough. The Demerol? No, that would leave him too groggy in the morning. After a moment's thought, he compromised by grabbing the Vicodin.

He knew which pill bottle was which by their location on the shelves, which never varied, but he double-checked by examining both the shape and smell of the tablets.

Yep, Vicodin all right.

"I thought that if I was patient enough," Heather continued, "you would let me in. That we'd take our relationship to the next level."

Matt didn't bother pouring himself a glass of water. He just popped two Vicodin into his mouth and chewed the tablets into a sour white powder.

It left a bad taste in his mouth.

"Then I realized . . . this *is* the next level."

Matt slid open a kitchen drawer to get at a white plastic bag filled with Epsom salts. He scooped up a handful and walked into the living room.

The spartan furnishings included what appeared to be a polished metal coffin, occupying the center of the room. In fact, the bizarre sarcophagus was a state-of-the-art sensory deprivation tank. Matt lifted the lid, hearing the tank's liquid contents ripple softly. He dropped the crystalline salts into the water and stripped off the rest of his leathers.

Heather's voice emanated from the kitchen. "Good-bye, Matt," she said mournfully. The message ended with the click of a phone being hung up.

Good-bye, Heather, Matt thought. He didn't even consider calling her back. Heather was a sweet and caring young woman. She deserved a boyfriend who didn't spend his nights fighting tooth and nail against the scum of the earth, someone who didn't stagger home, bruised and bleeding, in the wee hours of the morning.

Someone who could make her happy.

Matt sighed, emotionally and physically exhausted. He slid into the warm, soothing water and closed his eyes. The dissolved salts helped to alleviate his aches and pains. He savored a moment of pure, blissful silence—until he heard a gunshot, several blocks away.

No, he thought, more fatigued than alarmed. Unseeing blue eyes stared off into space. *Not another one . . .*

The distant shooting sounded as if it was taking place right in his living room. Matt heard the bullet strike its target, followed by the raspy moan of the female victim. She sounded young, perhaps in her early twenties. Matt's weary muscles tensed, but he didn't stir from the tank; he could tell he was already too late.

The nameless girl, perhaps the same age as Heather, spasmed once on the sidewalk. Her heartbeat fluttered weakly before falling completely silent.

Matt continued to float weightlessly in the tank. *It never ends*, he thought, but there was only so much that one man could do, even if that man was Daredevil. Trying to stanch the ceaseless cycle of crime and violence with his fists was like sticking a Band-Aid over a sucking chest wound.

Especially in Hell's Kitchen.

His strength spent, Matt surrendered to his aching

body. He reached up and pulled the lid of the tank shut, hearing it clank into place. The insulated casket shut out the perpetual screams and shouts of the world outside.

At least for tonight.

CHAPTER 8

The Fisk Building, located on several acres of Manhattan's most expensive real estate, rose like a towering steel-and-glass temple to unbridled wealth and ambition. By day, its massive shadow blotted out the sun over several surrounding city blocks. Countless panes of rectangular glass reflected back the morning's light, giving the building an almost supernatural radiance that served to hide the darkness lurking at its heart.

On the top floor of the skyscraper, a man stood before a panoramic picture window. At six foot seven, weighing more than three hundred fifty pounds, he was an immense African-American whose tailored silk suit had been custom-made to accommodate his imposing dimensions. A hand-picked rose adorned his lapel, while a gargantuan hand rested on the crystal head of an expensive walking stick.

Despite his scale-tipping weight, this man was in no way obese or out of shape. His nearly four hundred pounds of muscle radiated confidence, power, and menace—all with good reason.

Wilson Fisk, the undisputed master of the Fisk

Building and much else beyond, smoked an imported cigar as he looked out over the city below.

His city.

He turned away from the window toward his desk, where a copy of today's *New York Post* rested. The front-page headline read: KINGPIN OF CRIME— MAN OR MYTH?

Fisk chuckled to himself, not worried in the least.

Still, he thought calmly, *some action is required. If only for appearance's sake.*

A throat cleared nearby, and Fisk looked up from the newspaper to acknowledge the presence of his chief attorney and aide, Wesley Owen Welch, who was standing respectfully a few feet away from the desk.

Welch was a lean and angular man in his early forties, with an expensive haircut and designer eyeglasses. Although lacking Fisk's commanding proportions and magnetism, the dapper attorney nevertheless exuded a certain degree of bravado and arrogance, all wrapped up in a two-thousand-dollar suit.

"You've seen the papers?" Welch asked unnecessarily.

Lawyers, Fisk knew, were fond of rhetorical questions. He nodded and exhaled a stream of blue smoke. No-smoking ordinances were the least of the laws he ignored.

"Somebody's been talking," Welch continued.

Fisk stepped away from his pristine obsidian desk. "Somebody always does," he said, in a basso profundo that seemed to well up from somewhere deep within his capacious chest. Cane in hand, he crossed the spacious office toward a closed door on his right.

Welch followed without being asked, as though caught in Fisk's gravitational wake.

Two suit-clad bodyguards, both only slightly less colossal than Fisk himself, flanked the exit. Their stony gazes were fixed straight ahead, as they diligently paid no attention to the matter under discussion.

In theory, at least.

Fisk smiled as he approached the door. Was that a drop of sweat he saw oozing down the crew-cut brow of the guard to the right? Had the other guard's Adam's apple bobbed just a tad, as if he was struggling not to appear nervous?

It doesn't matter, Fisk thought. He already knew what he was going to do.

"You know, Wesley," he observed casually, "in ancient times, you'd cut your guard's tongue out on his first day on the job, just to guarantee his silence. . . ."

His relaxed tone held no hint of what was in store. In an instant, he grabbed one of the guards by the throat. Powerful fingers crushed the startled guard's windpipe as easily as though it were a paper cup. The murdered guard crumpled to the floor, but Fisk spun toward the second guard before the first one even hit the carpet. Fisk savagely brained the guard with his cane, shattering his skull with a single blow.

The second guard joined his companion on the floor, and that was that: two men dead in a matter of seconds.

Not a bad morning's work, the Kingpin thought. He had assassins who could handle this sort of chore, of course, but sometimes the hands-on approach was more satisfying—and effective. *The rest of my employees will think twice before speaking to the press.*

Welch reacted to the altercation with admirable aplomb. He plucked a silk handkerchief from the front pocket of his suit and handed it helpfully to Fisk, who used it to wipe a few messy flecks off the crystal setting of his cane.

"Your eleven o'clock is here," the lawyer said evenly. He stepped over a still-warm corpse to open the door to the adjoining conference room, where the Kingpin saw a familiar face awaiting him.

"Niko, old friend," Fisk boomed expansively. His broad smile held nothing but warmth and hospitality.

Nikolas Natchios—a silver-haired gentleman whose lean, well-groomed features were well known to the city's society pages—sat at the conference table. He had come accompanied by two of his own bodyguards, who remained outside. The Greek tycoon's eyes widened in dismay as he spotted the dead bodies lying on the other side of the doorway.

Fisk entered slowly, letting Natchios get a good long look before closing the door via a convenient remote control device. *A picture is worth a thousand words,* he thought with a smile, *particularly if there's a corpse or two in the frame.*

A well-stocked bar ran along one wall of the conference room. Fisk poured himself a brandy as Natchios looked on, the image of the executed guards no doubt sinking into his mind.

"Would you like a drink?" Fisk asked.

Natchios shook his head. Worry deepened the lines on his face, aging him visibly. "I don't drink anymore."

Fisk turned away from the bar, glass in hand. "You don't do *anything* anymore." Despite their pleasant tone, his words carried a definite edge. "Do you, Niko?"

The older man shifted uneasily in his chair, taking

a second to work up his nerve. "I'm getting out, Wilson," he said finally. "I *am* out."

Fisk chuckled, unconcerned.

"You think this is funny?" Natchios snapped, his temper flaring. "Have you been reading the paper? The *New York Post*—"

"The *Post*?" Fisk raised an eyebrow, as though disappointed by his colleague's taste in reading material. "Really, now."

Natchios ignored Fisk's patronizing air. He lowered his voice and looked around fearfully, leery of hidden ears or listening devices. "They're writing about the Kingpin. They're going all the way back to the beginning. . . ."

"I'm aware of the stories," Fisk conceded patiently, bored and slightly embarrassed by the Greek's emotional display. He glanced back at Welch, who was standing a few paces behind him. "What do they call them, Wesley?"

" 'Urban Legends of New York,' " the lawyer answered on cue. He sniffed archly, like a connoisseur of fine wines forced to open a six-pack of beer. "It's a series."

Natchios wouldn't let the matter rest. "This reporter, this Ben Urich, he must have a source. Someone close to you."

"Impossible," Fisk stated flatly. No one would dare, especially after the example he had just made of those two loose-lipped guards. "You're worrying yourself over nothing."

Natchios sagged back against his seat, looking haggard and worn down. "I'm tired of looking over my shoulder," he confessed. Wrinkled pouches beneath his eyes hinted at sleepless nights. "I want to put that behind me now."

A folder full of legal-sized documents rested on the gleaming chrome-and-glass tabletop in front of the old man. He patted the papers with a bony hand. "I want you to buy me out. My lawyers have drawn up the contracts. I'm sure you'll find it's a very generous offer."

Narrowed brown eyes looked up at Fisk expectantly. *It's sad*, the Kingpin reflected, *to see a once-valued ally reduced to this*. Nikolas Natchios had been a formidable businessman back in the old days, iron-willed and ruthless when he had to be. *A shame that such strength has succumbed to the passing of the years.*

"So?" Natchios coaxed him, painfully eager to put his dubious past behind him. "What do you say?"

It was fortunate that Fisk knew just which button to push to keep Natchios in line.

"How's your daughter?" the Kingpin asked.

The stricken look on the old man's face was a thing of beauty.

BARROOM BLITZKRIEG! screamed the front page headline, above a grainy black-and-white photo of a low-life bar that looked like a herd of buffalo had stampeded through it. Foggy Nelson read the accompanying article to his partner as he and Matt had their morning coffee at their favorite diner on Twenty-third Street. They faced each other across a booth near the front of the restaurant.

" ' . . . police are still investigating,' " the portly lawyer intoned dramatically, as though presenting a case to a jury. He looked up from the paper to see if Matt was listening. His partner's dark glasses and lifeless expression made it hard to tell. "I bet they are," Foggy commented. "Check this out: 'Witnesses say Quesada was singled out by the demonic vigilante known as Daredevil.' "

This is great stuff! Foggy thought. *The folks at the* Post *must be in tabloid heaven.* Too bad the juicy story seemed lost on his partner; Matt was in a definite funk this morning, distracted and morose. If Foggy didn't know better, he'd think his longtime buddy had been out carousing all night. *Probably still beating himself up over the Sutton case,* Foggy guessed. *Never mind that Jose Quesada has apparently come to a bad end anyway. . . .*

Matt rubbed his temples wearily. His face was pale and bore a nasty-looking cut on one cheek; Foggy suspected that, beneath Matt's black glasses, there were dark purple shadows under his eyes. *Did he sleep at all last night?*

"Foggy. . . ." he sighed.

Foggy was well aware of his partner's skepticism where a certain infamous vigilante was concerned. "There must be something to these Daredevil stories. We've been hearing them for years."

Matt snorted dismissively. "Yeah, like the alligators that live in the sewers."

Foggy smiled in relief, glad just to have gotten Matt talking. "That's true about the alligators," he argued cheerfully. "I'm serious. I've got a friend in sanitation."

He glanced down at his copy of the *Post*. Next to the snapshot of the wrecked bar was an artist's rendering of Daredevil himself. The sketch depicted a grotesquely horrific gargoyle that looked like something out of H. R. Giger.

"There's a picture here," Foggy said.

"There's a picture?" Matt asked hesitantly.

"An artist's rendering. Boy, I'd hate to see this guy's therapy bills," Foggy remarked, before turning his attention back to Matt. "Speaking of bills, we got our first payment from Mr. Lee this morning."

"Great," Matt said, without much enthusiasm. "Could you pass the sugar?"

Foggy reached automatically for the sugar container, then hesitated. Matt still sounded blue. *Maybe a good old-fashioned practical joke will lighten his mood,* Foggy thought, *like it did back in college.*

Instead of the sugar, as requested, Foggy unscrewed the lid to the salt container and slid it over to Matt. "Actually, it's not great," he said. "He paid us in fluke. That's a *fish,* Matt. Did you know that? Because I sure didn't."

Foggy grinned slyly as Matt unsuspectingly poured the salt into his coffee.

"He goes fishing on weekends," Matt said matter-of-factly, as though attorneys were routinely compensated with several pounds of raw seafood.

"And I go salsa dancing," Foggy replied. "But you don't see me *dancing* to pay my bills."

"And a grateful city thanks you," Matt said, with a trace of his usual spirit.

Oh, yeah? Foggy thought. He covertly squirted ketchup into Matt's creamer. "Look, we can't keep taking these pro bono cases." Foggy hated to be the voice of crass reality, but somebody had to say it. "We need better clients."

The humor drained out of Matt's voice. "Define 'better.'"

"Guilty rich people," Foggy said bluntly. "Cream?"

He repressed a chuckle as the blind lawyer poured a pinkish mixture of cream and ketchup into his already salted coffee. At the same time, he kept on trying to reason with Matt.

"Remember back in law school how they taught us to create a 'moral vacuum' so that we could represent clients who might be not completely innocent?"

"Yeah?" Matt said warily.

"You got no vacuum, Matt." Foggy waited eagerly for Matt to take his first sip of the polluted coffee. "You're *vacuumless*."

Matt attempted a wry smile, only to wince in pain. He casually touched the ugly cut on his cheek, which finally provoked Foggy to address the injury. "What happened to you?"

"Walked into a door," Matt answered.

Foggy nodded, not really buying it. "How many times?"

Matt started to answer, then abruptly sniffed the air. To Foggy's surprise, some unexpected aroma had an immediate effect on Matt. Whatever he was smelling lifted Matt's spirits visibly. The color came back into his face, and his whole body language changed, becoming alert and energized for the first time all morning.

Foggy couldn't smell anything unusual himself, but he had a pretty good idea what had awakened his previously inert partner; he had witnessed this bizarre olfactory phenomena before. "Where, where, where?" he asked.

"Front door," Matt reported, without a trace of doubt.

Foggy glanced over his shoulder but saw nothing remarkable near the open entrance of the coffee shop.

"Soon . . ." Matt promised.

Sure enough, a moment later one of the most beautiful women Foggy had ever seen stepped into the restaurant. She was tall and athletic, with dark eyes and a flowing mane of curly, dark brown hair. Although she was dressed casually in a light blue denim jacket and matching jeans, something about her radiated exoticism and privilege, like a glamorous foreign princess traveling incognito.

How does he do it? Foggy marveled, unable to tear his eyes away from the incandescent goddess now gracing the coffee shop with her presence. For as long as Foggy had known Matt, his friend had always been able to sniff out beautiful women—literally.

"Tell me," Matt requested. Despite his astounding sense of smell, he still relied on Foggy to find out what exactly the newcomer looked like. Foggy felt a pang of sympathy, sorry that his friend couldn't fully appreciate the staggering feminine beauty on display.

"You want the truth?" he asked.

"And nothing but," Matt insisted.

Despite the legal phraseology, Foggy wasn't exactly under oath. "She's *hideous*," he testified.

Matt grinned, both of them knowing full well that Foggy had just perjured himself. Foggy picked up his spoon and used it to check on his reflection, all the while giving Matt a slightly distorted eyewitness description of the mystery woman. "I can't tell if that's a fungus or some kind of congenital defect, but as your attorney, I must advise against any further action in this matter. . . ."

But when Foggy put down the spoon, Matt was already gone.

Matt switched the coffee cups while Foggy was distracted with his reflection, then wasted no time getting up and out of the booth.

The woman's intoxicating fragrance, a mixture of rose oil and her own natural scent, drew him across the coffee shop. He sensed her sitting alone at her own table, and he tapped his cane like any ordinary blind man before "accidentally" bumping into her table. "Excuse me," he said.

"Sure," the woman answered absently. Matt heard the rustle of a newspaper—the *Village Voice* from the smell of it—and could tell that she hadn't even looked up from her paper.

"Seems every time I get the lay of the land here," he improvised, "they rearrange the furniture."

"Umm-hmm," the woman murmured, refusing to be lured away from her reading. Paper rustled indifferently as she turned the page.

"I was looking for some sugar," Matt explained.

"Right in front of you," she said flatly.

"Could you be more specific?" he pressed.

Exasperation colored her voice as she finally put down her paper. "What are you—?" she began impatiently, only to cut herself off with a mortified gasp. Matt imagined her eyes widening in surprise as she looked up at him for the first time.

" 'Blind?' " he supplied helpfully.

"Oh!" Matt felt the heat rush into her face as she blushed in embarrassment. "Oh, I'm so sorry. . . ."

He felt a twinge of guilt at taking advantage of his apparent disability this way, but, hey, all's fair in love and war, right?

He heard Foggy chuckle back at their booth. A moment later, Foggy sipped his coffee—and blew it across the table in surprise. He sputtered loudly enough to attract plenty of attention. Matt heard necks turn all over the diner, including the one belonging to the startled woman, and struggled not to laugh.

Her neck smelled wonderful. He couldn't help wondering what it felt—and tasted—like.

"Friend of yours?" she asked, perhaps observing the amused expression on his face.

"Never seen him before."

Matt could hear her smiling. Her taut muscles relaxed as she lowered her defenses somewhat. "Matt Murdock," he said, introducing himself. He offered her his hand.

She accepted his hand, and his whole body tingled as he felt her smooth, warm flesh press against his. She had a surprisingly strong grip. "Nice to meet you, Matt Murdock."

To his disappointment, she let go of his hand and got up from her table. She headed for the door, leaving behind a half-empty cup of mint tea, not to mention a stupefied blind lawyer.

"Wait!" he called after her. "I didn't get your name."

She glanced back over her shoulder. "That's because I didn't give it."

The scent of roses trailing in her wake, she left the coffee shop. Dumbfounded, he tapped his way back to his booth, where Foggy waited with the remains of his adulterated coffee. "Some people have no compassion for the handicapped," Foggy joked sympathetically.

A rueful smile crossed Matt's face. *Easy come, easy go,* he thought, before realizing that he wasn't about to give up on this woman so quickly.

Moving quickly, he snatched up his briefcase.

"Huh?" Foggy blurted in confusion. "Where are you going?"

"To file an appeal," Matt said decisively. He barely bothered to use his cane as he headed for the exit.

The woman's perfume still lingered in his nostrils. His palm was still warm from her touch.

A note of anxiety entered Foggy's voice. "We have to be at the courthouse at twelve o'clock."

"I'll be there," Matt assured him, not even slowing down.

"Twelve o'clock!" Foggy shouted after him.

For a second, Matt wondered if he was being crazy. After all, this woman was a perfect stranger whose name he didn't even know and here he was rushing after her.

But he couldn't help himself. Something about her stimulated his senses to an almost overpowering degree. He'd never felt so attracted to a woman before, not even with Heather.

Sniffing the air outside the diner, he tracked across the street. Horns honked and cabbies cursed as he jaywalked across Seventh Avenue. It wasn't easy, keeping track of one woman's perfume amid the smog and exhaust fumes, but he followed a wisp of roses in the air down the block and around the corner before the wind shifted uncooperatively. *Damn!* he thought, momentarily losing her.

"What do you want?"

Matt whirled around to find the mystery woman leaning against the chain-link fence of an inner-city playground, her arms crossed atop her chest.

She sounded pissed.

Matt hesitated, almost losing his nerve. Then he remembered what his father had always told him: *Don't be afraid. You can do anything if you're not afraid.* He smiled inwardly at himself as he stepped cautiously into the playground. *What's the good of being a Man Without Fear, as the papers keep calling me, if I can't even talk to a beautiful girl?*

"I just wanted to know your name," he said.

His explanation did not appease her. "I don't like being followed," she said coldly. "So don't."

She turned to leave.

"Hey, wait—" he protested, reaching instinctively for her arm.

To his amazement, she expertly caught his wrist in a flawless kempo lock. "And I don't like being touched."

Strangely, her display of martial arts prowess only emboldened Matt. "Why don't you tell me what you do like," he challenged her, "and we'll start from there?"

He collapsed her hold and reversed their positions as she gasped in surprise, simultaneously deflecting his guard.

Matt suddenly found himself losing his position as she flipped away from him. The two began to slowly circle each other testing the charged air between them, a dance both graceful and deadly: ballet meets kung fu.

"Are you sure you are blind?" she asked.

"Are you sure you don't want to tell me your name?" Matt responded.

They both removed their coats, continuing to size each other up. Suddenly, she launched a kick at Matt's face, which he expertly parried. Then he swiped at her with his cane. She deftly slipped underneath the strike, then ran across the playground to the teeter-totter. As Matt approached, she jumped down hard onto the other end of one teeter-totter, causing the rising end to catch Matt, knocking him backward toward another teeter-totter. Running to the second teeter-totter, she leapt onto the other end, knocking Matt backward again. Quickly recovering,

Matt found the upraised board and shoved down hard, launching her into the air and sending her flying into his arms.

"You're holding back," he accused her playfully.

"Yes," she said tersely. Then she spun away from him, launching a pair of lightning chops and kicks. A perfectly executed spring punch targeted his head, and he evaded the blow with a little old-fashioned bobbing and weaving.

The strikes came faster and more fiercely, requiring ever-greater effort to block and deflect.

An open-handed strike came at his face, threatening to ram his dark glasses back into his skull. He grabbed her wrist with his free hand and forced it away from his head, so that her high-velocity blow connected with nothing but empty air. She broke his grip within seconds and recovered by tossing a hostile kick at his head. Matt side-slipped out of the way of impact as the two performed simultaneous backflips, both of them landing on either side of the teeter-totters, straddling them in perfect balance.

A group of neighborhood kids, playing hoops at an adjoining basketball court, dropped their game in favor of watching the bizarre duel in the playground. "Whoa! You go, girl!" they hollered raucously, encouraging whoever had an edge at that particular moment. They pressed their rapt faces up against the fence. "Wow! Cool move, bro!"

If any of the kids found it odd that a blind man was holding his own against a sighted woman, they didn't mention it. *Must have seen all those Hong Kong action flicks about blind samurais and ninjas*, Matt guessed. *Or maybe they've just read too many comic books.*

At the back of his mind, he realized that he was

endangering his secret identity sparring in public like this. What if Foggy or one of their clients saw? But Matt didn't care. Whoever this amazing girl was, she was worth the risk.

"All this just to get your name?" Matt asked.

"Try asking for my number," she replied.

Matt smiled to himself. Their fight had grown more intense, but also more playful. Unlike last night's brawl at Josie's, which had been a grim, dirty business, offering only the most brutal of pleasures, this bout was exhilarating, almost sexual in its dynamic. They had anticipated each other's every move, connecting on a primal, instinctive level. Beneath his conservative courtroom attire, Matt's skin was bathed in a healthy sweat. His heart and blood were singing.

I wonder if she's half as turned on as I am. . . .

He had no chance to wonder any longer. The woman used Matt's own trick to turn the seesaw into a catapult, launching herself onto one board, causing Matt to launch into a side flip and land on the same teeter-totter as she was on.

The kids at the fence oohed in appreciation of the close call. "Hot damn! You almost got him, girl!" one kid shouted.

"Good save, man!" another teen yelled, jumping up and down on the other side of the fence.

"Nice," Matt said.

"Thanks."

The dark-haired woman didn't wait for Matt to regain his composure. Without missing a beat, she leapt at him, assaulting Matt with a high-powered lunge punch followed by an instant reverse punch.

Matt ducked beneath the lunge, then blocked the second blow with his cane. She countered with a strike at Matt's throat that he parried with his forearm.

The woman's scent and curvaceous contours were distracting him. He could feel her vibrant, passionate breaths, hear the hot blood racing giddily through her veins.

A crescent kick forced the cane from Matt's hand, sending it spinning across the playground, where it stuck into a picnic bench. A doubled-handed U-punch went after his head and stomach simultaneously, and Matt was forced to resort to an upper block lower push combo to fend off both attacks. *Talk about aggressive women!* he thought admiringly. *She's really keeping me on my toes.*

Matt sensed the park bench directly behind him and retreated a few steps more. He let the woman think that he was about to back into the obstacle when, at the last minute, he pushed off the heavy iron bench and slid past her defenses, wrapping his arms tightly around her and trapping her own arms against her sides.

Got you! he thought euphorically. They were pressed together, cheek to cheek, and the scent of her washed over him. He could feel her lithe, well-toned body, and hear her heart pounding almost in synch with his.

"Stop hitting me," Matt said.

The woman smiled. "Okay."

Just for a moment, he surrendered to the seductive sensations, relaxing his grip.

Big mistake.

The woman stomped hard on the bridge of his foot, then pushed him onto the bench. A roundhouse kick sizzled at Matt's face, stopping inches from his nose.

"My name is Elektra Natchios. I have to go." She
began to walk away.

"Wait . . ." Matt said, taking her arm and turning
her around. "Don't hit me. I don't want any more
trouble. Why do you have to go?"

CHAPTER 9

Water flowed everywhere within the Fisk Building, rising and falling mechanically behind walls and ceilings of translucent glass. From the lobby to the penthouse, the entire skyscraper was a veritable fountain, enclosed within a gigantic steel-and-glass frame.

Fisk liked that. The ever-present water conveyed an aura of cleanliness, of purity, that insulated him—and diverted attention from—the often squalid realities of his business. *No trace of dirt or blood must attach to me,* he thought, as he strolled confidently across the spacious lobby. Officially, Wilson Fisk had not a single arrest or conviction on his record, not even a parking ticket. *I remain spotless . . . untouchable.*

A pity the same could not be said of others.

"I want you to create a paper trail," he instructed Welch, who was sticking closely to his side, like a remora to a great white shark. "One that can be traced back to Natchios."

"Sir?" The lawyer sounded understandably puzzled. After all, he was more accustomed to burying evidence than manufacturing it.

"The press wants a Kingpin, so I'll give them a Kingpin." Fisk paused to take a puff on his cigar, before proceeding to the next item on his agenda:

one perfectly suited to tying up all loose ends in the Natchios matter, once and for all.

"Get me Bullseye."

The name on his passport was just a convenient alias. The passport's owner had left his real name behind long ago, preferring to be known by the highly appropriate sobriquet he had acquired over the course of his career.

Bullseye. The world's greatest assassin.

A dark nylon skullcap covered his shaved scalp, just above a pair of bristling brown eyebrows. Dark wraparound sunglasses concealed his eyes, while his black alligator-skin duster trailed behind him like a cape as he swaggered through the air-conditioned airport terminal, looking like a rock star who wasn't making much of an effort to go unnoticed. A plain black T-shirt and black leather pants matched his inky reptilian coat. A cocky smirk showed through his light brown mustache and goatee. Alligator boots conveyed him confidently toward the metal detectors ahead.

He waited patiently, in no hurry, behind a Japanese businessman at the security station. The traveling salaryman placed his keys and cell phone in a plastic basket before stepping through the metal detector, which let him pass by without so much as a single beep.

Bullseye expected to get through the security screening almost as easily—despite being armed to the teeth.

In a manner of speaking.

The guards posted at the station looked him over warily as he stepped forward. No surprise there. His sinister attire and obvious attitude made him look rather more suspicious than the average frequent flyer. "Step through," one of the uniformed guards instructed him, indicating the metal detector in front of Bullseye.

Why not? he thought calmly.

Beep, beep.

The guard gestured for him to step back. "Empty your pockets," she requested.

Bullseye smirked, unconcerned, as he emptied his pockets, producing nothing more incriminating than a paper clip, a pencil, and a solitary toothpick. Perfectly harmless objects.

For anyone else.

The guard scowled, visibly annoyed by Bullseye's cavalier expression and body language. "Try again," she said, watching closely as the black-clad traveler walked through the metal detector once more.

Beep, beep.

A second guard, larger and more imposing than the first, stepped forward. "Raise your arms," he ordered, brandishing a handheld metal detector of his own.

Bullseye complied readily, assuming a mock crucifix pose, complete with an exaggerated look of long-suffering patience. The two guards exchanged a suspicious look before the second guard waved his wand over and around Bullseye's body.

The wand beeped as it glided past his waist, and Bullseye lifted the hem of his T-shirt to reveal an ornate, star-shaped belt buckle. He shrugged casually—*oops, how did I forget about that?*—without the slightest hint of embarrassment. The impudent smirk never left his face, as though he was amused by a private joke.

The second guard made a few more passes with

his wand, but nothing beeped except the polished silver belt buckle. He glanced over at his partner, who had been carefully looking over Bullseye's passport and boarding pass. She shook her head and handed the documents back to Bullseye, apparently unable to find anything out of order with his papers.

"Go ahead," the larger guard said reluctantly.

Bullseye retrieved his paper clip, pencil, and toothpick before heading toward his gate. *What a bunch of losers*, he thought scornfully, recalling the guards' futile efforts to disarm him. *Like I'd really carry a gun or a blade into an airport.* The paper clip and his other belongings rattled comfortably in his pockets as he traversed the terminal. *I have all the weapons I need right here.*

A clock over the corridor caught his eye and his pace quickened, the alligator boots carrying him briskly toward his gate.

He had a flight to New York to catch.

CHAPTER 10

The neighborhood was officially known as Clinton, after nineteenth-century mayor DeWitt Clinton, but nobody called it that except greedy realtors anxious to shed the region's unsavory reputation. Some say that it was first christened "Hell's Kitchen" by an 1881 article in the *New York Times*, while others attribute the name to a world-weary cop called to the scene of a small riot on West Thirty-ninth Street near Tenth Avenue. Yet another account claimed that it was a deliberate mispronunciation of "Heil's Kitchen," a German-run restaurant that had once served as a notorious watering hole for the local Irish street gangs.

Regardless, this infamous locale remained one of New York's toughest addresses: more than twenty blocks of graffiti, litter, barbed wire, and winos. Broken glass and discarded cigarette butts carpeted the pavement while here and there isolated flower boxes fought back against the pervasive grime. Adult video stores shared the streets with scattered delis, Laundromats, and sidewalk vendors. Street crazies shouted obscenities at passing pedestrians, while kamikaze bike messengers risked their necks (and everyone else's) zipping up and down the traffic-clotted streets and avenues. The rancid smell of rotting garbage hung in the air.

Matt Murdock called it home.

"Where did you learn to fight like that?" he asked Elektra, as they walked up Ninth Avenue together. For once, the summer heat and humidity were not quite unbearable, and Matt was enjoying the walk thoroughly, which probably had a lot to do with the company—and the persistent fragrance of rose oil.

"My father," she explained. "He had me train with a different sensei every year since I was five years old."

Matt whistled, impressed by the regimen she described. "Sounds like he wanted to turn you into some kind of warrior." *Exactly the opposite of my own dad,* he thought, *who didn't want me to be a fighter at all.*

"No," she said, her voice growing more serious. Matt caught a hint of underlying sorrow. "Just not a victim."

On second thought, Matt thought, *maybe our dads weren't all that different after all. They both wanted to prepare us to overcome life's obstacles and dangers, no matter how hard they had to work us.*

They walked in silence for a block or so, lost in thought. Despite the obvious differences in their background, Matt felt closer to this woman than he ever had before to anyone else. They seemed two of a kind, sharing similar skills and secrets.

The sidewalk ahead was uneven and easy to stumble over, so he alerted her in advance. "Watch your step here."

Elektra gracefully avoided the crack in the pavement. "Thanks," she said. A note of curiosity entered her voice. "How do you do that? Back in the park, the sidewalk . . ."

Matt shrugged, as though it were nothing to write home about. "Growing up blind in the Kitchen, you learn to take care of yourself."

"You grew up here?" He could hear her turn her head, taking in the crowded city streets.

"Kitchen's like family," Matt said, unashamed of his roots.

They passed a dilapidated old brownstone, and as if on cue, angry voices escaped from one of the ground-floor apartments:

"You lazy, good-for-nothing bum. Why don't you get your fat ass off the couch once in a while?"

"Aw, leave me alone, you nagging witch! Go jump off the Empire State Building! See if I care!"

"Sometimes it's the Manson Family," Matt conceded, as the quarreling voices followed them up the avenue. "But we watch out for each other." A kid on a skateboard zipped toward them, and Matt adroitly stepped out of the way. "Or, in my case, listen."

"What do you hear?" she asked, sounding genuinely intrigued. She leaned toward him, her body language demonstrating her interest. He practically heard her pupils dilate. "When you listen?"

Matt paused on the sidewalk. An ambulance whizzed by, and he listened not to the siren but to where it was going. "Everything," he told her. "I hear everything."

The habits of a lifetime urged him to change the subject, to minimize his special gifts, but he found it hard not to open up to this woman, let her in to his secret world. *Besides,* he admitted to himself, *let's be honest. I really want to impress her, too.*

"Okay," she challenged him playfully. They continued up the street, going the same way as the ambulance. "So tell me, where are we now?"

Matt smiled, feeling a gust of hot air from a doorway to his left. This was too easy. "We just passed the Laundromat. It's another twenty-six steps to the corner." At the intersection, he waited briefly for the light to change before stepping onto the crosswalk. "Ten more to cross Thirty-second Street." At the other side of the street, he took a deep breath, refreshing his memory of the block ahead. He announced each shop at they passed it, like a bus driver conducting a guided tour. "Rose's Flowers . . . Manelli's for produce . . . Lung Fung's for bad Chinese food . . . Luis for the *Times* in Braille . . ."

The man at the newsstand handed Matt a paper. "Good morning, Mr. Murdock," he said cheerfully.

Matt handed Luis a dollar, then waited until they were a few steps past the newsstand before leaning over to whisper, "Aqua Velva."

Elektra laughed, suitably impressed. "You've got the whole city wired."

"Only the Kitchen," he insisted, fudging the truth a little. "Outside of that, I'm just another blind guy in New York."

He could almost feel her eyes examining him, looking deep into his soul. "Somehow," she said thoughtfully, "I find that hard to believe."

A delicious thrill ran through him as, once again, he experienced a profound sense of connection to this mysterious and strangely perceptive woman, who already seemed to understand him better than his closest friends. Matt had never believed in soul mates before, but he suddenly found himself entertaining an argument in defense of the proposition. *Is this what Dad felt, the first time he met my mother?*

He tried not to think about how badly that particular romance must have turned out. . . .

Squealing brakes intruded on his wistful reflections

as a gleaming black limousine pulled up to the side-walk, forcing its way across two lanes of traffic. The limo's back door swung open, and a man charged out of the car, stomping toward them. Matt's radar senses informed him that the stranger was a big man, at least two hundred fifty pounds, and mostly muscle.

An unexpected odor reached Matt's nostrils, and he abruptly stepped in front of Elektra. "Get back," he warned her urgently, gripping the shaft of his cane like the weapon it was.

"What is it?" she asked. To his surprise, she sounded more curious than alarmed. Her heart didn't miss a beat.

"He's got a gun," he said tersely. His muscles tensed for action as the armed gorilla approached. If necessary, he was perfectly willing to blow his secret identity to keep Elektra safe.

"He'd better," she said calmly, a touch of wry amusement in her voice. She laid a restraining hand on Matt's arm. "He's my bodyguard."

Bodyguard? Matt froze in place, his mental gears shifting more rapidly than his baffled reflexes could handle.

"I thought I lost him back at the coffee shop," she confessed, releasing a sigh of resignation before turning to address the hulking stranger directly. *"Ase me ese hi!"*

Now Matt was completely lost. His special senses did not include automatic translation from Greek to English.

The bodyguard tapped the face of his watch. *"Pame, Elektra,"* he scolded her.

"Malakas . . ." she muttered, with yet another sigh. Her slender fingers reluctantly let go of Matt's arm.

His mind was still struggling to catch up with this new development. "You need a bodyguard?"

Judging from the way she had fought back at the playground, Elektra was about the last woman he would have expected to have a hefty guardian angel shadowing her. *She needs a bodyguard*, he thought, *like I need color TV.*

"My father can be a little . . . overprotective at times," she explained. "Kidnapping's a big business back in Greece and"—she hesitated, and Matt guessed there was more to the story than she was letting on—"we're all we have left now."

Matt wondered what had happened to the rest of her family, to her mother. Had she lost a parent to murder, too?

Understanding dawned, as he belatedly fit two pieces together. "Natchios as in . . . Nikolas Natchios?"

Naturally, Matt had heard of the celebrated Greek tycoon. He seemed to recall reading something about the violent death of Natchios's wife several years back. *A drive-by shooting, wasn't it? Or maybe a car bomb?*

No wonder Natchios had taught Elektra how to defend herself!

"That's Dad," she admitted, a bit sheepishly. Her embarrassment faded as another thought occurred to her. "Wait a second. How did you know Stavros had a gun?"

Matt filed away the bodyguard's name for future reference. "I could smell the gunpowder," he said.

Her breath caught in her throat. *She believes me*, Matt realized.

Stavros interrupted the moment. "Elektra!" he barked impatiently.

"Na se pario diavelos!" Elektra shouted back, and Matt wondered if the looming bodyguard even spoke English. She turned toward him, her posture apologetic. "I'm sorry. I have to go."

"Can I see you again?" Matt asked quickly, before she could disappear into the limo. He was startled by how important this was to him, considering he had met her less than an hour ago.

Once more, he heard a note of sorrow in her voice. "I don't think that's a good idea," she began, then stepped backward in surprise. "What are you smiling at?"

"Your heart," Matt answered honestly. "It just skipped a beat."

"Meaning . . . ?" Wary, but interested, too.

"You think it's a good idea."

She didn't deny it, instead subjecting him to a moment of prolonged examination. Right then Matt realized one of the reasons he felt so comfortable in her presence: She never once felt sorry for him or underestimated his abilities just because he was blind.

"So you smell guns and hear heartbeats," she said finally. "Anything else I should know?"

Matt shrugged. "Just don't lie or shoot me and we'll get along great."

"You're a strange man, Matt Murdock," she declared, sounding intrigued despite herself. She glanced back over her shoulder at Stavros, who was tapping his size-ten foot restlessly on the cement. "I really do have to go. . . ."

Matt couldn't stand the idea of her exiting from his life forever. "How will I find you," he pleaded, "if you won't give me your number?"

"You won't," Elektra stated unequivocally, like a judge laying down a life sentence. Matt's heart sank until, just as she was stepping into the rear of the limo, Elektra commuted his sentence at the last minute. "I'll find you."

Matt watched, grinning like a madman, as the limo pulled away. *So long, Elektra*, he thought, feeling more stoked about the future than he had in a long time. The bruises and bitterness left behind by last night's mission of vengeance were forgotten now, replaced by the intriguing possibilities raised by Elektra's final promise. *I'll be waiting*, he thought eagerly. Waiting . . .

A sudden realization hit him, and he hastily reached for his wristwatch, flipping open the glass lid and feeling the Braille face with his fingers. He winced as he realized that it was nearly a quarter to noon.

"Shit!"

CHAPTER 11

Fourteen minutes later, after Matt took a frantic taxi ride downtown, Foggy and he walked as fast as propriety would allow through the busy corridors of the courthouse. "I told you I wouldn't wait," Foggy repeated, still steamed by his partner's late arrival. He glanced anxiously at his own wristwatch as they rushed to make their noontime appointment.

"I said I was sorry," Matt murmured. Frankly, he was just relieved to find Foggy here at the courthouse and not still waiting back at the coffee shop. "What more do you want?"

Foggy was too good-natured to hold a grudge for long. "Details," he demanded, and Matt could hear the puckish grin in his voice. "You owe me that."

Fair enough, Matt thought, *although I probably ought to leave out all that martial arts mayhem in the park.* "Her name is Elektra Natchios," he divulged.

"Sounds like a Mexican appetizer," Foggy replied, perhaps thinking ahead to lunch.

"It's Greek, genius," Matt told him. "Her father is Nikolas Natchios."

That stopped Foggy in his tracks. Despite their imminent tardiness, he came to a halt long enough to

make sure he was hearing correctly. "The billionaire?"

"Yeah," Matt confirmed.

Foggy took a deep breath and wiped his brow.
"Then as your attorney, I advise you to marry her.
Immediately."

"I'll take it under consideration," Matt promised.
He tugged on Foggy's arm to get them moving again.
As much as he would have preferred to fantasize
about his future with Elektra, they still had a potential client to meet. "What have we got?" he asked,
nodding toward the folder in his partner's hand.

At least Foggy had arrived in time to peruse the
file in advance. He gave Matt a quick rundown as
they marched down the hall.

"Daunte Jackson, ex-con from Queens, charged
with the August ninth murder of one Lisa Tazio,
your friendly neighborhood prostitute. The bad
news: Jackson was found passed out in an alley,
holding the murder weapon and with enough THC
in his lungs to get all of Staten Island high." Foggy
shook his head; clearly Jackson wasn't one of the
"better clients" he had been lobbying for. "Jackson
says he can't remember what happened the night of
the murder. Or for that matter, most of the nineties."

Matt had to admit the case didn't sound very
promising. "So what's the good news?"

Foggy delivered the punch line with the deadpan
understatement of a stand-up comic. "The fluke
wasn't bad."

Daunte Jackson was a scrawny black man with
elaborately coiled dreadlocks, faded tattoos on his
neck, and a worryingly stoned expression. Matt and
Foggy found him waiting for them in the holding

cell, seated behind a cheap pine table. Blank sound-proof panels covered the walls.

Jackson looked up as the two attorneys sat down across from him. He wore gray prison togs, courtesy of Rikers Island. "Who you?" he asked cluelessly.

"We're your lawyers," Matt explained. "If you're innocent." The stark, utilitarian decor of the holding cell offered few distractions, making it easy for Matt to zero in on the prisoner's heart rate. He listened carefully to see how Jackson reacted to his queries. "So, are you? Innocent?"

"Hell, yeah!" Jackson asserted, with more vigor than he had previously seemed capable of. To Matt's slight surprise, there was no indication that Jackson was lying; unlike Quesada on the witness stand, Jackson's heart was as steady as a rock.

"I believe you," Matt said.

"You do?" Jackson blurted. He sounded like he couldn't believe his ears.

"You do?" Foggy echoed, failing to conceal his own surprise and disappointment. He surely knew what was coming next.

Matt leaned across the table to offer Jackson his hand. "You've got yourself a defense."

Groaning, Foggy buried his face in his hands.

I can't believe I let Matt talk me into this, Foggy thought as he and Matt walked down Thirty-eighth Street on their way to check out the murder site. Bad enough that they had just taken on another hopeless disaster of a case, on behalf of a client who couldn't possibly afford their services. Now they had to track down a dead prostitute's address, too?

He sipped from a Styrofoam cup of coffee as they hiked past an auto body shop, just a few blocks south of the Lincoln Tunnel. It was midafternoon, and the humidity made Foggy long for the air-conditioned comfort of their office.

"I wonder what Jackson will pay us in?" he speculated. Despite Matt's handicap, Foggy had to hustle to keep up with his partner. "Free tattoos? Chronic?"

Matt greeted his partner's sarcasm with a sigh. "Foggy . . ."

Foggy couldn't keep quiet. He had to get this out of his system. "He's a three-time loser," he protested, "who was found holding the murder weapon a block away."

"He's also innocent," Matt insisted, his cane tapping on the sidewalk as they headed toward Tenth Avenue. The smell of fresh bagels emanating from the open door of a mom-and-pop bakery reminded Foggy that he hadn't had lunch yet.

"How can you be so sure?" Foggy knew there was no point in arguing; once Matt's mind was set, nothing could sway him. But he felt obliged to try anyway.

"Have I ever been wrong?" Matt asked.

"No," Foggy admitted. He sighed heavily, unable to deny that his partner had an uncanny gift when it came to weighing a defendant's guilt or innocence. Foggy wasn't sure exactly how Matt did it, but he couldn't question the results. Matt was always right about these things. "Which is really annoying, by the way."

Matt smiled sympathetically, but kept on tapping.

Foggy took another sip of coffee, feeling justifiably sorry for himself. Matt was a great guy, and the best lawyer Foggy had ever seen, but sometimes Foggy couldn't help wondering what his life and career would be like with a less crusading partner.

Water dripped on his head from a leaky air conditioner several stories above. *Then again*, he thought wryly, *how could I give up all this glamour and excitement?*

Matt halted in front of an old brownstone, and Foggy marveled at the blind lawyer's sense of direction. A makeshift shrine had been erected on the crumbling front steps of the building where Lisa Tazio had been murdered. Candles, flowers, photographs, and greeting cards were neatly arranged on the steps, and Foggy wondered briefly if Hallmark produced any cards specifically suited to this kind of situation. *When you care enough to leave the very best at the site of a ghastly killing . . .*

"This is it," he announced unnecessarily. He put his briefcase down on the sidewalk. "So now what?"

"We take a look around," Matt stated. Figuratively speaking, of course.

Foggy gulped down the last of his coffee before trying to reason with Matt one more time. "Look, I know you've got this built-in bullshit detector, but this time it's on the blink." He threw up his hands in exasperation. "I mean, let's say for argument's sake that Jackson is innocent—"

"He is innocent," Matt said with certainty.

Foggy ignored the interruption. "—so why would somebody go to all the trouble to set him up? Why the big cover-up in the death of a small-time prostitute?"

"We can't answer that," Matt said, "until we find out more about Lisa Tazio."

Foggy groaned like a D.A. faced with a hostile witness. "Too bad we don't have a key."

He watched forlornly as Matt tapped his way up the steps, carefully avoiding the accumulated candles and flowers. Foggy retrieved his briefcase and nervously followed Matt up to the front door of the apartment building. The paint was peeling from the metal doorframe, and a scribbled notice taped over the intercom indicated that the buzzer was out of order. Pushing through the door, the two began navigating the dingy halls of the building. They quickly located the murder victim's apartment. Yellow crime-scene tape was still stretched across the front door.

"Give me your pen," Matt said to Foggy.

"You're going to leave him a note?" Foggy asked.

Matt took the pen that Foggy produced from his briefcase, stooped down to the lock, and proceeded to pick it.

"What are you, MacGyver? I must have been sick the day they taught that," Foggy quipped. "Real estate law, right?"

Matt was too intent on his mission to acknowledge Foggy's joke. Foggy gulped as the door swung open, and Matt ducked beneath the yellow tape, with Foggy following right after him. Foggy shut the door behind him and switched on the light, revealing a small, one-bedroom flat decked out with cheap, thrift-store furniture. The TV set sat on top of a plastic milk crate packed with old videos. Comedies, mostly. Ashtrays were scattered around the apartment, and a neglected houseplant was slowly dying in one corner.

"What do you see?" Matt asked.

Foggy looked around the apartment. "High ceilings. Nice flow. Looks like we have hardware under here. Nice feng shui." The air-conditioning in the apartment had been switched off days ago, and the stuffy room felt like an oven. "You think they've rented this place yet?"

"Foggy," Matt said impatiently, his sense of humor definitely on hold.

"What?" Foggy shrugged; like all New Yorkers, he was constantly on the lookout for a more affordable residence. "I might as well get something out of this case."

Matt tapped his way to the center of the apartment, then took a deep breath, inhaling the apartment. Foggy watched attentively, having seen this before. He never failed to be amazed at what his partner's acute nostrils could pick up. He often teased Matt that he had a nose like a bloodhound.

"Ammonia . . . " Matt announced after a few seconds.

"So?" Foggy asked. He felt like a bumbling Dr. Watson watching Sherlock Holmes at work.

". . . over blood," Matt continued. He took another deep breath, then nodded decisively, having reached a conclusion. "I think Tazio was shot here, then dragged outside to make it look like some random robbery."

"By who?" Foggy asked.

"By someone with a lot to lose," Matt answered.

A wooden desk was wedged into one corner of the living room. Matt walked over to the desk and ran his fingers lightly over the pine tabletop. It was strangely clean, unnaturally so.

Foggy didn't care if Lisa Tazio had been a good housekeeper or not. "Matt, there's nothing there . . . let's go."

Matt seemed to feel otherwise. His alert fingers brushed the tabletop while his face maintained a look of intense concentration. "Get me a pen and write this down," he said abruptly.

What in the world? Foggy thought. He dug around

in his case until he produced another pen and a small spiral notepad.

"She wrote something with a ballpoint pen," Matt explained tersely, his fingers fluttering over the surface of the desk. "The imprint is still in the wood."

How about that? Foggy thought, his jaw dropping. Even though he had watched the whole thing with his own eyes, he was still astounded that Matt had somehow been able to detect the faint indentations in the pine. *I would've never noticed those in a million years.*

Matt stepped back and said to Foggy, "Mom, six-slash-eight."

Foggy's eyes widened. "I knew it!" he declared ominously.

"What?" Matt asked. He leaned intently toward Foggy, as if he were cross-examining a crucial witness.

"Her *mother* killed her," Foggy answered, sarcasm dripping from his tongue. As far as he was concerned, this whole breaking-and-entering routine had been a total waste of time. He glanced around nervously, worried that at any moment Lisa Tazio's neighbors might call the cops.

"Now can we get out of here," he pleaded, "before we need attorneys, too?"

Matt Murdock in court, building his case against
Jose Quesada.

Franklin "Foggy" Nelson,
Matt's partner, helps
prosecute the case.

A victorious
Jack "The Devil"
Murdock
triumphantly lifts
his son to his
shoulder.

Wilson Fisk,
aka the Kingpin.

The two faces of
Elektra Natchios:
daughter of a business
tycoon by day...

...and vigilante by night.

Bullseye, assassin extraordinaire.

Bullseye and the Kingpin get down to business.

Ben Urich, investigative reporter, picks up Daredevil's trail.

Daredevil leaves his mark, keeping the streets of Hell's Kitchen safe from crime.

Daredevil prepares to mete out his own brand of justice.

Bullseye on his motorcycle.

Matt and Elektra share a private moment.

Combining deadly grace with lethal agility, Elektra brings her sai into play.

Bullseye launches his deadly throwing stars.

Daredevil in battle.

Daredevil, the Man Without Fear.

CHAPTER 12

Thirty thousand feet above the ground, the man called Bullseye found himself trapped on the flight from hell. The dithery old lady sitting next to him had not stopped yakking since their plane took off from the runway.

"... and then my daughter, Susie, not the Susie from Buffalo—that's my son Larry's daughter from his first marriage—eloped with a semicolored fellow from London. What's that word? Mulatta? Let's just say he's got a little cream in his coffee. Anyhow, he does very well for himself on the Internet. Don't ask me to explain. They got me a computer last Christmas, but I won't use it because I'm afraid it will start a fire. ..."

Bullseye sank back into his aisle seat, doing his best to tune out the incessant chatter from his unwanted traveling companion. His Walkman, draped over his nylon skullcap, blared heavy metal into his ears, but enough of the old lady's rambling monologue leaked through to put his nerves dangerously on edge. The fact that he had shown absolutely no interest in anything she had to say—indeed, had gone out of his way to conspicuously ignore her—apparently made no difference whatsoever. The old bat just kept on talking, knitting as she spoke, as though he were hanging on her every word.

". . . Larry's second wife, Donna Marie, is picking me up at the airport. Of course, I'm perfectly capable of driving myself, but my children don't believe me. Just because sometimes I have to get out of the car and walk up to the intersection to see what color the light is, they think I'm too old to be behind a wheel. . . ."

He fiddled with a playing card, making the ace of spades dance across his knuckles, then disappear entirely, while he sullenly watched the old lady's lips move to the metal music of her knitting needles. Finally, he took off the headphones.

". . . and do you know what she said to me?" The elderly woman's knitting needles clacked noisily, weaving something revoltingly pink and fuzzy.

"*Would-you-shut-the-hell-up?*" Bullseye snarled with a distinct Irish brogue, his fists angrily gripping the armrests. Saliva sprayed from his lips, and his eyes blazed like a rabid dog's.

The oblivious old woman never looked up from her knitting. "No, she said, 'Come and visit, Mom.' But who can afford to fly these days?"

Frustrated, Bullseye yanked his headphones back on, just as an attractive flight attendant walked by and dropped a minuscule bag of peanuts onto his tray. He tore open the foil bag and a grand total of three peanuts rolled out.

Hmm, he thought, eyeing the garrulous geriatric to his left. A smirk crept across his face. *This has possibilities. . . .*

The yapping hag was too busy blathering to notice her own bag of peanuts. "But then my sister Marjorie called. . . ."

Bullseye rolled a single peanut under his forefinger, positioning it on the tray.

". . . and she said she has frequent flier miles that she can't use on account of her sciatic nerve acting up. . . ."

With a flick of his finger, Bullseye propelled the peanut into the plastic seat back in front of him. The tiny missile ricocheted off the seat and right into the old woman's mouth.

". . . and I said—*acccckk!*"

Right on target, the flying peanut lodged in the woman's windpipe, choking her. Bullseye watched with satisfaction as she tried in vain to draw a breath, her mouth working silently like that of a fish out of water. Her eyes bulged in horror and she clutched her throat with a withered arthritic hand until, with nothing more than a final choking rattle, she collapsed back into the window seat.

Bullseye licked the salt from his fingertip, then reached over to close the old woman's eyes. He calmly repositioned her hand as well, laying it peacefully in her lap. *That's better*, he thought, savoring the newfound silence. He figured he had done the entire plane a favor.

Not long after, the friendly flight attendant cruised by again. Seeing the old woman "resting" quietly, she leaned over Bullseye to drape a blanket over the sleeping passenger.

"Can I get you anything before we land?" she asked Bullseye after she had finished tucking the old lady in. She kept her voice low to avoid disturbing the elderly woman.

"More peanuts?" he requested.

The courtroom was grander and more impressive than the courtroom where Jose Quesada had walked free. Rich mahogany panels adorned the walls while the spectator's gallery was large enough to accommodate a sizable audience, if necessary. Lady Justice still presided over the proceedings, however, standing proudly behind the judge's elevated bench.

"Ladies and gentlemen of the jury," Matt began his opening statement, "I'm not here today to convince you that Daunte Jackson is a model citizen. He's been in and out of reform schools and prisons since he was twelve years old. But this isn't a court of character, it's a court of law. And in this case Daunte Jackson is innocent."

Matt heard the jury members shifting uncomfortably in their seats. No surprise there, considering that he was currently standing with his back to the jury.

"He's facing the wrong way," Jackson whispered anxiously to Foggy, who was sitting next to Jackson at the defense's table. Matt could easily hear their muted exchange.

"Don't worry," Foggy said. "Matt's got 'em right where he wants 'em."

"Right . . ." Jackson murmured dubiously.

Matt decided it was time to take both Jackson and the jury off the hook. Without warning, he suddenly spun around to face the jury box. "And that's what it's been like for Daunte Jackson. Like talking to a wall."

The jury members chuckled and sighed in relief.

The judge was distinctly less impressed, having seen this trick before. "Does this defense come with a two-drink minimum, Mr. Murdock?"

"No, Your Honor," Matt stated politely. "I just wanted to make a point. You see, justice is blind. But it can be heard. And today the truth will come out."

He turned his words back toward the jury. "Thank you."

Foggy scurried out from behind the desk to help Matt back to his seat. His assistance was entirely unneeded, of course, but the jury didn't know that.

Officer Robert McKenzie was the prosecution's chief witness. Unfortunately for the defense, he looked like the poster boy for an NYPD recruitment ad. According to Foggy, he was a fit-looking man in his forties, with clean-cut good looks and the face of a choir boy. *Just our luck*, Matt thought grimly.

"I was a block away when I got the call of shots being fired," McKenzie said confidently from the witness stand. "When I arrived on the scene Lisa Tazio was lying dead on the steps of her apartment building." He nodded toward the dreadlocked defendant. "I found Jackson passed out in the alley, still holding the murder weapon and Tazio's wallet."

As always, Matt listened intently to the witness's heart. To his surprise, the policeman's heartbeat was as steady as a metronome. *That can't be possible*, Matt thought, shaking his head in confusion.

Foggy noticed Matt's bewildered expression. "What is it?" he asked quietly.

"McKenzie," Matt whispered. "He's telling the truth."

"It happens sometimes in court," his partner said dryly.

You don't understand, Matt thought in puzzlement. His radar senses were more reliable than a polygraph, yet Jackson and McKenzie couldn't both be telling the truth. "Somebody has to be lying."

Foggy shrugged, unable to appreciate the full extent of Matt's dilemma. He glanced back over his shoulder at the rear of the courtroom. "Wonder what he's doing here," he commented absently.

"Who?" Matt asked. He had been concentrating so intensely on both McKenzie and the jury that he had paid little attention to the trial's meager audience. Despite the generous number of benches provided for spectators, the trial of Daunte Jackson had drawn few observers, the murder of a Hell's Kitchen hooker being not exactly big news.

"That reporter from the *Post*," Foggy replied. "Urich."

Matt frowned. Without needing to turn around, he directed his senses behind him. The wooden benches were largely empty, except for a solitary figure seated inconspicuously in the back row. Matt sniffed, picking up the telltale reek of nicotine. *A smoker*, he deduced. *Camels*.

This was worrisome. What was Ben Urich doing here? The death of Lisa Tazio barely rated a paragraph in the *Post*, but Matt was all too aware of Urich's ongoing coverage of Daredevil's one-man crusade against crime. The reporter, whose articles Matt had surreptitiously perused, had been showing way too much interest in Hell's Kitchen's resident vigilante.

Is he on to me? Matt fretted. Exposure of his nocturnal activities would torpedo his legal career, plus destroy Daredevil's effectiveness as well. Matt felt the reporter's inquisitive eyes on his back, and a trickle of sweat ran down his spine.

How much does Urich already know?

CHAPTER 13

Matt was still preoccupied with Urich's possible investigation as he walked home that evening. A long afternoon at the office, spent reviewing all the evidence and testimony in the Daunte Jackson case, had failed to turn up any sort of explanation as to how both Jackson and Officer McKenzie could be telling the truth. *I don't understand*, he thought, shaking his head. *My senses have never been wrong before.*

The night was hot and humid, with a tense electricity that made Matt's skin tingle. He sensed a thunderstorm approaching and quickened his pace to avoid being caught in a downpour.

Behind him, another set of footsteps quickened as well.

Matt's muscles tensed and he tightened his grip on his cane. Whoever was following him was in for a surprise; there was practically no way to sneak up on him undetected. He stepped around the corner of an old tenement building, ready to confront his shadow. *Just my luck*, he thought irritably. *It's probably that snoopy reporter again.*

Then a familiar fragrance reached him, and his spirits lifted. "Does this mean you want a rematch?" he asked with a smile.

Elektra marched around the corner to join him.

"How did you know I wasn't a mugger?" she asked.

"Muggers don't smell like rose oil," he replied.

A sultry breeze rustled through her hair. "I was in the neighborhood," she explained.

Matt gestured toward their surroundings, the motion encompassing the scattered garbage and graffiti. A few feet away, a homeless wino snored on the sidewalk. "On purpose?"

She laughed out loud. Busted!

Matt forgot all about Daunte Jackson and Ben Urich. Storm or no storm, tonight was looking a whole lot better all of a sudden. "Come on," he said enthusiastically. "I want to show you something."

Elektra looked around the lonely rooftop. At one time, it appeared, someone had used the roof as a makeshift gym. A deflated speed bag was still mounted on the skeletal frame of a dilapidated water tower. Exercise weights were scattered here and there on the tar-paper floor of the rooftop, along with cigarette butts and shards of broken glass. Obscene graffiti was scrawled on the surviving ribs of the old water tank, many of whose wooden slats had long since rotted away.

Not exactly the most romantic of settings, she thought, but there was something strangely magical about it nonetheless. *Like we're all alone on a deserted island, far away from the cares of the world.*

"Exactly how many girls have you had up here, anyway?" she asked.

Matt was seated beside her on the low stone railing, their backs to the street below. He had shed his jacket and tie and was now dressed more casually in a blue cotton shirt and slacks. It looked good on him.

"You're my first," he said.

She smiled, both sad and relieved that he couldn't see her face. "Good answer." She turned and looked out over the city. Lighted windows glowed like welcoming hearths amid the shadowed-haunted roofscape that seemed to stretch on forever. The steeple of a nearby church rose above the neighborhood, pointing toward the bright orange moon casting its tranquil radiance over the roofs of the city. In the distance, not too far away, the top of the Empire State Building blazed with its own electric illumination, shining brightly crimson against the hazy night sky.

"It's so beautiful, I—" she began, then caught herself, realizing that Matt couldn't possibly share the gorgeous scenery with her.

"Yeah. I remember," Matt said.

"I'm sorry."

"Why? It's okay," he assured her. "That's why I brought you up here. I wanted you to see it." His crimson cane lay forgotten at his feet, beside a pair of discarded black glasses. His sightless blue eyes stared past her, unoffended. "This was one of my favorite views when I was twelve years old. I've stored snapshots in my memory. I wanted to know how you see it."

"Okay, I'll show you," she said, her momentary embarrassment giving way to a rush of emotion. It wasn't fair that Matt couldn't see the enchanting spectacle he had brought her here to see!

She stood up, stepping closer to him, as she gazed out over the moonlit metropolis. "There are lights.

Millions of lights. So many, the city has been made of diamonds.''

Matt smiled, clearly picturing it in his mind. ''What else?''

''Taxis. But from here they line the streets. It could be a Christmas parade. And the moon is so huge and low,'' she continued, ''you'd swear you could touch it. Even though you know it's out of reach.''

A stiff wind cooled her shoulders, and to her chagrin, she saw a battalion of heavy black clouds rolling toward them, obliterating the moon.

Matt slowly reached out and touched her cheek, his fingers gently tracing her jawline, down to her neck, brushing against her necklace. ''What's this?'' he asked.

''It's a gift from my mother. A good luck charm,'' she said.

''A lucky charm? I need that. Do they make them in Braille?'' he joked.

Elektra smiled warmly, half lost in memory. ''My mother gave it to me right before she died.''

''I'm sorry,'' Matt said. ''What happened?''

Elektra's eyes, almost misty, suddenly cleared. ''No Greek tragedies, okay? Look . . . I should go.''

''Wait. You've got to stay. I want you to stay,'' Matt said. ''It's about to rain.''

''No, it's not,'' Elektra said.

''Yes, it is. Any second now. And when it rains I can hear the drops on all the surfaces. It's like a blanket on the world. I can see shapes and textures I usually miss. And for a moment, everything is clear. For a moment . . . I can see again.'' He turned his face toward her, his blue eyes as deep and mysterious as the Aegean Sea. ''I just want to see you.''

Elektra fell silent, moved by his words. "Okay," she finally said, her voice hoarse with emotion.

"Here it comes."

The rain bounced off Elektra like solid droplets of sound, showing Matt the outline of first her face and shoulders, then her entire body, in perfect silhouette. Glittering diamonds and starlight traced her every contour and curve, and the graceful symmetry took his breath away.

Heedless of the torrential deluge, she walked slowly toward him. She took his eager hand and placed it against her face, inviting him to "see" her even more closely. Matt slowly caressed her delicate features. Her skin was warm and soft to his touch, and he gratefully explored every subtle nuance of her exotic splendor. Cooling rain washed away the salty residue of her tears, running in rivulets between his fingers and her cheeks.

"You are so beautiful . . ." he breathed softly.

Matt bent forward to kiss her, and her lips met his hungrily. For a precious heartbeat, the rest of the world slipped away, and Matt luxuriated in the intoxicating taste and feel of her.

"Get away from me!"

The frightened shriek jolted Matt's senses. For one startled moment, he thought—insanely—that the jarring scream came from Elektra. He pulled away from her, only to realize that the cry was coming from somewhere beyond the rain-swept rooftop and that the fear-stricken voice belonged to a young boy, maybe five or six years old.

"What is it?" Elektra asked, confused.

The violent echoes of the boy's scream literally tore apart her sparkling silhouette. The enticing phantasm vanished, replaced by the naked panic of an endangered child.

"Matt?"

The boy was crying now, his frantic sobs sounding as though he were here on the rooftop with them, cowering at Matt's feet. "No! No! Leave me alone!" he implored, his childish voice filled with mortal terror.

"Matt? What is it?" She raised her voice anxiously, but Matt forced himself to tune her out, striving instead to locate the source of the little boy's panicky cries. He tracked the echoes off the roof, down the street, and through an open window about two blocks away.

"No!" the boy shrieked again, right before the window slammed shut, trapping the child inside with whatever menaced him.

"I have to go," Matt said tersely.

He didn't need eyes to imagine the hurt and baffled expression on her face. "Matt?"

"I'm sorry . . ." he mumbled weakly, wishing there was some way he could explain without exposing his other identity. But there was no time to even concoct a plausible excuse; for all he knew, the little boy was already under attack.

Drenched to the skin, he scrambled to retrieve his glasses and cane, then ran for the stairway, leaving Elektra alone on the rooftop in the pouring rain.

CHAPTER 14

The drunken father, reeking of booze and sweat, stumbled down the dark hallway, which was lit only by a single buzzing lightbulb overhead. "Where are you? Goddamn it!" he bellowed, his fists clenched at his sides.

He was a big, beefy man whose heavy tread reverberated down the hall. He passed an open window, letting in the sounds of the city (among other things), and the truculent anger in his voice grew. "Did I say you could open this window?" he hollered, slurring his words slightly.

A whimper emerged from beneath the stairs, where his petrified son huddled in terror, his tiny hands clamped over his ears in a futile attempt to block out his father's explosive wrath. Tears gushed from his eyes, and his child-sized heart thrummed like a toy locomotive. Choking sobs betrayed his hiding place under the steps.

The brutal dad closed on his terrified offspring. "Listen when I talk to you!" he raged, raising his fist.

That's enough, Daredevil decided. His arm snapped out of the shadows, grabbing the other man by the wrist. Gloved fingers locked onto the father's arm, halting its progress.

"What—?" the drunk blurted, and Daredevil twisted violently, causing the man to howl in pain. "See how it feels?" Daredevil said.

"Stop it!" the little boy screamed, and Daredevil automatically turned his head toward the sound.

Crack! The father elbowed Daredevil in the jaw, making his teeth rattle.

The jarring blow only fueled Daredevil's fury at the abusive parent. *Think you're a tough guy?* he thought vindictively, slamming the drunk against the wall hard enough to crack the plaster. *My dad had it rough, too, but he never beat me!*

Daredevil let the poor slob have it, holding nothing back, not even hearing the little boy continue to plead. Pile-driver fists hammered the drunk's face and body, shattering bone and cartilage. *Not so tough, are you?* Daredevil taunted silently, his knuckles punishing the other man's ribs. *When you're not bullying a defenseless kid!* Outraged by the drunk's heartless brutality, provoked and frustrated by his aborted date with Elektra, he unleashed all his unbridled anger on the drunken father until the once-threatening ogre was nothing but a crying, pathetic mess of a man, unable to stand up under his own power.

"I'm sorry . . . I'm sorry . . ." he blubbered through a mouthful of blood and broken teeth. "I love my son . . . I love him . . . I'm sorry. . . ."

Daredevil stepped back, letting the pulverized drunk collapse onto the floor. He turned to check on the little boy, who was still hiding in the dusty crawlspace under the stairs.

To his surprise, he discovered that the child's racing heart and laboring lungs sounded even more panicked than before. Whimpering pitifully, he had retreated into the crawlspace as far he could go, his arms wrapped protectively around his knees.

The boy sounded as if he was in a state of shock. With a start, Daredevil suddenly realized what a nightmarish image he must present to the poor kid. He imagined catatonic eyes staring in fixed horror at the grotesque crimson demon that had just attacked his father. "Hey," he said reassuringly, reaching out his hand.

The child flinched and scrambled backward. His galloping heart sounded ready to explode.

Daredevil's own heart felt a painful stab. The savage gratification of his victory over the brutish father evaporated, leaving a bitter taste in his mouth. He contemplated the wrecked remains of his victim and it dawned on him, with a sense of growing revulsion and remorse, that the pulped and bleeding carcass on the floor behind him probably bore an uncomfortable resemblance to Daredevil's own father in his final minutes.

Oh, my God. . . .

"I'm not the bad guy, kid," he tried to explain to the devastated child, but it was more of a plea than a statement. He stood silently in the hall for a moment, contemplating the awful aftermath of his mission of mercy, then disappeared out the window he had opened earlier.

The traumatized boy's sobs and whimpers followed him into the city streets, where he used a pay phone to make an anonymous call to the police, alerting them to the situation back at the blood-spattered apartment before taking a fire escape up to the rooftops. He raced across the soot-covered crown of the city, trying but failing to outrun his turbulent thoughts and emotions. *Did I do the right thing?* he wondered, leaping from roof to roof. *I saved the poor kid, sure, but did I also scar him for life?*

Finally, he arrived at the building he and his father had lived in years ago, where the decrepit water tower loomed as a monument to his childhood memories. Elektra was long gone, of course, and the driving rain had washed away any trace of her fragrance.

Daredevil pulled off his mask, and Matt Murdock stood alone in the rain, sick to death of the life he had made for himself. "I'm not the bad guy," he repeated forlornly.

But could he be sure?

The next day started with a cavalcade of aches and pains. Matt climbed slowly out of the flotation tank, his knees and shoulders popping and cracking like those of an old jock. Because he was no longer shielded by the soundproof solitude of the tank, the usual street noises assailed Matt. The strident honks and squealing brakes jabbed at his throbbing head like splinters in his brain.

He staggered over to the stereo and hit the POWER button. Nickelback's new CD blared to life, and Matt turned the volume all the way up to ten in hopes of drowning out the early-morning urban cacophony outside.

It worked, a little.

A hot shower helped bring him back to life. Matt stood in the stall, letting the pelting water massage his aching muscles. Something rattled in his mouth, and he reached in to remove a loose tooth. *What—?* he wondered briefly, then remembered the details of last night's violence. *Oh yeah, the elbow to my jaw.* He released the cracked molar, letting it fall. He heard it clatter its way down the shower drain.

After the shower, he wandered over to his closet, where his business suits were carefully labeled with Braille tags. He might have superhuman senses, but he still couldn't match a coat and pants for court without a little assistive technology. His fingers glided over the tags and he picked out his attire for today's hearing.

Once he was dressed, he moved on to the next part of his daily routine. He pulled out a kitchen drawer and removed several legal-sized envelopes marked in Braille. Each envelope contained dollar bills of a different denomination, and Matt replenished his wallet, folding a pair of twenties lengthwise, a ten in half, and dog-earing the corners of a couple of ones.

To be honest, he could probably tell the bills apart just by feeling the impressions of the ink, but the system of specialized folds spared him from having to pretend to fumble with his money. Besides, it was just easier.

Properly put together, he headed for the door. He passed a crucifix hanging on the wall, with a string of rosary beads draped over it. Matt pocketed the rosary and went out to face the day.

The Church of the Holy Innocents was empty at this hour of the morning. Matt had the pews pretty much to himself as he sat in the empty nave, the rosary in his hands.

An imposing antique pipe organ (mercifully silent now) towered behind the altar and sanctuary. Three tiers of polished brass pipes ascended a majestic two hundred feet, ending just below the ornate, stained-glass rose window overlooking the hushed interior of the church. Sunlight filtered through the hundreds of translucent color panels making up the elaborate circular design of the rose window, which was nearly twenty feet in diameter. Many stories below, a maintenance man diligently repaired the large mechanical choir elevator located to the right of the sanctuary. Incense scented the air, but not oppressively enough to offend Matt's keen nose.

Mild footsteps approached and a familiar voice greeted him from behind. "One of the strengths of the church," Father Everett observed dryly, "is its sense of community."

Matt knew the old priest was alluding to the all-but-empty pews. "Good morning, Father," he said courteously, not quite managing to muster a cheerful smile.

He had known Father Everett ever since he was a child. The kindly neighborhood priest had been instrumental in seeing that Matt was looked out for after his father's murder; he had spent many long hours trying to comfort Matt in the wake of that tragedy. Matt still burned with unquenched fury regarding his father's death, but he was grateful for the priest's compassionate efforts nonetheless.

"This may come as a surprise to you, Matthew, but we're open on Sundays."

"I like the quiet," Matt said.

"You like the solitude," Father Everett translated. He sat down next to Matt and sighed. "Do you find it here, Matthew?"

Matt listened to the relative peace and quiet of the cathedral. He wasn't entirely evading the issue when he suggested that a full Sunday service would not offer the same healing serenity he found on these private weekday mornings; the massive pipe organ alone would surely be hell on his amplified senses.

"Sometimes," he assured the priest, even as the distant wail of sirens encroached on the restful hush he so urgently craved.

The harsh, discordant noises sought him out, bringing the roar and yowl of a speeding fire engine blasting through the church, followed by an equally clangorous ambulance. Matt smelled the smoke rising from the engines of two wrecked cars, only a block and a half away, and listened with mournful resignation as the EMTs failed to restore a faltering heartbeat. . . .

"Sometimes not," he admitted.

Father Everett spoke to him with open concern and affection. "You don't have to go it alone, Matthew. My confessional is always open to you."

I wouldn't know where to begin, Matt thought, mordantly amused by the very prospect of divulging the details of his secret life. *Let's see. . . . Last night I beat an alcoholic, abusive father within an inch of his life, while simultaneously scaring an innocent child out of his wits. . . .*

The old priest seemed to sense Matt's reticence. "There are no secrets from God," he said. "And after thirty years of sitting in that box there's nothing that I haven't heard before."

Matt rose and crossed himself. "Let's keep it that way."

He slipped out of the pew and tapped his way toward the front entrance, feeling Father Everett's concerned gaze upon his back.

The law offices of Nelson & Murdock were not exactly Park Avenue. In fact, they were several avenues west, located between a check-cashing service and a Korean pet service named U WASH DOGGY.

A bell above the door jingled as Matt entered the office, where he was greeted by both Foggy and their secretary, a perky young blonde named Karen Page. "Your ears must be burning," she told Matt, handing him what felt like an embossed invitation of some sort.

Nice quality paper, Matt noticed.

"This just came by messenger," Karen explained, before Matt had a chance to examine the note. "It's an invitation to the Black and White Ball at the Grand Hotel. Plus one."

A hopeful chirp in her voice suggested that she hoped to be asked.

"Plus one? Sweet!" Foggy snatched the invite from Matt's hand, clearly oblivious to Karen's own aspirations to attend the gala event. Matt imagined the secretary's baleful glare.

Sometimes Foggy could be a little clueless. . . .

The three-room office was on the cramped side. Matt's and Foggy's law diplomas adorned the walls, along with a selection of framed testimonials from grateful clients. Karen picked up the coffeepot and offered Matt an empty mug. "Coffee?"

"No, thanks," Matt said and walked into his office. Behind him, he heard Foggy lift up his own cup.

"I'd like coffee," he declared.

Karen just went back to her desk.

"O-kay . . ." Foggy drawled, finally grasping his faux pas. Fleeing the antarctic chill now emanating from the pissed-off secretary, he followed Matt into his office, which was packed to the ceiling with all manner of junk: remote-control sailboats, leisure suits, action figures, boxes of shoes, sno globes, souvenir ashtrays, plastic lawn furniture, disposable diapers, and Girl Scout cookies . . . the dubious rewards of an excess of pro bono cases.

Matt weaved through the boxes and pressed a button on his specialized printer. Legal transcripts began printing out—in Braille.

Foggy perused the invitation instead. "When should I pick you up?" he asked casually.

"I'm not going," Matt said. After last night's multiple fiascos, he was in no mood for a party, no matter how exclusive.

"What?" Incredulity suffused Foggy's voice. "Are you crazy? That place will be crawling with people. Rich people. People who don't pay their fees in fish."

He sat down on the nearest box, balancing precariously on the corner of a crate of smoked halibut.

"Then you go," Matt stated. He lifted the first page from the printer and brushed his fingertips over it.

"I'm a Plus One," Foggy protested. "Plus Ones can't get into anything by themselves."

Matt put down the transcript impatiently. He didn't have the time or the inclination to debate this with Foggy. "Are you finished?" he demanded brusquely. "Because we have to be ready for court in one hour."

"What's eating you?" Foggy asked, sounding more concerned than offended.

Matt immediately regretted snapping at his partner. Foggy was a good friend who deserved better. "Had a bad night," he said vaguely.

"Wanna talk about it?"

"No." Matt appreciated the offer, but if he couldn't confess to Father Everett, he wasn't about to open up to Foggy over coffee—or the absence thereof. *Why does everyone want me to bare my soul this morning?*

Foggy plucked a Nerf basketball from the piles of accumulated debris. Matt heard Foggy slap his forehead in sudden realization. "This is about Elektra, isn't it?"

Matt realized, to his chagrin, that Foggy knew rather more about his personal life than Father Everett. "No," he insisted.

But Foggy was too busy putting the pieces together to be squelched now. "Natchios owns the Grand Hotel. *She's* the one who invited you to the ball."

Matt had figured that out already, not that it made him feel any better. "She's out of my league," he said glumly, unable to comprehend why Elektra would even want to see him again after he ditched her on the roof last night. "You know that. It's better to end it before it starts."

Foggy mulled that over for a second. He shot the Nerf ball at the wastepaper basket, but it bounced off the rim. "That's got to be some kind of record," he said finally. "You completely bypassed the relationship phase and went straight to the break-up." He whistled appreciatively. "What a time saver."

He retrieved the ball from the floor and lobbed it at Matt. "Ball."

Matt caught the ball easily, then smoothly sank it in the basket. "We're from two different worlds," he argued reluctantly. Foggy meant well, but Matt wished he'd drop the subject. "Besides, she's not really my type."

Foggy wasn't buying it for a minute. "You know, I've always wondered . . . what happens to that lie detector of yours when it detects your *own* bullshit? It must really bury the needle, huh?"

He shot an air ball while Matt stood there speechlessly, like a crooked witness caught lying under oath.

"Swish," Foggy said. Matt smirked as his partner walked over and dropped the Nerf ball on his desk. "Ball."

Matt picked up the spongy rubber ball, regarding it as though it were a crystal sphere foretelling his future. Maybe Foggy had a point. "Plus One?"

He tossed the ball again. Foggy grinned as it hit nothing but net.

CHAPTER 15

The Grand Hotel was a luxurious, old-school hotel located in the heart of Manhattan. The palatial architecture was done in the Spanish-Italian Renaissance style, with just a hint of Art Deco as well. Foggy described the decor to Matt as they entered the lavish ballroom where the gala event was being held.

Crystal chandeliers hung from the hand-painted thirty-foot-high ceiling. Ornate balconies, separated by imposing marble columns, looked down on the main floor of the ballroom, where men and women in formal attire met and mingled. A live orchestra provided music for the elegantly clad couples gliding across the dance floor. In keeping with the ball's "black and white" theme, the well-heeled partygoers had eschewed garish colors in favor of more monochromatic gowns and tuxedos.

All this tasteful opulence was wasted on Matt, who had only one overriding concern: *Where was Elektra?* His every sense was harnessed to the task of locating her amid the celebrating throng, but so far he was striking out; there were too many overheated bodies, sounds, and odors, from the fishy aroma of fresh caviar to the popping of champagne bottles.

Strolling beside him, Foggy had his own agenda. "Do

you know how much money is here?" he whispered in awe. "One client and we could be set for a year."

Whatever, Matt thought. He sniffed the air, hoping to detect a whiff of rose oil, but caught a puff of cigarette smoke instead. And not just any cigarette, he realized, with a twinge of anxiety. *Camels.*

"Matt Murdock?" Ben Urich said, approaching him. The vertically challenged reporter wore a cheap rental tuxedo that didn't fit him very well. No doubt he had wielded his press pass to gain access to the exclusive event. "Ben Urich with the *Post.*"

I know who you are, Matt thought, taking Urich's hand reluctantly. *But how much do you know about me?*

"You write those urban legends stories," Foggy recalled, shaking the reporter's hand as well.

"Among other things," Urich said. His voice had a distinctively New York nasal quality.

"Maybe you can settle this," Foggy said hopefully. "You know those alligators that live in the sewers?"

Urich sighed wearily, as though he was asked that question way too often.

"I read your piece on the Kingpin," Matt stated, changing the subject to something of greater interest to him. "Another urban legend, Ben?"

Urich paused, perhaps eyeing Matt curiously. "I think some legends, if you look back far enough, are based in fact," Ulrich said. "Why?"

"I hear stories from time to time from some of our clients. Usually somebody who knows somebody who knows the Kingpin. That sort of thing."

"Sounds like you're a skeptic."

"One man who runs all of the organized crime in New York?" Matt asked. As Daredevil, he had heard lots of stories about the Kingpin, but had never uncovered definitive proof of his existence. "Sounds far-fetched."

"Yeah," Urich admitted. "But then so does a vigilante that dresses up like the devil."

Matt froze, struggling to maintain a poker face. He thanked heaven for his dark glasses, which helped to conceal his perturbed reaction to the reporter's words. *Is he deliberately trying to provoke me?*

Foggy, of all people, came to his rescue. "They're huge now, right? The alligators?"

"That's a myth, Foggy," Urich informed him.

"Oh," Foggy said, crestfallen. Matt was just grateful for the distraction.

"Give me a call when you get the chance," Urich urged Matt. "There's something we should talk about." He attempted to hand Matt his card, but somehow managed to "accidentally" knock Matt's cane out his hand.

"Sorry," he muttered, bending over to retrieve the cane. "Interesting color," he observed, inspecting the burnished red walking stick, which, no surprise, just happened to be the same color as Daredevil's billy club.

Matt hastily took the cane back before Urich could stumble onto any of its special features. "I wouldn't know," he said.

"Right," the reporter acknowledged wryly. He fished around in his pockets for another cigarette. "Enjoy the party."

Matt repressed a sigh of relief as the prying reporter wandered away. Urich was trouble all right. Matt tried to push his concerns regarding Urich aside so that he could return to the challenge of locating Elektra, only to be distracted by a heavy basso heartbeat only a few yards away.

Who? he wondered, impressed by the booming reverberation of the stranger's powerful heart, which sounded like a bass drum. Matt had never heard anything like it.

"Wilson Fisk is in the house," Foggy announced, his own heart speeding up in excitement. He tugged on Matt's arm. "Come on, I might never get this chance again."

"Foggy, wait. . . ." Matt tried to slow his partner down, but he was too late. Foggy was already making a beeline toward Fisk, whom Matt guessed to be the source of the prodigious heartbeat.

He had never met Fisk before, but the business magnate's colossal wealth—and dimensions—were well known. *Even still*, Matt thought, reluctantly following after Foggy, *nobody ever told me he was really this big!*

Fisk loomed like a mountain among the assorted guests, exerting an almost gravitational attraction on Foggy, who hurriedly offered Fisk his business card. "Mr. Fisk," he introduced himself, "Franklin Nelson from Nelson and Murdock. It's a real pleasure."

Foggy shook Fisk's hand enthusiastically, while the mammoth businessman towered over him, as solid and immobile as one of the marble columns lining the ballroom. A rumble of amusement emerged from Fisk's gargantuan chest.

"I'd just like to say," Foggy continued breathlessly, "that if we can of service in any way, please don't hesitate—"

A smaller man, smelling of expensive cologne, interposed himself between Foggy and Fisk, clearly acting as gatekeeper. He peered disdainfully at Foggy over the tops of his wire-rim glasses. "If you wish to speak to Mr. Fisk," he said frostily, "you'll have to make an appointment—"

But Fisk overruled his subordinate, apparently having no objections to Foggy's overtures. "Nelson and Murdock," he said pleasantly, his voice as deep and sonorous as any Matt had ever heard. "I've heard about you. The blind lawyer from Hell's Kitchen."

An unaccountable chill ran down Matt's spine at the sound of Fisk's rotund intonations. Something about it stirred long-buried memories and emotions. . . .

"He's the blind one," Foggy clarified, gesturing toward Matt as Matt caught up with his partner. This close, Fisk registered on his radar senses like a huge geological formation. Matt found himself strangely reminded of the iceberg that sank the *Titanic*.

Fisk chuckled, a sound like boulders rolling downhill. His oily myrmidon backed down, allowing Matt and Foggy to draw nearer to the gigantic tycoon.

"Give him your card, Wesley," Fisk instructed. "I'm always on the lookout for new blood."

Fisk's haughty lieutenant handed Foggy a card, which Matt's partner read aloud: " 'Wesley Owen Welch.' " Foggy tucked the card into his pocket and offered Welch his hand. "Nice to meet you. Franklin Allan Nelson. And this is my partner, Matthew Michael Murdock."

Welch harrumphed testily, unhappy at being mocked, but Fisk himself chortled once more. "What do you think, Mr. Murdock?" Fisk asked amiably. "Are you ready to make the move uptown?"

"I don't think we'd be a good fit," Matt said diplomatically. He'd heard rumors about Fisk's underworld connections. Nothing definite, but enough to make Matt—and Daredevil—think that there had to be something to the stories. There was an old saying: Behind every great fortune usually lies a great crime.

"Why is that?" Fisk asked evenly.

"Yeah, why is that?" Foggy echoed, aghast. He sounded like he couldn't believe his ears. "Buddy?"

Matt felt sorry for his long-suffering partner, who was doubtless envisioning a bleak and penurious future filled with nothing but cheap plastic knickknacks and raw fish, but he wasn't going to duck the truth. "We only represent innocent clients," he said.

Foggy gasped, and Welsh hissed, and even Fisk seemed taken aback for a second. But the massive billionaire rapidly regained his composure, chuckling at Matt's impertinence.

"If there's one thing I've learned in my years of business," he declared, too confident in his power to be troubled by Matt's implied accusation, "it's that nobody is innocent. *Nobody*." He turned away from them, seeking fresher divertissements. His departing footsteps echoed like seismic tremors. "Enjoy the party."

"We'll be in touch!" Foggy called after Fisk and his attorney. His shoulders sagged as he admitted the unlikeliness of their ever hearing from Fisk again. He turned woefully toward Matt, more regretful than aggrieved. "You okay?"

"Yeah," Matt replied, "I'm fine."

Foggy's jaw dropped at the sight of something above and behind Matt. The enticing fragrance of rose oil, layered over a scent even more distinctive and intimate, caused Matt to spin around suddenly, his mouth going dry and his pulse quickening.

Elektra.

He reached out with his senses, locating her at the far end of the ballroom, at the top of the steps leading to the second tier of the vast party space. All thought of Fisk's dubious reputation and smug self-assurance fled from his mind as he confirmed that she was really, truly there.

"—I wish I could give you my eyes for the night," Foggy said wistfully.

"Like that, huh?"

"Like that," Foggy confirmed, unable to tear his gaze away from her. Transfixed, he stared wide-eyed at the beautiful young woman atop the stairs. She had been stunning in the coffee shop the other day, but tonight, her lithe form sheathed in a glittering silver dress, she looked absolutely breathtaking. An elegant silver necklace sparkled around her swan-like neck.

Foggy felt a twinge of envy. *How come gorgeous Greek heiresses never fall for me . . . ?*

Elektra was scanning the crowded ballroom below her, no doubt looking for Matt. Foggy didn't think she'd spotted them yet.

"Want me to take you over?" he volunteered, but when he looked away from Elektra to address his partner, he discovered that Matt was already gone.

Don't go away! Matt entreated her urgently as he hurried toward the stairs. Wielding his cane as delicately as a surgeon's scalpel, he zigzagged across the packed ballroom. His nostrils flared as he desperately strove to keep a lock on her scent, despite the myriad other odors competing for his attention. A cloud of cigarette smoke, followed by a tray of spicy appetizers, attempted to lead him astray. The people he passed gave off their own distracting pheromones, every drink and snack called out pungently, yet Matt refused to let go of the fragrant trail guiding him toward Elektra. He climbed the wide marble steps in a hurry until, at last, she was there right in front of

him, the smell and sound of her shutting out everything else in the world.

"And now I've found you," he said softly, alluding
to their encounter in Hell's Kitchen the day before.

She reached out and touched his face, gasping in
amazement at the way he had tracked her down despite the crush of the crowd. She stepped closer to
him, so that their faces were only inches apart.

"I'm sorry about last night," he began. He felt
flushed and out of breath. "I wish I could explain. . . ."

"You're here now," she said, granting him blissful
absolution. Silver tinkled gently around her neck as
she took his hand and guided him toward the dance
floor. "That's all that matters."

At the bar, Wesley sat sipping an icy martini.
Foggy approached him, spotting Wesley's polished
cuff links, engraved with the initials W-O-W.

"Wow, engraved cuff links? It's your initials, Wesley Owen Welch."

Wesley turned to face Foggy, clearly annoyed. "Let
me cut to the chase. If this were up to me, and it is,
do you really think that for one moment the Fisk
Corporation would hire some pro bono storefront
Hell's Kitchen lawyers, let alone a blind one?"
Welch's voice dripped with condescension. "I've already filled the quota of handicapped employees for
the year, thank you very much." Wesley reached into
his pocket and retrieved Foggy's business card. "So
why don't you enjoy the party . . . Franklin Nelson?"

With that, Welch slid the card back into Foggy's
jacket pocket and patted him, hard, confirming the
point that he wanted Foggy to stay the hell away
from him. Then he turned and walked away.

*   *   *

On the dance floor, Matt and Elektra danced gracefully across the floor, gliding in perfect step, comfortable in each other's arms.

"Why do you wear those glasses?" Elektra asked him.

"To let people know I'm blind. So they can see me coming down the street."

Elektra narrowed her eyes, looking at Matt knowingly. "Why do you wear them . . . really?"

Matt paused, then answered, "It makes people uncomfortable when you can't look them in the eye."

Elektra reached up and gently removed Matt's glasses. "I think you see me perfectly."

Matt's fingers slid slowly up Elektra's back to her neck, once again tracing the chain of the necklace that she always wore. "What are you wearing?" he asked.

"A cartouche. It spells my name in Greek."

"Do they come in Braille?" Matt asked, as Elektra threw her head back and laughed, her thick tresses spilling around her shoulders.

Nikolas Natchios watched his daughter enjoy a slow dance with a handsome young man in a black tuxedo. The well-groomed youth had been wearing dark glasses and appeared to be blind, yet seemed to be getting by nonetheless. Natchios smiled sadly, touched to see Elektra happy at long last.

Wilson Fisk stepped onto the balcony beside him, his immense presence instantly filling the older man with dread. "I haven't seen her smile like that since before her mother was killed," the Kingpin said casually. "Poor girl. Right in front of her eyes."

"Why must you bring that up?" Natchios said unhappily. *Can't I be allowed a moment's escape from the past?*

"History has a way of repeating itself," Fisk said, looking out over the dancing couples below, Elektra included.

Natchios nearly had a heart attack. "What—what are you saying?" he asked anxiously, overcome by a sudden sense of panic. "What do you mean?"

"Just saying good-bye, old friend." Fisk bent over low to kiss Natchios once upon the cheek. "Just saying good-bye."

He exited the balcony, leaving the distinguished Greek in a state of extreme agitation. Natchio's hands trembled uncontrollably, and his pulse fluttered alarmingly as he watched the Kingpin of Crime depart.

Oh dear Lord, he thought. *Elektra!*

CHAPTER 16

The music carried them across the dance floor, and Matt savored the sensation of holding Elektra within his arms. Dancing was not something he usually looked forward to, but right now, at this moment, it beat diving off rooftops hands down.

He made a mental note to thank Foggy for holding his cane while he danced, then felt a peculiar tremor pass through Elektra's body, as though she was fighting back a sob. He felt her mood shift perceptibly as she laid her head on his shoulders. Her eyes moistened, and he heard her blink away tears.

"What is it?" he said gently, whispering into her ear.

"Good things don't happen to me very often," she said. "And when they do, I get scared."

Matt had to wonder what had instilled this abiding fear of the future. *Her mother's death?*

"Nothing bad is going to happen," he assured her, vowing to do whatever it took to lift these dire specters from her wounded spirit. He lifted her face to his and kissed her passionately. "I promise."

* * *

It looked like any other English-style pub. Ceiling fans spun slowly, churning the smoky haze. The evening patrons lined up along the polished mahogany bar, across from the numberless bottles of spirits stacked neatly in front of a long, frosted mirror. A TV set, with the sound turned off, was mounted above the jukebox and video poker game, while framed newspaper clippings, celebrating various World Cup victories, adorned the wood-paneled walls, along with autographed photos of minor celebrities. A list of appetizers was scrawled on a green chalkboard propped up behind the bar, and the polished brass taps gleamed beneath hanging lamps with translucent green shades. Ashtrays, napkins, matchbooks, ketchup bottles, and plastic stirrers were all generously provided on the counter.

To Bullseye, it was an armory.

Every eye in the pub was turned toward him as he raised a dart while carelessly sipping from the pint of beer in his other hand. Without even looking at the target, he hurled the tiny missile at the dartboard, which already had five previous darts stuck in the bull's-eye.

Thunk. The sixth dart came to rest right on top of one of the earlier five. The entire pub gasped in astonishment, and a drunken Englishman, whose name Bullseye hadn't bothered to remember, dropped his head in stunned disbelief, having just lost a very sizable bet.

Kid's stuff, Bullseye thought. He smirked, enjoying the Brit's dismay, until his pager beeped for his attention. He checked it quickly, then downed the last of his pint. "Keys," he demanded, extending his hand toward the soggy Brit.

"Two outta three!" the drunk suggested pathetically, but Bullseye merely glared in response. With a petulant scowl, the soused Englishman reached into the pocket of his motorcycle jacket and handed Bullseye a pair of keys.

Time to get to work, Bullseye thought and headed for the door. As he was leaving, however, he heard the stupid Brit try to get the last word in.

"Irish piece of trash," the man muttered audibly.

Business can wait, Bullseye decided. He turned around to confront the loudmouthed idiot and pulled off his nylon skullcap. A collective gasp and shudder went through the pub as all present got a good look at the literal bull's-eye carved into the assassin's forehead. He reached into his coat and the Brit's eyes bulged in alarm, doubtless expecting Bullseye to pull out a knife or a gun.

Instead Bullseye produced a paper clip.

The Englishman laughed, visibly relieved, as Bullseye straightened the tiny metal wire. The unsuspecting Brit was caught totally off guard when Bullseye expertly flicked the straightened paper clip right into the man's throat.

The perforated drunk screamed in pain and fright, the miniature steel spear jutting from his Adam's apple. Before he had a chance to do more than shriek, Bullseye fired off three more paper clips, turning the Brit's neck into a pin cushion.

You should have kept your fat gob shut, the glowering hit man thought pitilessly. *You didn't know who you were messing with, you snotty-nosed little shite.*

Blood streaming from his throat, the terrified Englishman ran madly for the back door of the pub. Clutching his throat, which looked as if it had been attacked by a metallic porcupine, or perhaps a homicidal acupuncturist, he stumbled down the alley behind the bar. A dented Dumpster, overflowing with trash, offered refuge of a sort, and he crouched behind it, cowering in fear.

Bullseye stepped out of the bar, holding a dart he had snatched from the dartboard. *This won't take long*, he thought, scanning for his prey.

A trail of blood, leading down the alley and around the corner of an old Dumpster, would have tipped Bullseye off to the Englishman's hiding place, even if he hadn't heard the wounded man's pathetic moans and whimpers. The Brit's jagged breaths whistled in and out of his punctured windpipe.

Time was short, so Bullseye didn't bother trying to get a straight shot. He just hurled the dart with tremendous velocity and watched with satisfaction as, at the last second, the missile curved *around* the corner of the Dumpster.

"Aaaahh!" An ear-piercing howl came from behind the rusty trash receptacle, followed by an ominous silence. Bright arterial blood spread across the dirty asphalt.

Bullseye laughed cruelly. The Englishman's keys jingling in his hand, he walked around the side of the pub until he came to the snazzy Harley-Davidson motorcycle parked outside.

Enough of that, he thought, climbing onto the bike, whose original owner definitely wouldn't be needing it anymore. *Fun's fun, but I've got a job to do.*

The song came to an end, and Elektra lifted her head from Matt's shoulder. He felt her stiffen in surprise as she spotted something beyond the dance floor. Matt directed his senses in the same direction and detected an older man heading rapidly for the exit. He was flanked by a pair of larger, heavier individuals who Matt assumed were bodyguards. The whole party seemed to be fleeing the ballroom with unseemly haste.

"Something's wrong . . ." Elektra murmured, sounding alarmed. She pulled free of Matt's embrace.

"What is it?" he asked.

Apparently there was no time to explain. Taking Matt's hand, she left the dance floor, hurrying after the middle-aged man and his strapping guardians. "Papa?" she called out, and Matt grasped that the departing gentleman was none other than Nikolas Natchios.

They caught up with Natchios near the exit of the ballroom. "Go back to the party," he told his daughter firmly. Matt heard Natchio's heart pounding wildly in his chest and realized that the older man was scared nearly to death.

"What is it?" Elektra demanded anxiously. "What's going on?"

Natchios tried to present a sturdy facade, despite the frantic racing of his pulse. "Stavros will take you home," he declared sternly. Matt recognized one of the bodyguards as the impatient bruiser who had surprised him and Elektra in Hell's Kitchen the other day.

The two bodyguards escorted Natchios out of the hotel, where a purring limousine was waiting out front. Matt and Elektra followed them onto the sidewalk,

Elektra and her father argued in Greek, while Matt stood by, uncomprehending. *What's this all about?* he wondered, certain only that the elder Natchios was in fear of his life. Matt's apprehension increased as he heard the bodyguards' guns click loudly. "They're taking their safeties off," he warned Elektra.

Matt's announcement only magnified Elektra's concern. "What's happening?" she shouted at her father.

"Go back inside!" Natchios ordered. Stavros opened the back door of the limousine and the frightened billionaire climbed into the waiting car.

"I'm going with you!" Elektra insisted. She forced her way into the limo after her father, then looked back at Matt from inside the car. "I'm sorry," she said, her voice full of fear and regret.

Stavros glared warningly at Matt before clambering into the backseat as well. The second bodyguard joined the driver up front, and without any further adieu, the limo pulled away from the curb. The deluxe-sized car sped away, leaving Matt standing on the sidewalk in front of the hotel.

But not for long . . .

Parked on a side street alongside the hotel, Bullseye watched the limo depart as well. *Right on schedule*, he thought smugly and fired up his newly acquired Harley-Davidson.

He took off after the limo.

Within the luxurious interior of the limo, Stavros drew out his Glock automatic. He rode shotgun at the rear of the car, while Elektra and her father sat side by side on the plush leather couch facing the built-in bar and television. Elektra could tell the vigilant bodyguard was anticipating trouble.

But what kind?

"What's going on?" she pleaded with her father once more. She had hated leaving Matt behind like that, but sensed that something terrible was happening. "Tell me. . . ."

Her father's face was pale, and he looked far older than his fifty-some years. She had never seen him look so stricken, at least not since the horrible day her mother died. "New York is not safe tonight," he said curtly. He kept glancing nervously out the tinted windows, as if fearing an ambush. "That is all you need to know. . . ."

Traffic was heavy, slowing their progress more than either her father or Stavros would have liked. Elektra heard the roar of a powerful engine behind them and turned toward the window. She saw a large black motorcycle closing on them, the glare of its headlight obscuring her view of the driver. *Who?* she wondered, feeling an icy chill clutch her heart.

Crash! Something smashed through the driver's window, striking the chauffeur in the throat. Elektra's eyes gaped at the sight of a silver fountain pen jammed into the driver's windpipe.

The wounded driver gurgled blood and lost control of the wheel, causing the speeding limo to swerve wildly from its lane. Stavros barked in Greek at the other bodyguard, Christos, who hurriedly grabbed hold of the wheel. "Get down!" Stavros shouted at Elektra and her father.

Amid the chaos, Elektra felt a pang of fatalistic despair. *I tried to warn you, Matt,* she thought bleakly. *Good things never last. . . .*

Two stone angels perched on the roof of an old bank building, gazing down on the busy avenue below.

A devil crouched between them.

Daredevil gripped his cane, which Matt had swiftly retrieved from Foggy, and sifted through the sounds rising from the street. His head jerked upward as he heard the squealing tires of a limousine hurtling out of control. It careened down Fifth Avenue, barely missing a double-decker tour bus. Frightened pedestrians ran for cover.

"Elektra . . ."

He surged into action, terrified that he might already be too late. He hacked into the granite neck of the angel on his left and pulled himself around the statue. Adrenaline powered his legs as he ran along the length of the narrow ledge, nearly two hundred feet above the pavement, and leapt across Thirty-ninth Street to the next building over.

Hang on! he mentally entreated Elektra. *I'm on my way!*

Kneeling on the floor of the limo next to her father, Elektra peered upward through the tinted window at the towering high-rent buildings rushing by. She had no idea when or from where the next attack would come. *A fountain pen?* her mind boggled in disbelief. *What kind of assassin uses a fountain pen as a murder weapon?*

Scanning the rooftops for snipers, she was stunned to see a bizarre figure, dressed in a dark red devil costume, chasing after them, jumping fearlessly from building to building.

Bullseye pulled a leather strap from his coat and, winding it around the bike's throttle, locked the throttle in place. With his hands free, he nimbly leapt onto the bike's seat, literally surfing the rocketing motorcycle down the street, deftly maintaining balance while reaching down to his belt.

His fingers found the middle of his star-shaped belt buckle, and after he pressed down on it, a stack of razor-edged shuriken were released into his palm. Snapping off five of the deadly throwing stars, Bullseye positioned them between the fingers of first one of his gloved hands, then the other. Maintaining his balance on the surging bike, Bullseye hurled the shuriken in a two-handed cross-throw, sending the lethal projectiles through the windshield of the limo, embedding them into the necks of both the driver and Stavros.

With no one controlling the wheel of the limo, the car careened out of control, smashing violently into a newspaper delivery truck and grinding to a screeching halt. Copies of the *New York Post* fluttered down into the street.

Bullseye dropped down onto the seat and brought the bike to a skidding halt, looking back over his shoulder to the crash site with a cruel grin. The smile suddenly froze on his face as a dark figure dropped down into his field of view. . . . *Daredevil.*

With a look of astonishment, Bullseye snapped off the last of his shurikens and launched it at Daredevil's head. Hearing the whistling of the heavy blade through the air, Daredevil deftly avoided the throwing star, which sailed past his head and skittered away down the street.

Bullseye sneered. "You made me miss. . . ."

Steam spouted from the crumpled hood of the limo, and Bullseye grinned maliciously. He looked back and forth between the car and Daredevil finding himself faced with a dilemma: go after his designated target or finish off the sodding wanker who had spoiled his shot?

Ego won out over professionalism. With a feral snarl, he yanked the Harley around and drove it straight toward the man in red. . . .

Daredevil heard the motorcycle bearing down on him. *Coming in for the kill*, he realized. Daredevil felt the heat of its headlight upon him, but he didn't budge. A blind man never flinches.

And a Man Without Fear *never* backs down.

He waited, every muscle tense and wired, until the oncoming bike was just about to crash into him. At the last minute, he sprang into the air, running up the front fender of the Harley and spin-kicking the driver right off the stampeding motorcycle!

The bike crashed into a squat yellow fire hydrant, as its owner tumbled onto the street. *Couldn't happen to a nicer guy,* Daredevil thought sarcastically, landing on both feet a yard and a half away, between the fallen desperado and the wrecked limousine. To his relief, he heard two sets of heartbeats still beating inside the limo, one of them clearly Elektra's.

Thank God, Daredevil thought.

He reached confidently for his billy club, ready to pay the would-be assassin back and then some, only to discover that the holster was empty. *What the—?*

A wicked laugh called his attention to the motorcycle's bloodthirsty driver. The nameless killer rose to his feet, brandishing a familiar weapon. Daredevil recognized the smell of his own billy club and realized, to his utter amazement, that the other man must have snatched the club from him in midair!

"Thanks for the stick," the gleeful psychopath mocked, spitting out a mouthful of blood. His jeering voice had an unmistakable Irish brogue. "I owe you one."

Behind him, Daredevil heard Nikolas Natchios, still alive and mobile, pull Elektra out of the crumpled limo. Sirens keened in the distance, zooming down Fifth Avenue toward the crash site, and the middle-aged tycoon frantically waved his arms in the air, trying to attract help. "Here! Over here!"

Get down! Daredevil thought in alarm. Natchios was making himself a target.

The Irish assassin whipped the stolen billy club at the Greek billionaire.

"No!" Daredevil cried. He leapt for the billy club, desperate to abort its murderous flight, but the telltale whistle of the hickory baton was suddenly overpowered by the strident howl of an arriving police siren. Daredevil reached out blindly, but his outstretched fingers just missed the rocketing club.

The siren fell silent as the police car pulled up to the scene. Daredevil listened in abject horror as his club rocketed across a full city block before striking Natchios in the chest, piercing his heart. Standing only a few steps away, her torn dress rustling in the breeze, Elektra screamed hysterically.

"Bull's-eye," whispered the anonymous killer, before bolting into the shadows of an adjacent alley. Daredevil wanted to go after him, but his bleeding wounds and spinning head convinced him that he was in no shape to pursue the escaping hitman, let alone subdue him. He had taken too many serious falls and cuts tonight.

This isn't over, he solemnly informed the unknown Irishman, before turning to check on Elektra.

One minute her father was there beside her, helping her clamber out of the demolished limousine, now holding the lifeless bodies of Stavros and the others. Still in shock, Elektra had barely processed the gruesome deaths of her three countrymen, when, without any warning, some sort of wooden nightstick came hurtling out of the night, impaling her father right before her eyes!

An anguished scream tore from her lungs, and she

dropped to her knees to cradle her father's violated body. Blood gushed from the gaping wound in his chest and she tried futilely to stanch the flow of blood with her hands. A dark crimson pool spread across the pavement beneath her, running into the gutters at the curb. The dying man twitched spasmodically in her arms, his ragged breaths growing weaker and weaker, as his life slipped away forever.

"No . . . no . . ." she sobbed, mentally reliving her mother's death as well. *Not again!*

He choked one last time, a trickle of blood seeping from the corner of his mouth, and his breathing rattled to a halt. Glassy brown eyes stared lifelessly up at the hazy night sky. Elektra looked away in despair, her tearful eyes searching for the cause of her father's death.

The man in the devil costume stood alone in the middle of the street. The empty holster on his hip made it all too clear where the fatal baton had originated.

Grief gave way to all-consuming rage, and Elektra looked about avidly for a weapon. Her gaze fell on Stavros's Glock, lying on the floor of the limo, and she lunged for the pistol, then opened fire. The sound of gunfire shattered the night, driving back both curious bystanders and the newly arrived police officers.

Die! Elektra thought savagely. Her torn silver dress was stained with her father's blood. *Die, you murderous bastard!*

But the crimson devil reacted with maddening speed. Moving like lightning, he dodged her bullets, jumping over a parked yellow cab. He hurled himself into the air, grabbing onto a streetlight like a gymnast, and swung onto the roof of a nearby building. He ran along the slender ledge while Elektra fired wildly after him, blowing out a row of top-floor windows with a hailstorm of hot lead. Broken glass rained down on Fifth Avenue, which was mercifully free of passing pedestrians thanks to both the crash and the gunfire.

The devil retreated across the rooftops, disappearing from sight, but Elektra kept squeezing the trigger until the clip was empty. With a frustrated cry, she flung the useless pistol away and slumped to her knees on the bloodstained pavement. Hot tears streamed down her face, while violent sobs rocked her trembling body.

Damn you! she thought ferociously, the image of the horned assassin burned into her memory. *You won't get away with this. I'll make you pay, devil, even if I have to follow you all the way back to hell!*

Ben Urich arrived on the scene just as the forensic unit was bagging up Daredevil's billy club. Still clad in his rented tuxedo, the reporter watched in stunned disbelief as the weapon, broken and bloody, was dutifully preserved as evidence.

His newsman's eye took in every detail: the crashed limo, the broken glass, the blood on the pavement, and the chalk outline where Nikolas Natchios's body had breathed its last. *Daredevil did this?* Urich thought, shaking his head. *I don't get it.*

Detective Manolis wandered over to where Urich was standing. The overworked cop didn't look half as bewildered as Urich, just worn-out and disgusted. He didn't even crack a joke about the reporter's penguin suit.

"Looks like you got your story," Manolis said.

CHAPTER 17

Fisk surfed the news channels as his private limousine drove him to his office that morning. Outside the deluxe bullet-proof limo, storm clouds were brewing over the city. The threatening sky matched the ominous tones of the TV news anchors as they reported on the grisly events of the night before:

". . . a scene of carnage last night as a wild car chase ended in the murder of the Greek shipping mogul Nikolas Natchios—"

". . . the breaking *New York Times* story will identify Nikolas Natchios as the so-called 'Kingpin of Crime.' Files found in Natchios's private office seem to implicate Natchios in a myriad of ruthless crimes which have terrified this city since—"

". . . Daredevil, New York's self-styled vigilante, was said to be the prime suspect in the murder—"

Fisk leaned back against his king-sized seat, chortling in amusement. He took a puff on his expensive Cuban cigar. The news couldn't have been better if he had scripted it himself—which, in a sense, he had. *Checkmate*, he thought.

Arriving at his building, he took an elevator directly to his office on the top floor. As ever, crystal-clear water flowed through the walls and ceiling of his headquarters, as though washing away the evil and corruption born there.

He stepped inside his inner sanctum, to be greeted by an unexpected whirring sound. He scowled momentarily, unhappy at being surprised in his own office, then strode forward like a mountain on the move.

"How did you get past security?" he asked calmly.

Bullseye sat behind the Kingpin's desk, his alligator boots resting on the pristine glass desktop. He drew a yellow No. 2 pencil out of an electric sharpener and walked it across the back of his hand, like a magician performing a card trick. "You mean that guy?" he asked, pointing to the floor, where the lifeless body of a dead security guard rested on the tiles. A straightened paper clip was embedded in the watchman's throat, while a half dozen sharpened pencils protruded from his chest. Blood streamed onto the otherwise spotless white floor.

Fisk frowned. This was the third dead bodyguard this week, counting the two loose-lipped dolts he had personally executed a few days ago. Personnel would not be amused. . . .

"Was that necessary?" he sighed.

"No," Bullseye admitted. The target-shaped scars on his forehead were plainly visible. His bald pate shone beneath the bright halogen lights and his goatee and mustache needed trimming. "But it was fun."

Oh, well, Fisk thought. There was no use crying over spilled blood. Besides, he still needed Bullseye.

He strolled over to the bar and poured himself a drink. "You've exceeded all of my expectations," he told the Irish assassin. "Even managed to implicate Daredevil in the process." He fished an olive out of a handsome crystal canister. "You should be pleased."

Bullseye snarled at the mention of Daredevil's name. "He made me miss," he said poisonously.

Hit a nerve? Fisk thought, amused and intrigued by the sheer bile in the other man's voice. He smiled to himself, pleased to have discovered Bullseye's weakness; it would make him easier to manipulate.

"Too much pride can kill a man," he cautioned Bullseye. The target etched on the assassin's brow struck Fisk as a foolish affectation; he would never be so reckless as to advertise his criminality.

Fisk lifted a plump green olive, preparing to drop it in his drink. He let go of the olive, just as Bullseye suddenly flung his pencil with amazing speed.

The yellow missile zipped across the room, spearing the falling olive and pinning it neatly to the back of the bar.

"The Devil is mine," he insisted.

Fisk had no objections to Bullseye's vendetta. The costumed vigilante had become a nuisance, interfering with underworld activity in Hell's Kitchen and elsewhere. From what he had heard of Daredevil, however, he suspected that Bullseye might find him a more difficult target than most. "Then you'll have to answer a question," Fisk advised. *"How do you kill a Man Without Fear?"*

Bullseye had the answer already. "By putting the fear in him," he snarled.

The Kingpin nodded in approval. "Very well. But first . . ." He plucked a fresh red rose from the lapel of his ice-blue silk suit and handed it to Bullseye. "I want you to give Elektra my best."

Given a choice, Foggy Nelson would have rather bungee-jumped naked off the Empire State Building than cross-examine a defendant in front of a skeptical judge and jury. He was good at paperwork and finances and tracking down obscure precedents; courtroom theatrics were his partner's specialty.

So where the hell is Matt?

Sweat soaked through Foggy's navy blue suit as he tried to guide Daunte Jackson through his testimony. ". . . and what happened from there?" he prompted his client, who so far had made a less than favorable impression on the jury.

"Man, I was so wasted," Jackson recalled under oath. The dreadlocked defendant seemed hazy and confused; Foggy half suspected that Jackson had somehow managed to score some dope in prison and was even now under the influence. "It's kind of hard to remember everything. . . ."

Foggy tried desperately to keep the examination on track. "But you remember where you were until ten-fifteen." He tugged uncomfortably at the collar of his suit, praying that Jackson would just repeat his testimony the way they had rehearsed. *"Remember?"*

"Yeah. Sure," Jackson mumbled. A respectable gray suit, provided by Nelson & Murdock, made him look slightly less like one of society's problem children. "Where was I again?"

Kill me now, Foggy thought. He ruffled clumsily through his notes. "Um . . . where is—here—you said you were in Chumley's Bar until ten-fifteen. And then you went to meet a friend—"

"That's right," Jackson said, perking up momentarily. He smiled broadly, like a game show contestant who had just won a chance at the jackpot. "Turk. I was going to meet Turk." He nodded, the details coming back to him. " 'Cause he owed me some money."

Foggy wished he could call on Turk to support

Jackson's alibi. Unfortunately, as far as the defense was concerned, Turk had turned out to be a small-time crook with a long list of arrests and convictions. If anything, Turk was an even less reliable witness than Jackson himself.

"Yes. Good," Foggy said, having no choice but to soldier on. "And you talked to Turk outside his apartment on Thirty-ninth, a block from Lisa Tazio's apartment. There you passed out from drinking, correct?"

"Smoking weed, mostly," Jackson supplied helpfully.

Foggy wondered if it was too late to switch to dentistry. "Thank you for clarifying that." Was it just his imagination, or was the prosecutor actually chuckling at her table? Lord knows some of the jury members seemed to be snickering at Jackson's testimony. "Now, Officer McKenzie testified that he found you holding a handgun at that time."

As in the holding cell a few days ago, Jackson only truly came to life when he was protesting his innocence. "That's a lie," he stated emphatically.

"In fact," Foggy prompted, "you don't even own a handgun, do you?"

"No, sir," Jackson declared.

Foggy started to feel the testimony going their way. Maybe they weren't dead yet. "Have you ever owned a handgun?"

"No, sir," Jackson insisted again.

That's more like it, Foggy thought, breathing a sigh of relief that the exam was almost over. "Thank you—" he began.

But Jackson wasn't through talking. "Can't hit nothing with a handgun," he volunteered.

Oh, no! Foggy thought. In a panic, he tried to shut Jackson up. "That's all. Thank you—"

Alas, Jackson was warming to his subject. "But a shotgun, that's a whole different thing."

"Thank you, Mr. Jackson!" Foggy exclaimed, before his clueless client could breathe another word. He resisted an urge to leap into the witness stand and silence Jackson physically.

"Shotgun has these little things called buckshot and it sprays everywhere. . . ."

"I have no further questions, Your Honor."

The judge banged her gavel, ending Foggy's misery, at least for the moment. "Court's in recess," she announced, then turned a forbidding eye on the mortified defense attorney. "Mr. Nelson."

Foggy crept up to the bench like an abashed school kid whose homework had allegedly been eaten by a dog. The judge looked down on him in dour exasperation.

"For your sake," she intoned gravely, "I hope your partner comes back soon."

Foggy couldn't have agreed with her more. "Me, too," he said weakly, all the while wondering just what had become of the latter half of Nelson & Murdock.

Where are you, Matt?

Nikolas Natchios was buried in a Greek Orthodox cemetery on Long Island. Matt stood at the back of a small crowd of mourners. The turnout was unusually light for the funeral of such a prominent man; Matt guessed that the scandal surrounding Natchios's death, plus all the incriminating press coverage, had scared away many of the billionaire's former friends and associates.

Elektra stood a few yards away, watching her father's casket being lowered into the ground beside her mother's weathered headstone. Matt heard her veil rustle and imagined her dressed in black, her exotic face beautiful even now. To his slight surprise, he never once heard her sniffle or sob. She seemed paralyzed by grief, as still and silent as one of the marble angels adorning her parents' tomb.

First her mother, now her father, Matt thought, trying to imagine what she must be feeling. *And to think I promised that nothing bad would ever happen to her. . . !*

He waited patiently for the ceremony to conclude before approaching Elektra. He heard her bid farewell to a few distant relatives, then walk toward one of the waiting limousines

"Elektra," he called out, stepping forward.

A glowering bodyguard, whom Matt had never met before, moved to block Matt but Elektra waved him off, murmuring something in Greek.

The dry grass crackled beneath his feet as Matt joined Elektra by her limo. "I've been trying to reach you," he began.

"Matt, please." Her voice was cold and dead, and Matt was startled by the change in her. She didn't sound at all like the passionate and dynamic woman he had come to know.

"I know how you feel," he said.

She hesitated, and for a moment, Matt thought he was getting through to her. When she spoke again, there was a trace of uncertainty, of vulnerability, in her voice. "You don't know how I feel. . . ." She clenched her fists so tightly that Matt could hear her nails digging into her palms. "I want justice," she proclaimed, her voice ringing with pent-up rage.

"You can't get justice. Not like that," he told her.

That was the wrong thing to say. He sensed her shutting down emotionally as an ominous chill came over her. The last thing he wanted was for Elektra to go after that murderous Irish hit man. Even if she survived, the bloodshed and violence would leave their indelible mark on her soul.

Matt was about to urgently try to reason with her. Then he realized the bitter irony of what he was saying. *Counselor, advise yourself,* he thought mordantly. Didn't he spend nearly every night seeking justice as Daredevil, finding only a never-ending procession of cracked skulls and bruised knuckles?

Thunder rumbled overhead, and a cold rain began to fall. Matt couldn't help remembering the last time it had rained for them, on the rooftop of that old brownstone. That seemed like a hundred years ago. . . .

The rain fell harder. Once again, the bouncing droplets outlined her features, letting him "see" her with his radar senses. He reached for her face, wanting only to stroke her tender cheek and perhaps bring some comfort to her wounded spirit. Instead, unexpectedly, her graceful silhouette transformed into that of a coffin!

"I won't be a victim again," Elektra said from inside the spectral casket.

Matt started in surprise, then figured out what he was sensing. *An umbrella,* he realized; Elektra had opened an umbrella, shielding herself from the rain— and from Matt. No longer allowing herself to be seen.

Before Matt could protest, she stepped behind her ready bodyguard and into the limousine. Sheets of rain ran down the car windows, like the cleansing tears she refused to shed.

"Drive," she told the chauffeur hoarsely.

Matt watched the luxury sedan carry Elektra away from him. Intent on her painful departure, he failed to notice the gargantuan businessman until the other man approached the grave, his monumental tread crushing the freshly mowed lawn. Fisk plucked a flower—a rose, it smelled like—from his lapel and dropped it onto his colleague's casket.

As he heard the flower drop, a memory stirred within Matt: another rose left behind on the bleeding corpse of a murdered prizefighter. . . .

"Hello?" Matt barked, whirling around to face Fisk. Twenty-year-old memories came together with snatches of underworld gossip in his mind, birthing a dreadful and momentous suspicion. Matt's blood simmered, despite the pouring rain, and he gripped the shaft of his cane like a club. "Hello?" he called again, determined to get Fisk's attention.

The mammoth billionaire had walked back to his own limousine. He paused by the open back door and glanced back at Matt, seeing only a helpless blind man standing in the graveyard, pitiful and unimportant.

He didn't even bother to acknowledge Matt. Wordlessly, Fisk climbed into the limo and drove away. Matt impotently watched the powerful business tycoon leave him behind, just as Elektra had. Bile collected at the back of his throat as he brooded silently in the rain, angry and frustrated but not quite alone.

A cigarette butt landed at his feet, sizzling as it hit the rain-drenched grass. Matt smelled the now-familiar stink of Camel cigarettes.

"Why are you following me?" he demanded harshly.

A nasal voice addressed him from behind. "Matt, it's Ben Urich—"

"I know who it is," Matt snapped. The last thing he needed right now was this infuriating reporter

snooping around again. "What do you want?" Matt
demanded, in no mood for sly hints or innuendo. "If
you've got something to say, just say it."

"I think your client is innocent," Urich said.

Matt blinked in surprise. He had been so used to
thinking of Urich as a threat that it had never occurred to him that maybe, just maybe, the reporter
might be on his side.

Have I misjudged him? Matt wondered suddenly.

"I had a source for my Kingpin story," Urich explained. A steady heart rate vouched for his honesty.
"A source named Lisa Tazio."

Matt couldn't believe what he was hearing. "Tazio
had access to the Kingpin?"

Urich nodded, turning up the collar of his coat
against the pelting rain. "One of the Kingpin's men,
to be exact. Pillow talk in a hotel room. She sold the
information to me piecemeal, but I never got a
name."

Matt wondered if Tazio's boyfriend was now as
dead as she was. *Probably,* he guessed. "They said
Natchios was the Kingpin."

"Not my paper," Urich said with a snort. "The
other guys got it wrong, as usual. Tazio said that
Natchios was one of the Kingpin's business partners,
back in the day."

If the Kingpin had a motive to have Tazio killed, Matt
thought, swiftly grasping the full implications of
what Urich was saying, *that might weaken the case
against Daunte Jackson. Tazio's death was no routine
mugging gone wrong.*

"Will you testify to that?" he asked the reporter
forcefully.

Urich shook his head. "First Amendment and all
that. Story's still open as far as I'm concerned." He

shrugged his sloping shoulders apologetically. "Besides, I've got to protect my other sources."

Damn, Matt thought, but he knew better than to waste his breath arguing with the dogged reporter. "Is there anything you can tell me that will help my client?"

Urich lit a cigarette and took a puff. He scratched his chin thoughtfully as he exhaled a cloud of pungent smoke. "I got a cousin," he said eventually, "that manages a Mercedes dealership over in Hoboken. Said he just filled an order for a brand-new 500SL." He took another drag on his cigarette, pausing dramatically before delivering the punch line. "To a Robert McKenzie."

Matt recognized the name instantly. "Officer McKenzie . . ."

Urich nodded again. "That's three years of a cop's salary."

"But McKenzie was telling the truth," Matt recalled, struggling to reconcile what Urich was saying with his own resounding memory of the cop's heart beating as regularly as a metronome on the witness stand. "It doesn't make any sense. None of this makes any sense. . . ."

He paced back and forth across the soggy graveyard, flailing wildly with his cane as his thoughts tumbled madly out of control. McKenzie. Jackson. Natchios. Elektra. Foggy. Fisk. *What's the good of having all these special gifts*, he lamented silently, *if I can't even make sense of my own existence?*

"Hey, hey!" Urich said, sounding alarmed by Matt's visible agitation. "Take it easy."

But Matt was too upset to calm down. Doubts and questions spilled out of him, like rose petals falling onto his father's body. "I used to think I had . . . I had a gift," he blurted in confusion, not caring who heard. The echoes of countless screams and heartbeats bounced back and forth inside his skull. "But it's more like a curse. . . ."

"Calm down, will ya?" Urich pleaded anxiously. He laid a restraining hand on the younger man's shoulder. "You're gonna give yourself a heart attack."

Matt froze.

"What did you say?" he asked

Urich stepped back, baffled by the sudden change in Matt's tone. "You're gonna give yourself a heart attack," he repeated dutifully. "So what?"

Matt's jaw dropped. Suddenly, all the pieces came together, the discordant, seemingly incompatible notes merging to form a single cohesive melody. The truth, now that he had worked it out, was, well, blindingly obvious.

"Son of a bitch," he muttered.

CHAPTER 18

It was after midnight when Officer Robert McKenzie stumbled out of the topless bar down by the East River. His silver Mercedes convertible was parked out front, gleaming in the moonlight, and the off-duty cop took a moment to admire his sporty new roadster.

The 500SL was a thing of beauty, with stylish black leather upholstery and polished maple trim elements. A powerful eight-cylinder engine lurked beneath its snazzy silver hood, capable of going from zero to sixty in less than six seconds, with a maximum speed of over a hundred fifty miles per hour. Brand-new, it still had the sticker on its windshield, and best of all, it was all his, for a mere ninety thousand clams.

This is the life, McKenzie thought smugly, pleasantly buzzed by the beers he'd consumed in the bar, not to mention a couple of primo lap dances. He beamed triumphantly at the Mercedes. *Have I hit the big time or what?*

"Don't you just love that new-car smell?"

The sarcastic voice caught him by surprise. McKenzie whirled around to discover a tall man wearing dark glasses standing right behind him. It took him a sec to recognize Murdock, that blind lawyer from Jackson's trial.

What's he doing here?

Before the startled cop could react, Murdock reached into McKenzie's coat and yanked out his handcuffs. He swiftly slapped one end of the cuffs around McKenzie's wrist.

"What the fu—?" he blurted, but Murdock was too fast for him. He yanked open the convertible's door and shoved McKenzie into the passenger seat. The other end of the cuffs snapped shut around the door handle, trapping him in the seat.

With the cop securely cuffed to the door, Murdock climbed into the driver's seat. His nimble fingers explored the controls. "Never driven a stick before," he commented nonchalantly

McKenzie started sweating, unsure what upset him more: the cuffs or the prospect of a blind man behind the wheel of his new Mercedes. He gulped loudly as Murdock deftly hot-wired the car, starting up the engine.

"Stop it!" he hollered. *This wasn't funny!*

Murdock's voice took on an accusing tone. "Where'd you get the car, McKenzie?"

What is this? the cop fumed. *A cross-examination?*

"Lots of cops got Mercedes these days," he muttered.

"I'll bet they do," Murdock said caustically. He gunned the car—in reverse! The convertible slammed back into the brick wall of the bar, tearing off its rear fender. The shriek of tortured metal filled the night.

"Jesus Christ!" McKenzie shouted. Murdock threw the car into drive and the roadster lurched forward abruptly, throwing the hysterical cop back against his seat. "Stop it!" He tugged frantically on the cuffs, trying to get free, but the unyielding steel bracelet bit into his wrist, refusing to let go. "Stop the god-damn car!"

The base of the Brooklyn Bridge ran along the southern wall of the sleazy strip club. The right side of the Mercedes scraped against the heavy concrete abutment, throwing off a trail of sparks and screeches. McKenzie winced as the passenger side mirror snapped off.

"Crazy son of a bitch!" he ranted, groping wildly for the steering wheel with his free hand. Murdock batted his hand away with a vicious blow that left the cop's arm smarting.

"Now the tough part," the blind attorney said. "Parallel parking." Yanking hard on the wheel, he threw the Mercedes into reverse again, this time backing into a solid metal Dumpster—hard. The jar-ring impact hurled McKenzie into the dashboard, knocking the wind out of him, but before the shell-shocked cop could even catch his breath, Murdock was accelerating the convertible forward once more.

He charged right into a large cement block at the southwest corner of the parking lot. With a tremen-dous crunch, the Mercedes' elegant front end crum-pled into so much scrap metal. *My car!* McKenzie wailed in mental agony. *My beautiful new car!*

"What do you want?" he shrieked at the lunatic lawyer.

Murdock turned on McKenzie. Despite the attor-ney's dark glasses, McKenzie could tell the other man was seething. "I want to know why your *heartbeat* never changed this entire time!"

My heartbeat? the cop thought, blinking in confu-sion. *What's this got to do with my heart?*

Murdock let go of the wheel and grabbed McKen-zie's shirt, tearing it open with his bare hands. A long, ugly scar ran down the center of the cop's chest, and Murdock smiled coldly as he traced the scar with his fingertip.

"When did you get the pacemaker?" he asked.

This was getting nuttier by the minute. "Three years ago!" McKenzie bawled. "So what?"

Murdock nodded to himself, as if all this insanity made sense somehow. "You lied in court," he accused McKenzie, as though he had him under oath. "That's perjury."

"You're crazy!" McKenzie snapped. There was no way this screwball lawyer could know that!

Murdock didn't argue with him. "You're right. I am crazy." Who knew what kind of homicidal glare was hidden behind those dark, concealing shades?

Sweat poured from McKenzie's body. His hands shook like a junkie in withdrawal.

Murdock spun the wheel and floored the gas pedal, slamming the brutalized Mercedes back into the bar. Gleaming silver metal ruptured, and McKenzie started to wonder if Murdock was really blind; he sure had no trouble hitting things with McKenzie's ninety-thousand-dollar car!

"You think I'm the only one?" the cop taunted Murdock spitefully. "Take me down and there's a hundred more just like me waiting to take my place."

Murdock got the message. "Tell me who he is."

"I don't know who he is," McKenzie asserted. "He's too smart for that."

Murdock's expression darkened. "How many other cops does he own?" he demanded grimly.

McKenzie laughed harshly. "You think this is about cops? That's just a part of it. He owns the judges that try your cases. The politicians you vote

for. The banks that pay your mortgage. He's everywhere. Like a *cancer*." After what Murdock had put
him through, McKenzie was happy to slap the self-
righteous attorney in the face with a cold, hard dash
of reality. "If he asks you to join, you join for life.
Or end up like Natchios."

"What are you talking about?" Murdock snarled
He grabbed McKenzie roughly by the collar.

"The Kingpin doesn't just kill you," the cop explained hurriedly, willing to tell Murdock anything
just to get the insane lawyer out of his face. "He kills
your entire *family*."

Murdock froze, a look of utter horror coming over
his face.

He whispered a name: "Elektra."

The spacious dining room had once been used for
entertaining, but no more; with her father dead, Elektra was interested only in vengeance, not hospitality.
The antique banquet table and chairs had been
cleared away within hours of her father's funeral,
giving her more room in which to train.

Sandbags hung suspended from the ceiling rafters.
The pear-shaped bags were blank and featureless, but
to her mind's eye, every target bore the face and
form of a leering demon in red. Newspaper articles,
all of them about Daredevil, covered every available
inch of wall space. DEVIL ON THE LOOSE! read a typical
headline, above a police artist's conception of what
the wanted vigilante might look like. HERO OR KILLER?

For herself, Elektra had no such doubts. Daredevil
was a killer; she had seen that with her own eyes.
She still saw that hateful horned figure, in fact, every
time she closed her eyes.

There was only one way, she knew, to exorcise this

particular demon from her mind. *I will never forget you, Devil,* she thought feverishly, her dark eyes flashing with unquenched hatred, *until I've sent you back to hell.*

Elektra leapt and spun between the hanging sandbags, striking out at the bags ferociously. She wore sweat-soaked black workout wraps and gripped a lethal-looking sai in each hand. The tridentlike weapon was of classic Okinawan design, with a long central shaft flanked by two smaller prongs. It was her favorite martial arts implement, versatile and deadly. She looked forward to spearing Daredevil on its pointed tines.

She expertly spun the twin sai in her hands, as skillfully as a majorette twirling a baton, while simultaneously battering the nearest sandbag with a brutal round kick. *Feel that, Devil?* she thought savagely. Without missing a breath, she segued from the completed kick into a flawless front kick/side kick combination. *Feel that, and that!* The first bag came swinging back at her and she deftly sidestepped out of its way, then hammered it in the side with the blunt end of her sai's hilt, striking hard enough to crack the skull of any man or devil. With her second sai, she stabbed another swinging bag. Powdery white sand bled onto the scuffed teak floor of the chamber.

Her wrists ached from wielding the three-pound metal blades, and her back and shoulders protested the vigorous workout as well. Her spinning, snapping, kicking legs felt as if they were weighed down by solid lead restraints, but Elektra kept on lashing out at the heavy sandbags, imagining each and every blow was punishing Daredevil instead. *I hope you put up a fight, Devil,* she thought mercilessly. *I don't want to kill you too quickly.*

Elektra finished off the bleeding sandbag with a spinning back kick. Nobody who hadn't witnessed their own mother blasted apart before her eyes, or felt their father's hot blood stream past her fingers, could. . . .

In Greek mythology, the character Elektra endured the treacherous murder of her father, Agamemnon, and cried out to the gods for retribution. She waited bitterly for years, until her brother, Orestes, finally returned to Greece to avenge their father's death.

But I have no brother, Elektra's modern-day namesake thought grimly. She slashed at the empty air with her razor-sharp sais, while dodging the frenzied blows of an imaginary billy club. *So the bloody task of killing my father's slayer falls upon me alone.*

She had always known that she could not escape her family's guilty history of murder and revenge. There was no room for love and happiness in her life; like a member of the cursed House of Atreus, to which the mythical Elektra had belonged, she had inherited a legacy of never-ending sin and bloodshed.

I'm sorry, Matt, she thought sadly, remembering the stricken look on her handsome suitor's face when she turned away from him back at the funeral. *But I tried to warn you. You're better off staying far away from me. . . .*

She ran through an entire range of advanced kobudo and jujitsu exercises, pushing herself to the brink of exhaustion. A sheen of slick perspiration coated her body, and her abused muscles drowned in painful fatigue poisons. Soon, perhaps, she would be tired enough to drop instantly into unconsciousness as soon as her depleted body dropped onto her waiting bed. That was the only way she could sleep these days, and even then her dreams were haunted by nightmarish images of a wooden rod plunging deep into her father's chest—and of the crimson devil who had snatched away her last hope of happiness.

The words of the mythical Elektra, drilled into her as a child, echoed inside her troubled mind, driving her to push herself ever harder:

"If the hapless dead is to lie in dust and nothingness while the slayers pay not with blood for blood, all regard for man, all fear of heaven, will vanish from the Earth. . . ."

Her eyes zeroed in on the artist's sketch of Daredevil, pinned to the wall on the other side of the converted dining room. She whipped her right arm up and flung one of her sai with all her strength.

The chrome-plated short sword flew across the room like an avenging fury, landing with a heavy thunk into the inky black-and-white portrait of Daredevil. The center blade sank in deeply between the Devil's inhuman eyes.

Elektra nodded in satisfaction. *Soon, Devil,* she promised, her heart as cold and hard as the forged steel sai.

Soon.

CHAPTER 19

The lights were on late at the offices of Nelson &
Murdock, where Foggy was burning the midnight
oil. Not literally, of course, although he wouldn't
have been surprised if there was an old-fashioned oil
lamp buried somewhere amidst the heaps of clutter
stacked around the office. Lord knows they had
every other kind of junk crammed into the corners.

Foggy sat at his desk, poring over his notes as he
searched for an edge in the Daunte Jackson case. *I
can do this,* he thought, impressed by his own energy
and determination. Transcripts and legal briefs were
spread out atop the desk. *I'm in the zone. . . .*

Still no word from Matt, alas, even though Foggy
had left several messages on his partner's home answering machine. Perhaps Matt was off consoling
Elektra somewhere, after the tragic death of the elder
Natchios? *Poor Matt,* Foggy thought sympathetically.
He no longer envied his partner's good fortune in
landing the orphaned Greek heiress. *Just his luck to
get involved with a woman whose father turns out to be
the Kingpin of crime!*

"You need more coffee," Karen observed as she
stepped into his office. Their invaluable secretary was
working late, too. Foggy hoped that meant that she

had forgiven him for squeezing her out of an invite to the Black and White Ball. To tell the truth, he had a bit of a crush on the shapely blond secretary.

She took his cup for a refill, as Foggy flipped through his notebook on the Jackson case. He paused as he came to the hidden message Matt had uncovered at Lisa Tazio's apartment:

MOM 6/8.

Foggy scratched his head, unable to figure out what, if anything, the cryptic inscription had to do with Ms. Tazio's murder. Matt had seemed certain it meant something.

Karen reentered his office, bearing a fresh cup of steaming coffee. Foggy accepted the much needed caffeine gratefully.

"Thanks," Foggy said. "Did you get ahold of Matt?"

"Don't worry. He'll call," Karen said.

"You should go home."

"I'm fine. How's it going? Your mom coming to town?" she asked.

"Hmm?" It took Foggy a second to realize she was referring to the mysterious message. "Oh, no. Matt thought this might mean something for the Jackson case."

Karen cocked her head, examining the page from a different angle. "When was the night of the murder?" she asked.

"August ninth," Foggy said. "Why?"

She leaned over him rather distractingly and turned the notebook around. "Maybe you're looking at it the wrong way."

Foggy forcibly diverted his attention away from Karen's tantalizing proximity and back onto the page. His eyes widened as he stared at the inverted message:

8/9—WOW.

Karen sauntered out of the office, leaving Foggy alone with the transformed clue. He mulled it over for a moment or so, an idea gradually forming in his mind, then slapped his forehead in exasperation at his own slowness. *Of course!* he realized, hurriedly fumbling through his pockets to retrieve an expensive-looking embossed business card, which Foggy had just happened to acquire the other night at the Black and White Ball.

He held the card up to his eyes, reading the name inscribed there:

Wesley Owen Welch.

Foggy sagged backwards against his chair, totally flummoxed by his discovery. "Well, I'll be damned . . ." he muttered.

Not surprisingly, the hallway outside the city morgue was uncomfortably chilly. Somebody had the air-conditioning turned up to the max, although Urich doubted if the stiffs inside appreciated the dramatic relief from the heat.

"This better be good, Kirby," he said, slapping a hundred-dollar bill into the palm of his favorite forensics assistant, a hip-looking young man with horn-rimmed glasses and a scruffy black beard.

"I'm always good," Jack Kirby insisted, pocketing the money. He wore a rumpled white lab coat whose assorted stains Urich chose not to speculate about. "You know that."

He led Urich into a private room, where the enterprising morgue employee unlocked a drawer and pulled out a plastic bag containing a bloodstained wooden rod. He opened the bag and laid the fractured baton onto a gleaming metal counter, beneath the concentrated glare of a set of high-powered operating lights.

Urich recognized the splintered baton as the murder weapon responsible for the death of Nikolas Natchios. He had no doubt that it was also Daredevil's infamous billy club, having heard the fearsome weapon described by any number of talkative hoodlums, most of them with busted skulls and concussions.

"I've seen it," he said, unimpressed.

Kirby grinned impishly. "You haven't seen this."

He removed the club from the plastic bag and pressed a hidden stud on the wooden shaft. *Chik-chik!* The ends of the club extended automatically, transforming the bloody rod from an intimidating truncheon to a blind man's cane.

Urich's jaw dropped, and he almost lost the cigarette dangling from his lip, as his astonished eyes recognized the trademark red cane of Matthew Murdock, attorney-at-law.

"You said to look out for anything weird," Kirby reminded him, visibly enjoying the reporter's dumbstruck reaction. "This is some pretty weird shit, man."

Urich shook his head in disbelief. "You have no idea. . . ."

A jarring ring from the cell phone in Urich's pocket startled both men. The reporter shrugged ruefully as he answered the call. "Urich."

A familiar voice entered his ear. "Ben, it's Foggy Nelson."

Talk about awkward timing! Urich thought. He wasn't ready to talk to Murdock's partner just yet, not before he'd had a chance to mentally process everything the peekaboo red cane implied. "This isn't a good time—" he mumbled into the phone.

"It's about Lisa Tazio," Nelson blurted, rendering the reporter's protests academic.

Suddenly, the eager attorney had Urich's full attention.

CHAPTER 20

Daredevil stalked restlessly through the grimy back alleys of the Kitchen, consumed by the need to find this Bullseye character before the murderous Irish assassin carried out the hit on Elektra. A spare billy club was strapped to his thigh, to replace the one Bullseye had used to murder Elektra's father, and the scars left by the killer's throwing stars still smarted every time he moved. Daredevil's overriding concern for the orphaned heiress's safety was only heightened by the terrifying realization that Elektra was doubtless searching for Bullseye as well.

Somebody has to know something, he reasoned. Somewhere in the city's fetid underworld, there had to be someone who could point him toward Bullseye. *All I have to do is find the right hoodlum—and shake the truth out of him.*

He sniffed the air and, to his surprise, caught the tantalizing scent of fresh rose oil.

Her scent.

Galvanized by the beckoning aroma, he pushed off the narrow walls of the alley, the soles of his boots smacking against the graffiti-covered brickwork, before leapfrogging up onto the rooftops. He landed on the level roof of an old brownstone, where he discovered a huge collection of fresh laundry strung out to dry.

Damn, he thought. The hanging sheets and towels and such created a veritable linen labyrinth, confusing his radar senses. *Where are you, Elektra?* he wondered, anxious to catch up with her before she found Bullseye—or vice versa. He listened carefully for her heartbeat, but heard only the usual street sounds rising from below, plus the bells of the Church of the Holy Innocents, only a few blocks away.

An alert nose searched the late-night breeze, and his nostrils flared as he detected another faint whiff of rose oil. Fabric rustled directly ahead of him, and he thought he sensed a vaguely feminine shape. He stepped forward cautiously. "Elektra?"

Perhaps it was not too late to talk her out of her perilous quest for revenge. . . .

The maze of fragrant laundry frustrated him. Elektra could not have devised a better way to elude him even if she had known all about his hypersenses. But, no, he reminded himself, there was no way she could know that Daredevil and Matt Murdock were one and the same.

He reached out a gloved hand, drawing aside a hanging beach towel and ducking beneath one of the crisscrossing clothes lines.

Flap! Flap! Flap! A clamorous fluttering of wings overwhelmed his ears as a flock of disturbed pigeons flew at him. He threw up his hands to protect his face as a storm of feathers and warm, compact bodies engulfed him. The frenzied racket of the birds' tiny hearts was almost as deafening as their wildly flapping wings.

Stomping his foot and waving an arm, he shooed them away impatiently. None too soon, the agitated pigeons took to the skies, taking the worst of the distracting pandemonium with them. Despite the raucous avian exodus, he quickly relocated that intriguing feminine silhouette and reached out for it urgently.

Elektra?

His fists closed on empty fabric. A limp cotton dress, hanging from a pair of clothespins.

Not Elektra.

Then where—?

A heavy leather boot came out of nowhere, slamming into the back of his head. Daredevil hit the floor of the roof hard. His skull ringing, he turned his ears and nose toward his assailant, probing outwardly with his senses.

Elektra stood over him, her scent and carriage unmistakable. He heard sleek, oiled leather brush against her skin and realized that she was dressed to kill. A low-cut leather vest barely blocked her angry heartbeat, while a matching choker vibrated against the pulse of her throat. Tight leather pants were belted below her midriff. Glossy leather armbands embraced her athletic biceps. Fingerless leather gloves protected her clenched fists, while a pair of metallic weapons jangled at her sides. *Sais,* he guessed, recalling her martial arts training.

In all, she was clad very differently from the way Matt had known her to dress before. Naturally, he had no idea what color her fighting gear was. For all he knew, it could have been lustrous black or brilliant bloodred.

"Remember me, murderer?" she asked venomously.

Before Daredevil could answer her, before he could even begin to explain what had really happened to her father, her powerful legs lashed out at him, triple-kicking his face, stomach, and balls. Six-inch heels dug into his flesh.

He rolled away instinctively, grunting in pain. Somehow he managed to spring back onto his feet even as Elektra circled him menacingly, keeping up her attack. A rapid-fire series of bone-jarring strikes and kicks drove Daredevil back across the rooftop, away from the hanging laundry. A driving forefist punch made his teeth rattle, but when she threw a spinning side kick at his head, he caught the oncoming foot in an ankle-lock.

"I didn't kill your father," he insisted rapidly. If only he could make her see the truth . . . !

"Liar!" she screamed. Her free foot flew upward and kicked him forcefully across the face. He staggered backward, tasting the coppery tang of his own blood, while she completed a gravity-defying backward flip, landing squarely on her feet less than two yards away.

He heard her whip out her lethal sais. The sharpened blades sliced through the air as she twirled them adroitly in her hands.

Reluctantly, he drew out his billy club as well, snapping it apart so that he wielded a baton in each hand to counter the twin sais. *I have no choice*, he realized, even though he feared that the sight of the clubs, identical to the one that had impaled Elektra's father, would only add fire to the blazing fury consuming her.

His concerns proved all too prophetic as Elektra lunged at him, slashing out with both sais. Fire-hardened hickory blocked the three-pronged swords as the two leather-clad warriors feinted and parried atop the downtown brownstone.

This fierce duel was nothing like their carefree sparring match in the playground. That had been fun, flirtatious even, with no real intent to inflict serious damage on the other fighter. In contrast, this battle was in deadly earnest, with at least Elektra determined to make a fight to the death. She threw a right palm-up punch at his stomach, which Daredevil blocked with a downward swing of his left club.

He kicked out defensively, trying to drive her out of striking range. But Elektra took advantage of the sudden distance between them to draw back her arm and hurl a sai at his head. The pointed trident whistled through the air, and Daredevil barely jerked his head out of the way in time, so that the sai thudded into the mortar of the brick chimney behind him.

He tried one more time to convince her. "It was a man named Bullseye," he called out.

"I know it was you," she spat back at him, her husky voice dripping with corrosive hatred. "I saw you there."

She leapt toward him, tossing the second sai as she did so. Daredevil spun his bisected billy club like twin propellers, deflecting the flying blade. He ducked beneath her headlong charge and grabbed her in a classic kempo elbow lock.

The diverted sai clattered to the rooftop several feet away, leaving her weaponless. Daredevil swiftly wrapped his arm under her throat, his own leather sleeve chafing against her embossed choker. He pulled her close against his chest and heard their hearts beating only inches apart.

"I'm not going to fight you," he insisted. The intoxicating smell of her hair filled his nostrils, and he realized that he was holding her exactly as he had back in the park that day, right before she finally trusted him with her name. The scent of her hair, the feel of her body within his arms, took him instantly back to that rapturous moment, flooding his soul with a profound sense of loss and hopeless yearning. They belonged together, but not like this. *Is it the same for her?* he wondered painfully. *Can she feel it, too?*

Maybe not.

"Then this will be quick," she retorted, savagely jabbing her elbow into his stomach. He doubled over, gasping for breath, and she pulled away from his grappling embrace. The rattan-wrapped hilt of her sai protruded from the brick chimney behind him, and she reached and wrenched it free from the crumbling mortar. No romantic flashbacks appeared to be cramping her style, as she whirled around and violently thrust the point of the blade into Daredevil's shoulder.

Searing pain erupted from his shoulder, radiating out along his screaming nervous system, as over a foot of sharpened steel pierced through leather, skin, and muscle. Daredevil bit down hard on his lower lip to keep from crying out in agony. He dropped to his knees on the sooty rooftop, blood streaming down his chest. His club slipped from his fingers.

With a vicious twist, Elektra yanked the sai from his shoulder, triggering a fresh gout of blood. She pounced on him like a jungle cat and pressed the tip of the bloody sai against his throat. "I want to look into the eyes of my father's killer as he dies," she said icily.

Her fingers dug roughly under the edge of his mask, scratching his face with her nails, and peeled back the cowl so abruptly that his neck was wrenched back hard enough to give him whiplash.

The humid night air kissed his exposed face, and he heard Elektra's heart skip a beat as she suddenly realized the truth.

"No . . ." she whispered.

Matt realized it was too late to try to preserve his secret with some lame-ass explanation. "So now you know," he said gravely.

The point of the sai fell away from his throat, and Elektra let go of his cowl as though it were on fire. She kneeled down to his side, unable to accept the face beneath the mask. "No . . . not you . . ."

"I was trying to protect you," he told her haltingly. Surely, she couldn't still think that he was responsible for her father's execution, could she?

"Oh, God . . . oh, Matt. . . ." She stared at the blood on her sai, on her hands. Matt's blood.

He tried to stand up, but he had lost too much blood and too quickly; his head spun and he collapsed back onto his knees, his pierced shoulder burning like the fires of hell. "Elektra . . ." he whispered, reaching out for her.

"Forgive me," she whispered hoarsely. For the first time since her father's funeral, tears leaked from her eyes. The salty smell of the tears was almost lost amidst the torrent of fresh blood flowing across the rooftop.

I forgive you, Matt thought. He tried to speak, but his mouth was too dry and numb. His limbs felt like rubber, and her anguished voice seemed to be coming from very far away.

For a moment, they were frozen that way, trapped in an ironic tableau out of some tragic grand opera. Elektra stared down at him, her heart pounding in horror, while Matt fought to stay upright and conscious, unable to cross the daunting yards between

them, but wanting nothing more than to hold the
woman he loved, the woman who had nearly killed
him. . . .

A sardonic voice intruded on their private heartbreak. "Oh, Daaaaaredevil . . . ?"

Matt instantly recognized the voice, remembering
both its accent and its callous, mocking tone. *Bullseye!*
Footsteps clanged up the old brownstone's metal fire
escape, the shock and danger jolting Matt back to
full alertness.

"It's him," he tried to warn Elektra. "Bullseye."

He heard her body stiffen abruptly, forcibly dis-
carding the softness and vulnerability she had only
just rediscovered. When she spoke again, her voice
was flat and emotionless. "He has to pay for what
he did," she said.

No! Matt thought. This was exactly what he had
wanted so much to prevent. There was no way the
Elektra he loved could survive her confrontation with
Bullseye; she would become either a killer—or a
corpse. "Don't . . ." he whispered, trying and failing
to get up off his knees. "Don't go. . . ."

She bent toward him. Slender fingers brushed his
face. "I'll find you again," she promised.

Her lips found his, and they kissed each other hungrily, a fervent kiss of passion and pain and remorse.
Then she gently pulled his mask back down over
his face.

Helpless to stop her, he heard her walk away.

Elektra retrieved her second sai, then waited, her
fingers wrapped around the hand-crafted hilts of her
weapons, as Bullseye stepped off the fire escape onto
the roof.

He was a stranger to her, a smirking interloper

with a bald head, a dirty brown beard, and eyes like those of a mad dog. Gold rings dangled from his pierced earlobes. Like her, he was dressed entirely in black. A scaly alligator-skin coat flapped behind him in the breeze and equally reptilian boots trod upon the grimy rooftop at a relaxed, unhurried pace.

She checked out his hands first—oddly, he appeared to be unarmed. Then her eyes were drawn to the grotesque scars cut into his forehead: three concentric circles overlaid by the cross hairs of a gunsight, every line clearly inflicted by design. *Bullseye*, she thought grimly. *Matt said the real killer was named Bullseye*. A bitter smile lifted the corners of her lips. Not much chance of mistaken identity here; this *had* to be the man Matt meant.

Looking into the true assassin's feral eyes, she felt a pang of guilt for ever having suspected Daredevil.

"You killed my father," she accused the stranger. She angled away from the drying laundry so that she had a clear shot at Bullseye.

"Yeah," he admitted with a marked Irish brogue; despite his empty hands, he seemed strangely unworried. Cocky even. "But you gotta admit that was a hell of a toss."

Nightmarish images of her father's final moments, the bloody club jutting from his ruptured chest, flashed through her mind. She remembered kneeling in her father's blood, struggling in vain to keep his life from gushing away . . . and watching his coffin being lowered into the earth.

The fevered words of the mythical Elektra echoed inside her skull: *O home of Hades and Persephone! O Hermes of the shades! O potent Curse, and you, dread daughters of the gods, Erinyes, you who behold when a life*

*is reft with violence—Come, help me avenge the murder of
my father!*

An unearthly wrath, like none she had ever
known, rushed through her veins. Like her mythical
namesake, she craved a daughter's vengeance: blood
for blood, a life for a life. *I want you dead*, she silently
cursed the gloating assassin. *I want you dead—now!*

Unassuaged grief and hatred fueled her muscles as
her arm shot up, hurling her right sai at Bullseye.
The blade had already tasted Daredevil's blood,
through her own confusion and misjudgment; let it
now, she prayed ardently, find her true enemy at last.

The sai soared unerringly toward that tempting
target on the assassin's brow. Elektra held her breath,
waiting for the sword to strike home. *The hunt is
almost over*, she thought, feeling an oppressive burden
begin to slip from her shoulders; perhaps, with her
father's murder finally avenged, she could begin to
rebuild her life, maybe even with Matt. . . .

To her surprise, Bullseye did not even try to duck
or dodge the oncoming sai. He just stood there, grinning confidently, until the trident was just about to
spear his skull. Then, in an astonishing display of
lightning-fast reflexes, he reached up and caught the
triple prongs of the sai between his fingers!

Elektra's jaw dropped. *That's not possible!* she
gasped silently. While her dumbstruck eyes were still
trying to reconcile what she had just witnessed with
reality, Bullseye twirled the captured sai and fired it
back at her.

"A throwing weapon," he observed, watching the
purloined sword zoom back at its mistress. "I
approve."

Something cold and unyielding pierced her palm.

Crying out in pain, she stared in stunned horror and amazement at the sight of the sai stuck through her hand. A sticky red stream flowed down her wrist, dripping onto the tar-papered rooftop.

He had stabbed her with her own weapon! A shiver of fear shook her soul, but not enough to extinguish her insatiable thirst for revenge. With brutal efficiency, she yanked the sai free of her hand, then quickly bandaged the gaping puncture wound with a black silk wrap.

Exuding an air of infuriating nonchalance, Bullseye waited patiently for the injured woman to recover from his surprise attack. He leaned casually against the brick housing of the brownstone's elevator equipment, showing no sign of concern where his victim's revenge-hungry daughter was concerned, nor any trace of repentance either.

Elektra didn't keep him waiting for long. With the implacable tenacity of one of the ancient Greek furies, she leapt at Bullseye, kicking him across the face while frenziedly slashing at him with both sais. *All right, you murderous psychopath*, she thought. *You drew first blood, but I'm still going to kill you—or die trying!*

Ducking and weaving, Bullseye dodged the sword strikes. Sparks flew as the steel blades scraped against the brick elevator housing. Elektra lashed out at him in rage and frustration, duty-driven to return all her pain and suffering to its diabolical point of origin.

She sprang into the air, targeting his head with her heels, but Bullseye rolled beneath the flying kick, jabbing her in the back with his elbow as he did so. She grunted briefly, pushing away the pain, and swung her right sword at his elusive form, keeping him on the defensive. *He can't dodge me forever*, she reasoned. *All I need is one good slice with a sai . . . !*

At the back of her mind also was the chilling realization that, should she fall in battle, Daredevil would be left alone on the rooftop, injured and unable to defend himself, with Bullseye. *I have to win*, she understood completely, *or Matt will be this killer's next victim.*

The weighted pommel of a sai smashed into a wall, turning aging brickwork to powder. Still seemingly unarmed, Bullseye effortlessly eluded her blades, blocking Elektra's unremitting strikes and kicks with perfectly executed countermoves.

A roundhouse punch slammed into her head, but she shook off the blow, retaliating with a combination left-handed lunge with her sai and crescent kick to his ribs. He absorbed the kick and blocked the hilt of the sword with his forearm, then sidestepped quickly to avoid a follow-up stab from the right.

That's it, she thought hopefully. *Keep him on the run.* Slowly but surely, never letting up the attack, she drove Bullseye backward across the roof. She chased him past TV antennae, fans, and sooty turbine vents until, finally, she had him backed up against the ledge, with nothing but a four-story drop behind him.

She smiled in anticipation. Beyond the cornered assassin, she saw the steeple of a Gothic cathedral silhouetted against the moon. The upraised cross inspired no feelings of mercy in her. "Anything to say before you die?" she asked coldly.

Trapped and defenseless, Bullseye still flaunted an arrogant smirk. Like a stage magician, he held up an empty hand and—voilà!—a solitary playing card suddenly appeared between his fingers.

The ace of spades.

"Pick a card. Any card," he quipped.

Elektra blinked in confusion. Before she could even begin to guess what Bullseye was up to, the assassin threw the card with astounding force and precision. The edge of the card struck her exactly a millimeter below her leather choker, slicing her throat!

She dropped her sais, frantically clutching at her neck. A ghastly sensation of déjà vu came over her as she felt her own blood seep between her fingers, just as her father's had. *No!* she thought desperately. *It can't end like this . . . it's not right. . . .*

Bullseye was supposed to die tonight, not her.

"You're good, baby," the victorious hit man conceded. He strolled away from the ledge, the back of his reptilian duster dragging across the shallow brick railing. Holding one hand over her throat, she groped clumsily for one of her fallen sais, but Bullseye calmly walked over and kicked it up into his own hand. He admired the gleaming tips of the trident as he gripped the hilt firmly. "But I'm *magic*."

Elektra refused to surrender her life easily. She tore off the sash from her arm, tying it around her neck like a tourniquet to stanch the bleeding from her throat. *You haven't won yet, killer,* she thought, her dark eyes flashing defiantly. Her wounded hand still burned where the stolen sai had impaled her, and blood spurted from her palm as she clenched her fists. *I'll kill you with my bare hands if I have to!*

But her body lacked the strength and endurance of her spirit. Bullseye grabbed her throat by the choker and brutally yanked her to her feet. Elektra looked into his insane, bloodshot eyes and realized that her time had run out. *Forgive me, Poppa,* she thought mournfully. *I tried my best to avenge you*

Bullseye grinned. "And now, for my next trick. . . ."

Half kneeling, half sprawled on the floor, Daredevil listened anxiously to the volcanic combat taking place only a few yards away. He tried feverishly to get up, to aid Elektra in her life-or-death duel against Bullseye, but his depleted body declined to cooperate. Blood still flowed from the agonizing stab wound in his shoulder, and despite the humid summer heat, his body was racked by debilitating chills. All he could do was listen in excruciating suspense as the woman he loved single-handedly battled a master assassin.

Hang on, Elektra, he thought fervidly, marshaling his strength for another attempt to get back on his feet. His billy club, still divided into two segments, rested uselessly on the ground nearby, just out of reach. *Just give me one more minute . . . !*

But the end came too quickly. Daredevil sensed the heated clash turning against Elektra. He heard her suddenly gasp in pain and fear, smelled her blood spill from her pulsing throat. A metallic clang alerted him to the fact that Bullseye had stolen one of her sais, and Elektra's leather garb squeaked alarmingly as Bullseye jerked her to her feet. "And now, for my next trick . . ." the killer smugly announced.

With a savage thrust, he jabbed the sai into Elektra's stomach, loudly tearing through defenseless skin and muscle. The central blade went all the way through her, its bloody tip poking out of her back. Daredevil's radar senses allowed him to grasp the entire gruesome silhouette, although, at this awful moment, he would have given anything to be truly and completely blind. *Oh, my God . . . Elektra!*

"No!" he screamed.

Bullseye's lips smacked wetly as he bestowed an ironic kiss upon his skewered victim, then threw her contemptuously onto the floor. Almost as an afterthought, he reached into his coat pocket and drew out a single fragrant rose. He chuckled cruelly to himself as he dropped the fragile flower onto the crumpled form at his feet, where Daredevil heard it land softly, its delicate petals barely disturbing the air.

A rose? Daredevil reacted with a start, his memory involuntarily leaping back to the night of Jack Murdock's murder. And, as well, to the solitary bloom that had been dropped onto Nikolas Natchios's lowered casket. *Again, a rose!*

Bullseye wiped Elektra's blood from his hands. Before he could finish her off, however, or perhaps turn his psychotic attention toward Daredevil, the echoing *whirr* of a police helicopter drowned out Elektra's dying gasps. A blazing spotlight searched the rooftops, drawing ever nearer to the site of the disastrous three-way encounter. *A neighbor must have heard all the fighting,* Daredevil guessed, *or perhaps reported a suspicious prowler climbing the fire escape.*

The helicopter's sudden arrival annoyed Bullseye. He muttered foully under his breath as he retreated into the shadows, his long coat flapping in his wake. He left behind him two wounded combatants, both vanquished and bleeding atop the desolate rooftop.

Daredevil barely registered Bullseye's departure. All his senses were focused on the still and prostrate form of Elektra, whose heartbeat and breathing were growing fainter by the second. There was almost no way, he knew, that she could survive that fatal sword thrust through her abdomen, not to mention her freshly slit throat; the miracle was that she was still alive at all.

I'm so sorry, Elektra, he thought in heartsick despair. *I promised to protect you. . . .*

Then, incredibly, her brutalized body stirred once more. Beneath the cold white glare of the airborne spotlight, and to Daredevil's disbelieving ears, Elektra somehow climbed to her feet and began to stagger across the rooftop toward Daredevil. Tottering precariously, like a drunk trying unsuccessfully to walk a straight line, and with one blood-soaked hand pressed tightly against her perforated belly, she crossed the nocturnal battleground, leaving a trail of crimson droplets behind her.

Through sheer determination and stubbornness, she made it all the way to Daredevil's side before collapsing into his arms. He grabbed her as though she were drowning and was horrified by the icy coldness of her flesh. Elektra felt as though she were dead already.

"No . . ." he whispered in torment. He hadn't felt so helpless, so lost and abandoned, since the night he found his father's battered body in that alley.

Her fading strength all but exhausted, she turned her face toward his. Her eyes fluttered moistly as she slowly reached up and touched his cheek. Her breath bore the coppery scent of internal bleeding. "I told you I'd find you," she reminded him weakly.

It was too late to try to bind her wounds. The better part of her life's blood had already escaped through the gashes at her throat and stomach. Daredevil could only gently caress her face, just as Matt had during that magical night in the rain, and softly trace the sad smile on her lips as her heartbeat finally came to a halt.

CHAPTER 21

He longed to stay with her, to watch over her lifeless body, but the sound of pounding footsteps racing up the stairs toward the roof informed him that their somber privacy would soon be disturbed. *The police*, he assumed, realizing that he had to get away from there or face arrest for the murders of both Nikolas Natchios and his daughter.

Good-bye, my darling, he thought, laying her gently down on the rooftop. He kissed her one last time, tasting blood on her lips.

The emotional jolt of her death gave him the adrenaline rush he needed to get back on his feet. Wincing, he snatched up his billy club, snapping it back together, and thrust it into its holster. The sudden movement caused the pain in his shoulder to flare up with renewed ferocity. The world spun dizzily around him, but he fought against the nausea and vertigo, clenching his teeth until the dizziness passed.

And none too soon. The clattering footsteps had reached the third floor already. Daredevil knew the police would be invading the rooftop at any minute. He recognized the heavy tread, and pungent cologne, of Detective Nick Manolis on the stairs.

Daredevil hastily surveyed his surroundings, his mind racing to figure out his next move. More than anything else he wanted to go after Bullseye, to make the sadistic hit man pay for Elektra's murder, but common sense prevailed; he was in no shape to take on the assassin, not grievously wounded and losing blood. *Bullseye will have to wait,* he realized angrily. *First I need to find someplace to recover, regain my strength. . . .*

The summer wind lightly rang the bells of the Church of the Holy Innocents, only a couple of blocks away, and when, moments later, Detective Manolis burst through the doorway, leading a squadron of armed police officers, Daredevil was nowhere to be seen.

"Matthew?"

Father Everett carefully cradled the wounded hero's head. Matt heard the concern in the old priest's voice, along with his lingering surprise over the revelation of Daredevil's secret identity. The marble floor of the cathedral felt cold against his back as Matt reclined weakly within the sanctuary, only a few feet from the altar. Incense competed with the coppery smell of spilled blood.

He tried to speak, but his throat was too dry. He had to swallow hard to work up enough saliva to be heard. "This is my confession," he croaked, aware of the poignant irony at work. Was it only days ago that he had conversed with Father Everett in this very church, resisting the priest's kindhearted attempts to draw him out?

So much for my vow of silence, he thought mordantly.

Father Everett undid his clerical collar, using the loose cloth to stop the bleeding from Matt's shoulder.

Matt prayed that the well-meaning priest would not feel obliged to call for an ambulance. Even through the cathedral's high stone walls, he could still hear the whirring blades of the helicopter searching the neighborhood from above. Was there any chance of keeping the secret of his dual identity intact?

The priest must have seen the anxiety on his face. "God has infinite mercy," he assured Matt, keeping the wadded-up cloth pressed tightly against the injured shoulder, where the profuse bleeding was finally starting to slow. "All you have to do is ask."

Matt laughed bitterly, the exertion causing another jarring spike of pain. "Everything's been taken from me, and now I'm supposed to ask for mercy?" He coughed hoarsely, spitting up a mouthful of blood. "I don't ask for mercy. People ask me."

The last minutes of Jose Quesada, lying helplessly on the tracks of the oncoming 1 train, surfaced from his memory. In his mind, he could still hear the panicked mobster pleading to be rescued. . . .

"Maybe it's time you listened," Father Everett suggested gently.

Unsure how to respond, Matt started to speak, only to be interrupted by the noisy *thwack* of a metallic object slamming into the altar only inches from Father Everett's head. Daredevil instantly remembered the menacing throwing stars Bullseye had employed against him the night Elektra's father died, leaving scars that had barely begun to heal.

The cathedral's magnificent organ climbed the rear of the sanctuary. Retracing the trajectory of the deadly missile, Matt directed his radar senses upward, past the tiers of silent pipes to the majestic rose window overlooking the hushed interior of the cathedral. A steady heartbeat, cool and calculating, emanated from a shallow limestone ledge running along the bottom of the rose window.

"First one's a warning, Padre," Bullseye said ominously, looking down on them from more than two hundred feet above.

He must have followed my trail of blood across the rooftops, Matt guessed. The very presence of the assassin within this venerable old church struck him as an unspeakable sacrilege.

He pulled his mask back down over his face. "Is there a back way out?" Daredevil asked Father Everett.

The elderly priest's heart, already agitated by Daredevil's dramatic arrival, now fluctuated worryingly. He crossed himself defensively; he required no introductions to comprehend that Bullseye was dangerous in the extreme. "Yes," he answered quickly, staring up anxiously at the stranger above them.

"Take it," Daredevil said. "Call the police."

If they're not already on the way, he thought. He could still hear the helicopter hovering over the church. Detective Manolis, he knew, was only a few blocks away.

Father Everett tore his fearful gaze away from Bullseye. He softly gripped Daredevil's shoulder. "What about you?"

A decisive tone entered the hero's voice. A gloved hand fell upon the grip of his billy club, still secure within its holster. "I have to finish this."

For Elektra.

"You can't fight like this," Father Everett said, concerned for Matt's safety. He had a pretty good idea of just how badly the injured vigilante was hurt.

Daredevil rose to his feet anyway. He drew out his billy club, wrapping his fist around the baton. If nothing else, his brief respite within the cathedral had given him a chance to recover a little of his strength, which would have to be enough. "Have faith," he instructed the apprehensive priest. "Isn't that right, Father?"

Realizing, perhaps, that there was no dissuading Daredevil, Father Everett turned away from the younger man and hastily exited the sanctuary. Looking back nervously over his shoulder, the priest ducked around the pulpit and scurried to safety. Daredevil breathed a sigh of relief as he heard the old man's footsteps recede into the distance. *One less potential victim to worry about*, he thought soberly.

Bullseye also seemed pleased to see the back of the priest. His grudge was with Daredevil, apparently. "Now then," he said breezily, "where were we?"

Daredevil wasn't interested in exchanging witty banter with this heartless sociopath. He backed up along the center aisle, keeping his senses locked on Bullseye every minute, until he was far enough from the sanctuary to get a decent running start. Then, club in hand, he charged abruptly up the aisle, launching himself up onto the first tier of ascending brass pipes.

Before he could reach Bullseye, however, the nimble assassin abandoned his lofty perch before the rose window. Clambering two hundred feet down the intricate woodwork housing the mighty organ and its pipes, he dropped into the sanctuary below.

Moving with unnerving speed, he snatched up a silver communion plate and hurled it at Daredevil like a Frisbee. The spinning plate struck Daredevil in the neck with a sickening *thwack!*

But that was only his first salvo. Even as Daredevil tottered uneasily, snatching up his billy club and throwing it at Bullseye, the assassin was on the move. Bullseye avoided the club as it ricocheted into the aisle. Then he leapt onto the first tier of the ornate pipe organ, out of Daredevil's range.

Daredevil ran down the rows of pews, picking up his billy club from where it lay in the aisle. Spinning around, he threw it at Bullseye, who nimbly caught the club from his perch on the organ, and whipped it back at Daredevil. The club whistled by and clattered against the pews, splintering wood. Once again, Daredevil turned to grasp his club and rejoin the attack, but as he did, Bullseye leapt from the organ.

Sensing the attack, hearing Bullseye's form hurtling toward him, Daredevil deftly spun out of the way, spin-kicking Bullseye off his feet. Grabbing the assassin, Daredevil flung him with all his might into the organ pipes, splitting the metal of some of the pipes and sending them clattering around the sanctuary floor with a tremendous clatter.

The booming bass tones struck Daredevil like a tidal wave, overpowering his hypersenses. His club dropped from his hand and he fell to one knee. He pressed his hands tightly against his ears, but there was no way to shut out the deafening ringing of the broken organ pipes. The sonic barrage was more crippling than any of Bullseye's brutal blows.

The ruthless hit man observed his opponent's distress with the greatest of interest.

A church, Nick Manolis thought sourly as his car pulled up to the curb outside the Church of the Holy Innocents. Heartburn seared his chest from the inside out, and he automatically tossed a handful of Tums into his mouth. *Of course, it would have to be a church. . . .*

Already the downtown cathedral looked as if it was under siege, which it basically was. An entire fleet of police cars was parked out front, spilling a bustling swarm of cops onto the street and sidewalks outside the church. Hastily deployed searchlights illuminated the weathered Gothic facade of the cathedral, while police sharpshooters were already getting into position, aiming their sights and nightscopes through the tall bay windows flanking the church's front entrance.

Manolis climbed awkwardly out of the backseat of an unmarked police car. He was already winded from running up and down the stairs of that decrepit brownstone a few blocks over. *What a waste of time and energy*, he thought irritably; despite his unaccustomed exertions, he hadn't caught so much as a glimpse of Daredevil and his unidentified playmates. The night was going badly and looking to get worse.

A rookie policeman, whose name Manolis couldn't recall, came running up to him. "We've surrounded the perimeter, sir," the uniformed kid reported breathlessly. "The doors are locked from the inside."

Naturally, Manolis thought, feeling his heartburn flare up again. Acid reflux ate away at the lining of his esophagus. *God forbid we should get a break tonight.*

"Break them down," he ordered.

The rookie wavered, looking as though he had just been asked to shoot a puppy. He stammered hesitantly. "It's . . . it's a church, sir."

Manolis gave him the stare he reserved for uncooperative skells and unusually clueless uniforms.

"Yes, sir," the rookie gulped. He hustled to carry out the detective's commands.

Spare me from fresh-faced baby cops, he thought, knowing full well it was a hopeless wish. He searched his pockets for another Tums. *And urban legends who dress up like the Devil.*

Bullseye was having a grand old time.

Seeing how Daredevil had reacted to the noise, he grasped a broken piece of pipe and was using it to bash the intact pipes on the organ. Daredevil grimaced in agony, his hypersenses battered by the relentless onslaught of sound. Every note hit him like a sledgehammer.

"Don't like my playing, Devil?" Bullseye asked cheerily, torturing Daredevil like a cat with a mouse. "Would you believe I've never had a lesson?"

He slugged Daredevil in the jaw, shoving the incapacitated hero against a nearby array of pipes. The collision spawned a burst of high-pitched chords that stabbed through Daredevil's skull like one of Elektra's bloodthirsty sais. His eardrums convulsed in pain as he slumped helplessly to the floor of the sanctuary, unable to defend himself.

Fighting through his pain, and hearing Bullseye rushing toward him, Daredevil managed to grab a colonnade behind him. He contorted his body and propelled himself up in a flip. Kicking out, he caught Bullseye and sent him careening down the hallway with a loud crash.

Regaining his balance, Bullseye ran around the corner and out of sight. Hearing his footsteps, Daredevil leapt after him. Just around the corner, Bullseye reached down and snapped off a half dozen shuriken from his belt buckle.

The lethal stars came spinning at Daredevil, who, a split second earlier, had lunged for his billy club. He grabbed the wooden baton and fanned it before him. . . .

Chuk! Chuk! Chuk! Chuk! Chuk! Chuk!

All six stars came to rest in the shift of the club. Bullseye gasped in disbelief.

Daredevil, rising swiftly to his feet, swung the club at Bullseye, hitting the assassin right in the middle of his forehead and knocking him against the wall.

As Daredevil approached him to take up the attack, Bullseye frantically looked around for another weapon to use against the relentless vigilante. Spotting some stain-glassed windows above, Bullseye grasped the ledge of a doorframe and swung his body up, kicking his feet against the glass and shattering the windows. Catching broken shards of glass as they rained down, Bullseye sent them at Daredevil with rapid-fire speed.

Hearing the shards whistle toward him, Daredevil eluded the whizzing glass, cartwheeling and back-flipping through the projectiles like a man dancing around raindrops.

Just as Daredevil was almost upon him, Bullseye noticed the rope from the bell tower hanging down to the floor just a few feet away. Running toward it, Daredevil launched after him—but was too late. Bullseye yanked the rope, causing the swinging bell to resound loudly in the cavernous space.

As the clapper hit the bell again and again, Daredevil grabbed his head in sheer agony, his acute senses assaulted by the violent sonic waves. Bullseye used the respite to snatch up a candelabra. Then he began to advance on the incapacitated hero.

"Man without fear," Bullseye chided. "Looks like I found something you're afraid of. Let's bring on the pain. Let's bring on the noise!"

With that, Bullseye smashed the candleabra against the base of the organ pipes, further rendering Daredevil helpless in a sea of sound. Smacking the pipes again and again, Bullseye broke the candelabra into a sharp point. He then turned to Daredevil, wielding the candelabra like a honed spear.

The police had the cathedral completely cordoned off. *About time*, Detective Manolis thought.

Sharpshooters wearing bulletproof vests ran up the front steps of the besieged cathedral. They aimed their rifles through every stained-glass window. Manolis crept up behind them, keeping his head low just in case Daredevil and his pal were armed with something more high-powered than fancy kung fu sticks. "Keep 'em in your sights!" he ordered the snipers.

"Which one?" one of the sharpshooters asked, never looking away from the sight of his rifle.

"Both of them!" he barked gruffly.

Incapacitated by sound, and worn down by the assassin's relentless attack, Daredevil rolled heavily onto the platform beneath an intact stained-glass window. Huge and ornate, it was known as the Rose Window, its design depicting the battle of good versus evil. Gallant angels wrestled with fearsome devils in an eternal struggle, with a passage from Romans 12:21 inscribed across its face: "Do not be overcome by evil. But overcome evil with good." It was through this window that the sharpshooters outside were taking aim.

Bullseye approached with the jagged candelabra in his hand. "Fisk said you wouldn't be easy. He was right," the assassin sneered.

"The Kingpin . . ." Daredevil uttered.

"Yeah. The whole rose thing—he's into that shite . . . not my style. He hired me to kill Natchios.

And to gut your sweet girlfriend, too." Daredevil's heart gripped tightly in his chest, the emotional hurt rivaling his physical pain. "But me?" Bullseye continued. "I'm going for the hat trick. The trifecta . . ."

Daredevil crouched there helplessly, unable to move against the ringing sound in his ears, crippled by the memory of Elektra.

"I told him that I'd do you for free," Bullseye continued to taunt. "You want to know why? Because you made me miss. And I never miss."

Bullseye raised the candelabra into the air, preparing for the final blow. "The devil is mine," he said with a wicked gleam in his eyes.

Daredevil heard Bullseye lift the candelabra over his head. He tried to spring up to stop him, but the harrowing storm of broken glass had taken its toll on his already overtaxed endurance. He didn't have the strength or the speed to overcome Bullseye on his own. Salvation would have to come from elsewhere.

His radar senses swept out in all directions, probing for the extra edge he needed. For the first time since his tussle with Bullseye began, he became fully aware of the extent of the police presence surrounding the cathedral. Every cop in Manhattan seemed to be outside, armed and ready to invade the embattled old church the moment the command was given.

Cha-chunk! Daredevil's keen ears zeroed in on a single sharpshooter down on the street below. The nameless sniper had a clear bead on Daredevil's head through the window. Judging from his jumpy heart rate and twitchy finger, Daredevil guessed that the trigger-happy police offer was only seconds away from firing his weapon.

A wild idea occurred to Daredevil. It was going to be tricky, but he just might be able to pull it off if he timed it perfectly. The margin of error ranged from slim to nonexistent, but what other options did he have?

A sharp intake of breath, taken in anticipation of breaking Daredevil's skull, alerted him that Bullseye was about to lower the boom on him with the candelabra. *Here goes nothing,* the bleeding hero thought.

The candelabra swung downward, whistling through the air above Daredevil's head, but he didn't move a muscle. *Not yet,* he cautioned himself. Concentrating as he never had before, a sweaty palm gripping his billy club, he waited for what felt like an eternity. *Not yet.* It wouldn't be enough just to block the candelabra with his club; to survive, he needed to halt the attack at precisely the right moment and location. Otherwise, one way or another, Bullseye would have his head for sure.

Daredevil held his breath, counting the microseconds. *Not yet.* The crushing candelabra plummeted toward his head, gaining speed and momentum as Bullseye propelled it with every last ounce of his murderous zeal. *Not yet.* On the street below, on the other side of the window, the overeager sharpshooter tightened his finger against the trigger. . . .

Now!

The billy club swung up to meet the candelabra, intercepting its lethal trajectory. Simultaneously, a gunshot rang out as Daredevil's unwitting accomplice squeezed the trigger.

Bullseye's hands were in exactly the wrong place at the wrong time. A single bullet tunneled through both his hands as the horrified assassin shrieked in pain and rage. The candelabra slipped from his grip, falling noisily onto the marble floor two hundred feet below them. "No . . . !"

Daredevil could just imagine the shocked look on Bullseye's face as the stunned assassin stared in horror at the gaping wounds piercing his legendary hands. Blood dripped from his open palms like the stigmata of a crucified saint. A despairing groan emerged from somewhere deep inside him as he grasped that his infallible aim had finally been taken away from him.

He backed away from Daredevil, his heartbeat galloping fearfully. "Remember what the Padre said," he reminded Daredevil uneasily, every drop of his former arrogance leeched from his quavering voice. "Have mercy, right?"

For you? the outraged vigilante thought. He remembered Father Everett's words all right, but he also remembered a bloodstained sai being driven through the body of a beautiful, passionate woman who deserved a far happier fate. *You expect mercy— from me?*

Snarling through clenched white teeth, he lunged to his feet and grabbed Bullseye. For an instant, their faces were only inches apart and the assassin got a close-up look at a devil's wrath. Then, with a violent shove, Daredevil flung Bullseye through the center of the rose window.

Stained glass exploded outward into a thousand ringing shards of light. His face and hands streaked by dozens of bloody cuts, Bullseye screamed like a banshee as he plunged toward the street fifteen stories below.

CHAPTER 22

Urich was driving fast enough to make a New York cabbie turn green. Racing down Ninth Avenue behind the wheel of his beaten-up old Mustang, he weaved recklessly through the sparse late-night traffic, occasionally tempted to jump the curb and drive down the sidewalk in his haste to get to the ongoing fracas at the Church of the Holy Innocents.

His police monitor kept him up to speed on the developing crisis, but he couldn't wait to get there in person. *Hell's Kitchen's own devil makes his last stand at a Gothic cathedral*, he thought, marveling at the copy-friendly drama. *Can the story get any more perfect than that?* The headlines practically wrote themselves. . . .

And that was only the tip of the iceberg. *Wait until Manolis gets a load of tonight's other hot tip*, the grinning reporter mused. *There won't be enough Tums or Rolaids in the world.*

With one hand on the steering wheel, and the other clutching a cup of hot coffee from a twenty-four-hour Korean deli, Urich pressed down on the gas pedal as he sped downtown, counting off the shrinking street numbers as he neared the neighborhood of the star-crossed church. A fuming Camel cigarette dangled from his lower lip, and he crossed his ink-and-nicotine-stained fingers, praying to the mercurial gods of journalism that the whole thing wouldn't be over before he got there.

Just a couple more blocks, he noted with relief, threading the Mustang between two yellow cabs that weren't speeding nearly enough for his purposes. *C'mon, Daredevil, old buddy. Hang on for only a few minutes more.*

His jaw dropped, and he almost lost his cigarette when he finally arrived on the scene. A blind man, he observed wryly, couldn't have missed the unholy spectacle surrounding the Church of the Holy Innocents; the timeworn cathedral appeared to have attracted dozens of heavily armed pilgrims in blue uniforms and flak jackets. M-21 sniper rifles were aimed at every stained-glass aperture, putting several stone gargoyles and grotesques at risk of becoming collateral damage. Urich spotted the stocky form of Detective Nick Manolis presiding as ringmaster over the entire three-ring circus, and his scoop-happy grin broadened. *Poor Nick,* Urich thought, enjoying the moment rather more than he should. *He must just be loving this!*

He circled the cordoned-off church, looking for a parking spot, and whispered a fervent prayer of thanks as he spotted an open space at the rear of the cathedral, directly underneath an impressive rose window. Ignoring the shouts and warnings of an irate uniform, he yanked hard on the wheel, pulling right up to the base of the church. He spotted a police sharpshooter aiming upward and followed the sniper's gaze up the towering limestone wall to the huge stained-glass circle. Through the tinted panes, he glimpsed the silhouette of two ominous figures grappling at the base of the gigantic rosette.

Hot damn! Urich thought exuberantly. *A front-row seat.* Front-page headlines flashed through his brain. *Guess I didn't miss all the excitement after all.*

Right on cue, a shower of colored glass rained down on the Mustang, immediately followed by the screaming body of a man in an alligator coat. Urich's car shook and he spilled his coffee into his lap when the falling man crashed into his windshield.

Okay, he thought, waiting for his heart to start beating again. *I didn't have to get that up-close and personal . . . !*

A cobweb of cracks covered the windshield, obscuring his view. He threw open the door and scrambled out onto the sidewalk. Staring up at the shattered window, he saw Daredevil looking down at his unconscious antagonist. In the shocked hush following the unknown bad guy's spectacular plunge, Urich could easily hear the crimson figure's final verdict on his foe.

"Bull's-eye," Daredevil pronounced.

The Kingpin stood by his office window, his massive silhouette reflected like a specter across the city below, across the empire he had created. Wesley, on the phone beside him, set the receiver back into the cradle and turned to face Fisk.

"There's been a problem."

"Bullseye failed," Fisk replied quietly.

"Yes."

A moment of silence passed between the men. "Then he will be coming here next."

"How do you know?" Wesley asked, a little nervous now.

"It's what I would do."

"We'll be ready for him."

Fisk took a long, deep draw on his cigar. "Send the guards home. It's time we settled this. Face-to-face."

Wesley was dumbfounded. "But, sir—"

"I'm from the Bronx, Wesley," Fisk cut him off. "I don't expect *you* to understand."

Wesley backed off. "Yes, sir," he said, then walked out of the Kingpin's office. Fisk turned to gaze out again at the city, as thunder crackled and lightning rent the dark sky above.

Urich watched as the EMTs loaded the unlucky fall guy into the back of a waiting ambulance. He was still breathing, but the reporter gave him only fifty-fifty odds of surviving the night. *With luck,* Urich thought, *he'll last long enough to give the police some sort of statement.*

The reporter's energetic brain was working overtime, trying to put together the pieces. The mystery man who had wrecked his windshield matched the description of the unidentified perp who had killed a British businessman the night of the Natchios murder, but what was his connection to Daredevil? The dead Brit's stolen motorcycle had been found at the scene of the Natchios hit, which suggested that there was definitely a link between the two murders. Urich recalled an unconfirmed rumor he'd heard, about some big-shot Irish hit man the Kingpin had imported from overseas, and he had a sneaking suspicion he knew who the John Doe in the stretcher was.

The ambulance pulled away, its siren wailing, and Urich spotted Nick Manolis standing nearby. The observant reporter noted an empty antacid wrapper at

Manolis's feet, among the scattered shards of colored glass.

The beleaguered detective groaned and rolled his eyes as Urich approached. He made a halfhearted effort at pretending he didn't see the reporter.

"We need to talk," Urich told Manolis.

The detective was in no mood to chat. "Give me a break, Urich," he growled.

A youngster in a blue uniform ran up to Manolis. "Doors are open, Detective!" he reported.

"Terrific," Manolis said flatly. "Just in time." The rookie cop winced at his superior's unimpressed tone. "I want both teams on that roof!" Manolis bellowed.

Too little, too late, Urich thought, figuring that Daredevil was already long gone. He guessed Manolis knew that, too, which probably accounted for his cheerful disposition.

The surly cop walked away from Urich, heading back toward the front of the church. The reporter trailed after him stubbornly. "Trust me," he called out to Manolis, "you wanna hear this."

The detective slowed down, emitting an impatient sigh. "You've got *ten seconds*," he warned Urich.

That's all I need, Urich thought confidently. "An anonymous source called with a tip about the Tazio murder—"

Manolis wasn't impressed; a dead hooker was the furthest thing from his mind. "Phone it into the station. I got bigger problems tonight."

"It leads to Wilson Fisk," Urich stated, playing his trump card.

Manolis froze in his tracks.

"The Kingpin," the reporter added for emphasis.

Now Urich definitely had the detective's attention. Manolis turned around, a skeptical look on his jowly face.

"I can prove it," Urich insisted. For the time being, he chose not to mention that the "anonymous" tip had come from Foggy Nelson, Matt Murdock's illustrious partner. "And with a little pressure, you just might plea-bargain your way into the collar of a *lifetime*."

Manolis eyed him suspiciously. "Why me?"

Urich sighed. "It kills me to admit this, but you're the only honest cop I know."

The storm suddenly broke over the city, pouring buckets of rain onto the city streets. To Daredevil, it seemed as though the heavens themselves were weeping for Elektra.

Several blocks east and a universe away from Hell's Kitchen, he stood on a rain-drenched rooftop, looking up at the towering steel-and-glass facade of the Fisk Building. The gleaming skyscraper loomed over him like an insurmountable mountain of brightly lit wealth and modernity. Fisk's private office sat at the pinnacle of the lofty structure, like Dracula's castle atop a craggy Carpathian mountaintop.

Daredevil thought of Elektra's butchered remains, lying lifelessly on the rooftop of another, less grandiose edifice. Had the police already carted her body away? He wondered who they would get to identify it, now that her immediate family had all been murdered.

Bullseye had been dealt with, but Daredevil knew that Elektra's murder, among others, was not yet fully avenged. The ultimate architect of his lover's demise, along with countless other ruthless murders, still awaited justice. *I'm coming for you, Fisk,* he thought. His gloved fist crushed an imaginary rose.

Breaking into the Fisk Building was child's play; in the stifling summer heat, it was easy to find an open window on one of the skyscraper's upper floors. Daredevil stalked through the empty corridors of the silent office building, his keen senses effortlessly letting him evade the occasional security guard as he prowled the cool, air-conditioned halls. The gurgle of water flowing behind the smooth glass walls was mildly distracting at first, but he quickly learned to tune it out.

Daredevil smiled coldly as his fingers read the plaque on the door of the utility closet. Just what he was looking for. *Care for a game of blindman's buff, Kingpin?*

One by one, floor by floor, the lights went out at the Fisk Building. . . .

Wesley Welch sat brooding over his third double martini at an upscale cocktail lounge. A peppy bartender eager to reel in a large tip stepped over to Welch and asked, "Care for another martini, sir?"

"No, I come here for the view, asshole," Welch bit back.

The bartender, trying to maintain his facade of hospitality, went about mixing another martini for Welch. A man approached Wesley from behind and, drawing near, sat down on the barstool beside him.

Wesley turned and blinked at Manolis in puzzled confusion.

"Wesley Owen Welch?" the detective inquired gruffly.

"Who wants to know?" Welch sounded more annoyed than alarmed.

"Detective Nick Manolis," the cop identified himself. A pair of uniforms accompanied him, just in case the pampered executive raised a fuss. "I'd like to talk to you about the murder of Lisa Tazio."

A flicker of apprehension passed over Welch's aquiline features, but he quickly regained his composure. "I want my lawyer," he declared coolly.

Manolis flashed a predatory grin. For the first time in weeks, he didn't need a Tums. "I haven't charged you with anything."

Welch maintained a poker face. "I won't talk without my lawyer present."

"Then I'll speak. You can listen," Manolis replied.

Wesley turned to the bartender. "Check." But after the bile that was thrown his way, the bartender was in no hurry to write it up. In fact, he was going to enjoy this scene a little.

"She put up a hell of fight," Manolis said. "Took two bullets to the stomach."

"Check please!" Wesley demanded.

"This killer was meticulous. He left no fingerprints. No witnesses."

"That's a nice story," Welch said. "Thanks for sharing."

Manolis pressed on. "But this killer left one thing behind."

"Oh really? What's that?" Welch asked.

"Himself," Manolis replied. "Right under her fingernails."

Welch froze.

"Like I said, she put up a hell of a fight."

Every nerve in Wesley's body was electrified. The hair stood up on the back of his neck. He had been careful . . . but not careful enough. Trying to think

quickly, he said, "You need a warrant for a DNA
test. . . ."

Manolis pulled a sheaf of papers from his coat
pocket. "Those aren't your judges anymore, Wesley.
Or your lawyers. Fisk is finished with you. You're
just a liability to him now."

Wesley's eyes glazed over with fear, and he broke
out into a cold sweat. "Okay. Let's make a deal."

CHAPTER 23

Daredevil found Fisk waiting for him in the Kingpin's private office. He shoved open a pair of heavy metal doors, immediately sensing Fisk's colossal presence at the opposite end of the spacious chamber. A booming bass heartbeat, unlike anyone else's, identified the Kingpin at once.

Despite the lateness of the hour, Fisk was fully dressed in a voluminous silk suit. The rose in his lapel gave off a flowery aroma that made Daredevil's blood nearly bubble over in rage, while the bottom of a king-sized walking stick tapped against the polished tile floor. Fisk's heartbeat was calm and steady, as though he was expecting Daredevil.

Which he probably was.

"Daredevil," Fisk said.

"Kingpin," he replied.

For an instant, Daredevil paused to take his bearings. The vast office was admirably clean and uncluttered, with little to distract his hypersenses besides the ubiquitous water flowing through the ceiling. Large picture windows looked out on the streets below; he guessed that the sparkling city lights gave Fisk just enough light to see by.

No matter, Daredevil thought. He wanted the insidious crime boss to see the devil who had finally come to make him pay for his sins. *Hell's Kitchen owes you big time, Fisk.* His hand rested on his billy club. *And so do I.*

He activated the club's grappling hooks and shot it at Fisk like a torpedo. *This is the end, Kingpin,* he vowed. *You're not destroying any more lives.*

For a seemingly immovable object, Fisk moved with unexpected speed. He swiftly raised his walking stick, wrapping the oncoming hook and grappling cord around the shaft of the cane. Then he yanked on the stick, jerking Daredevil off his feet.

The hero and the crime boss collided like a puma charging headlong into a grizzly bear. Daredevil's bones rang with the force of the impact; slamming into Fisk felt like diving headfirst into a brick wall. He jumped backward, taking advantage of his greater speed and agility, and gave himself a split second to clear his head before coming at the Kingpin again.

He disengaged the grappling cord, recovering both ends of the bisected billy club. Wielding them like escrima sticks, he mercilessly battered Fisk's mountainous flesh from every direction, darting in and out of the bigger man's reach like a matador tormenting an enraged bull. Superhuman reflexes and dexterity were pitted against sheer brute strength and mass.

Unfortunately, mass was winning. Daredevil's furious blows bounced off Fisk's gigantic head and shoulders with little effect. The Kingpin shrugged off the hammering attacks as though they were no more substantial than the raindrops falling outside. Frustrated, the vengeful hero whipped the baton against Fisk's head with enough force to crack a cinder block, only to hear the huge man chuckle in amusement.

Good Lord, Daredevil thought, aghast. *He's actually enjoying this!*

The storm intensified outside. Thunder rattled the penthouse and pelted the plate-glass windows with driving rain, drowning out the more placid gurgle of the tamed water flowing through the ceiling. A flash of lightning strobed across the night.

The violent tempest matched the cataclysmic fury of the battle inside the darkened skyscraper. Determined to bring the Kingpin down, Daredevil snapped the divided pieces of his billy club back together, then leapt onto Fisk's gargantuan back. He locked the club beneath the mobster's chin, trying to choke him into submissions. *Fall, damn you!* Daredevil thought vehemently. *Fall!*

But it was like trying to choke a redwood; Fisk was too strong. Without missing a breath, the Kingpin flipped Daredevil over his head and tossed him roughly onto the hard tile floor.

The hero hit the ground with bone-crushing force. The impact wreaked havoc on his radar senses, leaving him concussed and disoriented. He tried to snap out of it, to focus, but all he could feel was the pain racking his body, all he could hear was his own ragged gasps and groans.

He was as helpless as any other blind man.

Fisk stood over Daredevil like a victorious Goliath. He wasn't even breathing hard. "It's a shame you came wounded," he rumbled, prodding Daredevil's bandaged shoulder with the steel tip of his walking stick. "I would have liked to fight you in your prime. They call you the man without fear. So why are you afraid to show your face?" Fisk grabbed the rose off his desk and approached the vigilante.

Daredevil remained flat on the floor. Fisk had to

crouch several feet just to reach the fallen man's mask. He tugged the demonic red cowl off, exposing the bloodied face underneath, then took a moment to absorb what he found. "I don't believe it," he muttered, sounding genuinely surprised for the first time since Daredevil invaded his inner sanctum. He laughed out loud, the deep, reverberating guffaw sounding disturbingly similar to the thunderclaps shaking the city. "The blind lawyer!"

The Kingpin's merriment grated against Matt's ears. He summoned up enough strength to answer Fisk's coldhearted hilarity with a defiant retort: "You killed my father. . . ."

The resounding laughter subsided, and the Kingpin fell silent for a moment, as though searching his memory. *How many names,* Matt wondered wrathfully, *are inscribed in the annals of your crimes? How many innocent lives have you snuffed out without regret?*

"I've killed many fathers. Which one was yours?"

"Jack Murdock, you son of a bitch."

"The boxer's boy," Fisk remembered at last. "Of course."

"Why?" Matt demanded, the pain of his father's death suddenly as fresh as though it had happened mere hours ago. In his mind, he was back in that filthy alley again, his anguished fingers exploring the pulverized mess his dad had become. "Why did you kill him?"

"Business. Just business. He was supposed to throw a fight," the Kingpin revealed. His sonorous voice held a wistful touch of nostalgia, as if reminiscing about the good old days when he killed his victims personally. "He was supposed to stay down."

Fisk roared with laughter as he plucked the rose from his lapel and dropped it onto Matt's bruised and bloody form. "You're just like your father," he announced. "You should have stayed down."

Matt's fist closed angrily on the rose, crushing it to powder. Lying helplessly on the floor, barely able to track the Kingpin with his malfunctioning radar, he heard the storm raging outside. Thunder and lightning . . .

. . . and *rain.*

Fisk raised his crystal-headed cane, preparing to splatter Matt's brains all over the immaculately spotless floors, even as the endangered hero remembered another rainstorm, a few nights ago, and the magical effect it had created. *When it rains, it's like a blanket on the world,* he heard himself explaining to a woman whose loving heart no longer throbbed with life. *For a moment everything is clear. . . .*

Matt grabbed his billy club and hurled it upward, missing Fisk but striking the transparent water shaft in the ceiling. The glass exploded, unleashing a deluge of water onto the men below. Pure spring water sprayed down upon the office, startling the Kingpin, who lifted his bulky head in confusion. His upraised cane hung suspended in the air above Matt's head.

The blind man smiled. The artificial deluge illuminated the darkness, the falling droplets bouncing off Fisk's mammoth form and defining him in perfect silhouette—just like Elektra in the rain.

I can see you now, Kingpin, Matt thought.

Overcoming his momentary shock, Fisk swung his walking stick down, but Matt rolled out of the way just in time, so that the crystalline head of the cane slammed into the floor instead, cracking the expensive tiles. Fisk growled, no longer amused by his enemy's intransigence, and swung again. The solid-steel cane sliced through the air like a scythe.

But now Matt could hear the splashing of the Kingpin's ponderous footsteps, making it simple enough to dodge the heavy cane. Fisk stumbled on the slippery floor, further slowed by the soaked, waterlogged garments hanging on his lumbering frame. He swung wildly at Matt with his oversized fists, every titanic blow telegraphed by a sodden, dripping *swoosh*.

Matt slid like a sea lion through the spreading puddles, keeping a few feet ahead of the Kingpin's flailing fists and cane. He surveyed the enormous crime boss like a gem cutter inspecting an unhewn diamond. *Even a mountain has its weak spots,* he thought. Thanks to the lifesaving downpour, he could perceive his opponent in painstaking detail. *Every suit of armor has its chinks.*

Fisk swung and missed, the momentum of his sweeping assault almost sending him toppling over onto the floor. Grunting like a mountain gorilla, he struggled to regain his balance—just as Matt slid deliberately through Fisk's columnlike legs, kicking out with surgical precision.

Crack! Crack! A pair of well-aimed scissor kicks dislocated the Kingpin's kneecaps. *Timber!* Matt thought, as the indomitable crimelord fell at last, crippled at the knees.

"Aaahh!" Fisk shouted, his pain-filled shriek still remaining deep in the lower registers. His deadly walking stick went flying from his fingers as he joined Matt on the flooded tiles, where the two injured men exchanged a volcanic look. The Devil and his sworn nemesis, brought low by their long-destined conflict.

But Matt wasn't done yet. Slowly, awkwardly, he climbed back onto his feet, taking care not to slip on the inundated floor. He turned his head toward the Kingpin's huge cane, lying in a bloody puddle a few feet away; it was nearly as long as the metal pipe Bullseye had tried to kill Daredevil with.

Fisk saw where Matt was "looking." A look of sullen resignation came over his ebony face.

Matt pulled his mask back on, like an executioner preparing to man the gallows. The face of the orphaned lawyer disappeared, replaced by the unforgiving visage of a horned demon.

He picked up the hefty steel cane, weighing it in his grasp. It was heavier than his billy club, the better to bash the Kingpin's brains in. He recalled his father's brutalized features, beaten past recognition in a lonely alley nearly two decades ago.

"I've been waiting for this day," Daredevil said, his voice devoid of the roiling emotions churning inside. "Ever since I was twelve years old."

He raised the cane above his head as Fisk closed his eyes, waiting for the end.

"This is for my father. . . ." Daredevil swung the cane down with every fiber of his being, for his father, for Elektra, for the innocents sacrificed in the Kingpin's vile games . . . for himself.

Crack!

The mighty crash startled the Kingpin, who opened his eyes to look up at Daredevil, unhurt. The cane was shattered in pieces by Fisk's head. "I don't understand," Fisk said.

"I made a promise once. I intend to keep it," Daredevil replied. Outside, a cacophony of sirens grew near.

"They're coming for you," Fisk said.

"Not for me," Daredevil replied. "Haven't you heard? The word is out on Kingpin."

For the first time in his life, Fisk looked afraid. "I swear! I'll tell them who you are!" Fisk cried out.

"Yeah, who are you going to tell? The boys in Rikers? Tell 'em that you were beat by a blind man. It'll be like blood in water," Daredevil said.

"I'll get out."

"I know," Daredevil replied. "I'll be waiting." He threw the splintered remains of the cane down on the ground. "Justice is *served*."

Daredevil obtained the rose in the flower district, leaving behind the price of a single bloom. Now, several blocks southwest of the Fisk Building, he looked down on the abandoned husk of the Midtown Civic Center, where his father had fought and won his final battle—at the cost of his life. The graffiti-covered building was boarded-up and forgotten now, but the memory of Jack Murdock's untimely death was still fresh in the mind of his son. But tonight, for the first time in decades, his recollections didn't sting as much as they had before.

Bullseye was for Elektra, he decided. But the Kingpin's downfall was consecrated to the memory of another victim. "This one's for you, Dad," he whispered as he let go of the rose.

It fluttered slowly to the sidewalk below.

CHAPTER 24

The storm had finally passed, leaving clear skies and sunshine behind. A free man, Daunte Jackson celebrated on the steps of the courthouse. Wearing a set of fresh street clothes, he hugged first Foggy, then Matt, then both of them together. "Thanks, bros!" he exclaimed gratefully. "I ain't never going to forget you guys!"

Matt gracefully liberated himself from Jackson's enthusiastic embrace. "I hope you'll take this close shave as a warning," he advised in a friendly tone. "You might want to clean up your act a bit."

Jackson just shrugged and shook Matt's hand.

There were no guarantees, the lawyer knew. Jackson might well be back behind bars by the weekend, for a completely unrelated offense. Still, even flawed people were entitled to justice; for once the system had worked—with only a little assistance from Daredevil.

Jackson ambled away, perhaps to start a brand-new life, or maybe just to score some dope. *He's no angel,* the blind man thought. *But then again, neither am I.*

*   *   *

Matt and Foggy were back at their usual booth at their favorite diner, enjoying their morning coffee. Just like always, Foggy was transfixed by the day's headlines.

THE REAL KINGPIN? the *New York Post* screamed in its inimitable style, above a page-one mug shot of Wilson Fisk. A smaller headline, just above the fold, read: DAREDEVIL STRIKES BACK!

Foggy read the accompanying text with rapt attention.

". . . police say that although there were no eyewitnesses, they suspect Daredevil was the one to ultimately bring Fisk to justice."

As usual, Matt played devil's advocate. "See, no eyewitnesses."

"Don't tell me you're still a skeptic?" Foggy shook his head in weary disbelief.

"Even Bigfoot has eyewitnesses," Matt pointed out. He smiled faintly; although there was definitely something comforting about the familiar banter, part of his mind was elsewhere.

Perceptive as always, Foggy picked up on his friend's distracted state. "Hey, you okay?"

Matt gave Foggy a reassuring pat on the shoulder, not wanting to worry him. He slipped out of the booth and took hold of his cane. "I'm just going to get some air," he explained.

It was a short walk to the stoop of Lisa Tazio's apartment building, where Matt added a candle to the makeshift shrine commemorating her life and death. He lit the candle, finding a bit of much-needed closure. Lisa Tazio was beyond his aid now, but at least her true killers had been brought to trial. Neither Fisk nor Welch was likely to see daylight for a long time.

"Matt?" a voice addressed him from behind. Matt turned slowly to discover Ben Urich. For once, the persistent *Post* reporter was not accompanied by a noxious cloud of cigarette smoke.

"Ben . . ." Matt said warily. His body tensed; despite Urich's tip regarding Officer McKenzie, which had helped break open the Jackson case, Matt still regarded the tenacious reporter with suspicion. Urich had been showing way too much interest in Matt Murdock—and Daredevil.

Urich winced as he popped a stick of Nicorette gum into his mouth. "Promised the wife I'd quit," he explained. Matt found it difficult to imagine that Urich had a wife. "But the gum is gonna kill me quicker." His voice carried its characteristic nasal whine. "How are you?"

"I'm okay," Matt said.

Urich didn't seem bothered by the young lawyer's reticence. "I've still got people checking all the hospitals and morgues in town," he volunteered. "So far, no Jane Does that fit the description of Elektra Natchios. But she'll turn up somewhere."

"Thanks, Ben," he said sincerely. The mystery of Elektra's disappearance tugged at his brain. When he'd been forced to abandon her body on that laundry-covered rooftop, Manolis and his search team had been only footsteps away. He had just assumed that the police had taken custody of his sweetheart's remains, but apparently that wasn't the case. *So what happened to you, Elektra?*

"Don't thank me yet," Urich warned him. Something about the reporter's tone set off warning bells in Matt's mind, temporarily driving out his questions regarding the final disposition of Elektra's body.

Here it comes, he thought apprehensively. Unlike Bullseye or the Kingpin, the reporter's curiosity could not be subdued by a vengeful billy club.

"There's another story I've been following," Urich said, sounding uncomfortable. "And I wanted to alert you before it runs." His feet shuffled awkwardly on the sidewalk. "I know the truth, Matt." He nodded at the burnished red cane in the lawyer's hand. "Justice is blind."

A chill ran over Matt, and he felt a void open up at the pit of his stomach. Even knowing what Urich was going to say, it still came as a shock to hear the words spoken aloud.

"You run this and I'm finished," he said hoarsely. No more Daredevil. No legal career. Nothing.

Urich sighed and looked away from him. Matt could hear the grimace in his voice. "I'm a reporter, Matt. That's what I do."

I know, Matt thought glumly. He walked away, figuring there was nothing more to say. Urich let him go. Chewing his gum joylessly, the newsman lingered behind on Thirty-eighth Street, next to a shrine to a murdered prostitute.

The sun shone down on the rooftop of the old brownstone, warming Matt's face. A cool breeze carried the promise of autumn, and the hectic noises of the city, drifting up from below, sounded like old friends. A bittersweet sensation washed over his soul as he recalled that idyllic night with Elektra, the rain revealing her in all her grace and beauty.

I'll never forget you, Elektra, he thought, his throat tightening. *I wish we could have had more time together.*

Overcome with emotion, he turned to leave. But before he could exit the roof, a tinkling noise came from the direction of the old water tower.

Drawn by the metallic rustle, Matt walked over the ruined husk, where something dangled in the breeze from the wooden frame of the tower. He reached out curiously—and his breath caught in his throat as his fingers touched a delicate metal necklace.

Elektra's necklace.

Matt's heart sped up riotously, even as his mind could scarcely accept the wild hopes and fantasies cascading through his brain. *It can't be*, he thought, trying to protect himself from the heartbreak of having his most ardent desires and dreams crushed all over again. *I heard you die!*

His fingers shook as he detached the necklace from the rotting wooden supports. He handled it reverently, as if it was a holy relic, and slowly ran a finger along the back of the necklace, where Electra's name had once been engraved.

Her name was still there, but now it had been translated into a pattern of raised dots.

Into *Braille*.

Matt gasped in astonishment. He had never believed in miracles before, despite everything that had happened to him in his remarkable life, but all at once, here on this lonely rooftop, beneath the healing radiance of a bright new day, Matt found the courage to hope for the impossible

Elektra's last words, uttered with her final breath, echoed within his mind:

I told you I'd find you. . . .

EPILOGUE

It was nearing one-thirty in the morning as Ben Urich sat at his desk putting the final touches to the Story of the Century. A Styrofoam cup of coffee rested a safe distance away from the keyboard while a slow-moving fan sat on top of the filing cabinet behind Urich, stirring the stuffy August air. Crime photos and sketches were taped to every available surface.

"They say there's no rest for the wicked," he typed, quietly mouthing the words under his breath. "But what about the good?"

In a hospital bed on the other side of the city, an unidentified man lay trapped inside a full body cast. I.V. lines poked through the thick plaster cast and a plastic tube delivered oxygen to his nose. The heavy white dressings almost completely concealed the patient's identity; only the maniacal, hate-filled eyes peering out from the bandages revealed the seething mind locked inside the cast.

BZZZZzzzzz. . . .

A noisy fly buzzed around the hospital room, tormenting the immobilized patient. The insect zipped past his eyes, then landed on his nose, less than an inch away from the life-giving oxygen tube. Rabid

eyes glared at the fly until it took flight again, loop-
ing back and forth before his malignant gaze, as if
taunting him.

The battle against evil is never-ending, Urich wrote,
because evil always survives . . .

A hypodermic needle occupied a metal tray beside
the patient's bed. His groping fingers wriggled painfully toward the hypo, despite the aching soreness of
his injured hands. Gritting his teeth, he stretched out
his fingers until they finally came to rest on the waiting syringe.
BZZZZZZ—*thwip!*
The needle neatly pinned the fly to the wall.
Beneath the cumbersome plaster, Bullseye smiled.

. . . with the help of evil men.

The orange prison jumpsuit fit tightly upon his
frame, unlike the silk suits he was accustomed to.
Guards escorted Wesley Welch down the wide central hallway toward his cell. The dreary institutional
surroundings were a far cry from the pristine luxury
of his skyscraper.
At first, the other convicts looked on in silence.
Then, tentatively at first, the catcalls began.
Mocking laughter greeted the jibes, encouraging
the rest of the prison population to join in. Profane
and vulgar shouts followed Welch as he traversed
the lengthy corridor. He heard the guards snicker in
amusement as they closed the door to his cell.
A voice emanated through the bars from the adjacent cell.

"Oh, Wesley . . . tell me about your plea bargain."

Welch blanched. The Kingpin, his harsh laugh resounding through the prison halls, was in the very next cell.

Urich reached the end of his story. He leaned back against his chair, reading the finished text to himself.

"Now the world knows the truth. That there is a Devil living in Hell's Kitchen. A devil named Matt Murdock."

His words stood out brightly against the luminous screen of his computer monitor. A tad melodramatic, but effective nonetheless. He sipped thoughtfully from his coffee cup.

"After twenty years of reporting," he muttered softly to himself, "this remains the single most sensational story of my career. My Pulitzer Prize."

He glanced over at an open space on his bookshelf, where a Pulitzer trophy would fit perfectly. A nicotine-stained finger hovered over the PRINT key. *Boy, would I kill for a cigarette right now,* he thought.

With a sigh, he pressed the DELETE key instead, and watched his deathless prose disappear from the screen. "Shame nobody will ever read it."

Despite the lateness of the hour, he decided to step out for a breath of fresh air. He exited his apartment and strolled onto Twenty-sixth Street. Glancing up at the rooftops, he glimpsed a lone figure looking down on him from across the street. A devil's horns were silhouetted against the night sky.

"Go get 'em, Matt," Urich said with a nod.

He watched as the forbidding, yet strangely reassuring apparition disappeared into the shadows. Even though Ben was out walking Hell's Kitchen after dark, the savvy reporter had never felt safer, because he knew exactly who and what was watching over the neighborhood.

Daredevil.

The Man Without Fear.

About the Author

Greg Cox is the *New York Times* bestselling author of numerous *Star Trek* novels, including *The Eugenics Wars, The Q Continuum, The Black Shore,* and *Assignment: Eternity.* He has also written several novels based on such popular Marvel Comics characters as the X-Men and Iron Man.

He lives in Oxford, Pennsylvania.